AND THEN THERE WAS ONE

Visit us at www.boldstrokesbooks.com

AND THEN THERE WAS ONE

by

Michele Castleman

2024

AND THEN THERE WAS ONE

ISBN 13: 978-1-63679-688-8

This Trade Paperback Original Is Published By
Bold Strokes Books, Inc.
P.O. Box 249
Valley Falls, NY 12185

First Edition: June 2024

CREDITS
EDITOR: BARBARA ANN WRIGHT
PRODUCTION DESIGN: SUSAN RAMUNDO
COVER DESIGN BY INKSPIRAL DESIGN

Acknowledgments

· This book is for my parents, Geri Castleman and Michael Castleman, who have loved and supported me all my life. They have served as my first editors, critics, and (sometimes) my inspiration.

I also want to thank my editor, Barbara Ann Wright, for her guidance and feedback. She is right, I do use ellipses too often...I appreciate the efforts of everyone at Bold Strokes Books and am so thankful they took a gamble on Lyla'a story.

Many other friends and loved ones have also contributed to getting me and this novel to this point. I want to acknowledge the help of Holly Hoover, Amy Berger, Stacey Pistorova, Sandy Kimmel, Val Henderson, the Toledo-area writing group from SCBWI: in particular Candy Gremler, Marian Miller, and Judy Sobanski and the Ohio North SCBWI group—especially those who get up to write together at 5 a.m. once a week. I also want to thank Leah Pillegi and Kristy Hunter who provided valuable feedback on *And Then.* I am also grateful to the Highlights Foundation for building a wonderful space for children's authors to work. I want to thank my Highlights mentors—Lamar Giles, who challenged me to write something new at a time when I wasn't certain I would write again, and Clara Gillow Clark who championed this book when I revised it.

I want to thank the kitties who cuddled beside me or blocked my view of my laptop screen as I wrote and revised. Whether hindering or helping the writing process, I love you Frankie, Freddie, Click, Clack, and Salt an' Peppa. "Meow. Meow." Please assume any typos you find are the fault of a cat's need for attention.

Last, but certainly not least, I would like to thank you for reading this far. I have wanted to write and publish a book for you to read for years and years. I am so incredibly thankful to have finally gotten a book into your hands. Best wishes.

Dedication

For my parents: Geri and Michael Castleman.
I know I didn't become an astronaut, a lawyer, or a journalist.
But at least the murders I commit are all fictional!

CHAPTER ONE

In death, her face was ugly: translucent, puffy skin; sand-filled scrapes along the knees and the tops of the feet; lips blue with a white froth at the corners of the mouth and under the nose; brown eyes locked open and staring, pupils dilated; and the hair lanky across the forehead and twisting around the neck.

The pain of knowing my sister's eyes would never focus on me again, that her lips would never upturn in a smile both seared and froze me.

After dragging Skirty onto the beach, I swiped the long wet hair off her face as though that would bring her back to life, unclog the water from her lungs, and restore her soul to her body.

Lake Erie water and sunscreen stung my eyes. I beat her chest, wishing I'd paid closer attention on how to do CPR in health class. Where was the ambulance? Why wasn't it here yet? I needed someone to undo this. I whispered her name for the last time aloud and shook her shoulder, trying to wake her.

When the ambulance finally arrived, red and blue lights flashing and siren wailing, the paramedics didn't even try to resuscitate her cooling body. They knew what I wanted to deny: my sister was dead.

Because of me.

CHAPTER TWO

Six weeks later, the captain of the ferry watched with a bored expression as I struggled to pull my giant rolling suitcase from the boat onto the dock. He stood straighter than he had when we had first embarked from Sandusky, Ohio, making his small beer belly less noticeable. He now wore a dark valet hat and jacket and a name tag with *Weston* on it, as though he knew Mrs. Payne might be watching from the island's main house. He still didn't help me with my bag.

The island was small—less than a mile in circumference—and privately owned. The long dock led to a pristine path that ended at a looming mansion at the heart of the island. Everything here belonged to the Payne family, one of the richest families in the Midwest and distant relatives to my mom. Skirty and I had occasionally been invited here to amuse the youngest daughter, Charlotte, who was only a few years older than us. They only gave us access to the island when they had a use for us. In my case, it had been years since I'd been invited. In the case of my sister, Skirty had spent most summers here, nannying for Charlotte's young son, Rock.

With Skirty gone, I supposed I would be the poor substitute.

Finally, I pulled the suitcase over the edge of the gangplank and across the boards of the long dock, the plastic wheels whining between each shift from board to empty air and back.

A gray-haired white woman wearing all black and flats waited for me at the end of the dock. Ms. Eldonforth. As far as I knew, she didn't have a first name. She'd worked for the Paynes for longer than I had been alive, and if my memories from when I was allowed to vacation here were correct, had always worn the tight-lipped jowly expression covering her face now. She must have been in her late fifties, but something about her judgmental glare and pinched mouth made her seem older. She stood as though she carried a thick book on top of her head all day with ease and judged everyone else for not doing the same.

Her eyes shifted to take in my tiny jean shorts, tank top, and flip-flops. Her lips thinned, and her jowls deepened. I tried to pull down one of the legs of my shorts to cover another inch of skin. Skirty would have glared at me for dressing so casually to meet the vulture lady.

"Welcome back, Lyla," Ms. Eldonforth said without enthusiasm. "I think it's wise of you to try to return to normal."

I winced and adjusted my grip on my suitcase.

"Well." Ms. Eldonforth looked away from me. "You'll be in your usual room." She strode toward the mansion without looking back, clearly expecting me to follow the path to the main house: a three-story brick monster with ivy tickling its sides, a slate green roof, and more dark windows than I could easily count. When I was little, I'd always imagined it to be a sleeping dragon, guarding gold and hoping for an intruder to revive it and give it a reason to spew flames.

"Dinner will be at seven p.m. The usual dress code will be expected." That meant a dress or skirt. I shrugged one shoulder. Skirty had always fared better with the rules and expectations of the island. Probably why she'd been offered to nanny Rock.

Ms. Eldonforth hesitated, shifting only for a second to glare before resuming her march. "You'll start looking after Rock tomorrow," she continued. "He is still fixated on lake and ocean wildlife. I'll leave you reminders and expectations on the corkboard in the kitchen. Be sure to check it several times a day."

I hoped Ms. Eldonforth would only communicate via notes. I think I would prefer her that way.

"Charlotte will return to school in the morning," she continued.

I could sense Ms. Eldonforth running through the checklist of all she had to accomplish before the youngest of the three Payne siblings returned to OSU.

"She is taking an extra class to graduate by December, so she'll be staying on campus during most weekends. She's nervous about leaving Rock for so long, as any parent would be." She swiped at an imagined piece of lint on her shoulder. "So it falls to you to demonstrate he is in good hands. Understood?"

"Uh-huh." I switched hands to drag my suitcase over the gravel.

"Keep up."

"Yes, Ms. Eldonforth." I held my breath and counted in my head for a few moments. At no point had she mentioned that I had deferred college to be here, nor did she say, "I am sorry for your loss."

"Mrs. Payne will want to speak with you after dinner tonight," she added, leading me to the staff entrance that opened up to a long hall containing six closed doors that led to bedrooms and one shared bathroom.

"Yes, Ms. Eldonforth," I said, releasing the breath I'd been holding. In some ways, I could breathe again. In some ways, it was like a riptide dragged me farther down.

A few minutes later, I pulled my suitcase into our room.

My room.

The room Skirty and I always shared when we visited the island.

The small space contained two sagging twin beds, a wardrobe, and two nightstands, each with a small lamp on it. The same miserable brown-and-yellow flowered wallpaper greeted me, and a heavy beige curtain was pulled back to reveal the room's sole thin window near the ceiling. The bathroom was down the hall, and I would be sharing it with all the other house employees.

Despite the drab appearance, evidence of our history was written all over the room: Some of our childhood picture books leaned against the corner. Skirty had brought the books here over a year ago to share with Rock. Beside the wardrobe sat my sister's gray, shark-mouthed beach bag. Cloth teeth lined the long, zippered opening. A photo my sister had taken was taped to the wall. She'd taken the selfie at the end of our junior year in our school's cafeteria. Derek Steyer, aka. THE BOYFRIEND, as I always referred to him, smiled between me and Rose. Only Skirty had looked into the correct place on the camera, so she appeared to make eye contact with the viewer.

I resisted the urge to pull the photo down and instead powered on the old smartphone that my mom had tucked into one of the pockets of the rolling suitcase.

The image of the ancient books on the protective cover was marred by scratches. We'd never used lock screens, so it was only a couple of clicks to text my parents that I'd arrived safely. Next, I pulled up a text chain with THE BOYFRIEND. My fingers hovered. *What to say?* Eventually, I texted, *Made it*, and a smiley emoji, then immediately shut off the phone and shoved it into the top drawer of the nearest nightstand.

I sat at the head of *her* bed and reached under the duvet to grab the pillow. Holding it to my face, I inhaled deeply, searching for the scent of my sister's conditioner, hair spray, or something that was uniquely her. All I could smell was generic flowery fabric softener. The pillow fell into my lap. Our mom had washed her out of our linens in Sandusky too.

"Oh, hey. You must be Lyla." A girl my age stood in the doorway. She was white and wore all black just as Ms. Eldonforth had, but her outfit showed off her thin figure. Her dyed red hair was pulled back into a small bun. The vibrant red of her matching lipstick forced me to look at her mouth as she sang a familiar old tune at me and wished me a good morning while adding a flourish of jazz hands.

All I could think to say was, "It's not morning."

It's from *Singin' in the Rain*, she explained.

"Umm, you have a nice voice."

"Thanks," she said. The confidence in her tone gave me the impression she was used to receiving compliments on her singing. With her bright green eyes and expertly applied lipstick, I bet that her voice was not the only feature that earned comments. "Rock and Charlotte are so excited to have you here. Charlotte says you're the best at hide-and-seek."

I stood, pulling down the legs of my jean shorts.

"He says I sing too much," she continued with a smile. "I'm Gwen Verden, by the way."

"Hi, Gwen."

"I've only been here a few weeks. I'm actually a lowly maid." She curtsied. "But Charlotte has been asking me for help while she's been counting down the seconds to your arrival."

I hesitated. "Are you, by chance, a theater person?"

"What gave it away?"

Skirty had participated in a few of our high school's productions and dragged me to a couple of wrap parties, loud events punctuated by spontaneous singing. "Um." I didn't quite know how to say, *you seem dramatic*, without it coming out negatively. But before I could better articulate the thought, Gwen launched into a verse of, "Getting to Know You," and I guessed I didn't have to answer at all.

As she sang, I clenched my teeth. If she expected me to join in, she'd chosen to serenade the wrong girl. Skirty would sing, but she isn't—*wasn't*—tone-deaf like me.

Gwen cut herself off abruptly and smiled in a way that made my chest tickle. "I used to perform at Cedar Point. But Alex told me about this job, and this pays better."

"Alex?"

"The cook. You'll meet him soon. He's nice. We're old friends. We're so happy to have another young person here whose last name isn't Payne."

I nodded. The scent of her perfume had reached me. *Rose.*

We watched each other, silent. Before it got awkward, she said, "Let me know if you need anything."

"Okay." *Rose. Rose. Rose.* I'd missed this smell. *So much.* My calves tensed as I fought the urge to step closer, to breathe in deep. Instead, I held my breath.

"I heard you have to eat dinner with the family each night. You unlucky girl, you. I'll be the one carrying the food." And she shot finger guns in my direction before continuing down the hall.

Wow. I resisted the urge to peek into the hall to watch her walk away. She was vibrancy and light. It almost hurt to look at her since I dwelled in such a dark place.

With Gwen gone, I could hear the air-conditioner running through the vents and the tick of an ancient alarm clock marking the passage of each second in one of the wardrobe drawers. It was a trick of Skirty's. She'd always leave the alarm in a place where she had to get up to silence it, since she had trouble waking in the mornings.

I pulled it from the top drawer of the wardrobe. A faded unicorn sticker stuck to the side. Mom had tasked me with giving the sticker to my sister when we were little. A reward for having remained silent but adorable during a family dinner with Mrs. Payne.

I remember Skirty asking, "Didn't you get one too?"

I'd remained silent.

"We'll share," she'd said, and she'd put it on the clock so we could both see it.

My breath hitched at the memory. Two hours until dinner.

The logical choice would be to unpack. But the thought of opening the second drawer of the wardrobe where we'd written our initials in Sharpie did not appeal. I also didn't want to unzip my suitcase to see the old digital camera that I had brought, either.

Mom had made me pack it. "It's used by professional photographers," she'd said. "Perfect for the future artist. Not new, sorry, but barely used." It had been the most expensive gift a few Christmases ago. Mom still commented about it if she didn't feel like it was getting enough use.

We'd had it that day at the beach. Skirty had taken photos of windswept reeds emerging from small dunes of sand. There were still selfies on it from the day she'd died.

I'd wanted to leave it in Sandusky, but Mom had insisted: "Bring it. Pursue your passions. It's more important now than ever. It's what she would want for you. And the island is so beautiful. It's practically its own course on nature photography."

I set the alarm clock back in the drawer and slid it shut.

A movement caught my attention. At the top of the bedroom's thin window, the heavy beige curtain was held back with a knotted, beaded, decorative rope that swung in the breeze of the air-conditioning. I stood on tiptoe to inspect it. Cool air from the AC pushed against the side of my neck, and I shivered. The knot swung, making the faintest click as its beads repeatedly collided against the windowpane. It looked like a tiny noose.

I slid my index finger through the loop and pulled gently, watching as the skin surrounding the rope turned white. *Suffocating.*

Time for a walk, I thought, grabbing Skirty's old, shark bag and fleeing our room and the servants' wing.

CHAPTER THREE

It'd been years since I had walked the path to the Paynes' personal beach. *As though their indoor pool is not enough.*

I trudged across the expanse of manicured lawn, feeling small in the shadows of the old oak trees. My flip-flops thwapped with each step, and I held the shark-mouth beach bag a little tighter in my hand. The boathouse stood to my right. It didn't show its age; a fresh coat of paint had been professionally applied to the carved lattices. I hadn't ventured in there since Skirty had pursued me in a game of hide-and-seek when we were eight or nine. I'd wanted to climb into the speedboat that had rested in a stand but couldn't move after I'd noticed spiderwebs with very visible, very large spiders surrounded me. I'd huddled on the floor beside the boat, feeling lines of webs brushing against my skin as I'd held my breath, trying not to disturb them.

That had been how Skirty—She Who Did Not Fear Spiders— had found me. Only after she'd cut me free of the webs, giving me a way to escape the trap I'd gotten myself into, had I breathed in and tasted the damp and musty air.

There was nothing I wanted to see in that boathouse now. *Nothing.* I thwapped on, pulling the shark bag closer to my side.

Five-foot tall viburnum bushes hid the sole eyesore on the island: an ugly metal shack used for storing a couple of golf carts, snowmobiles, and gardening tools. The thin branches' dark green leaves whipped back and forth in front of the shed's door as though providing defense against would-be intruders. Those weapon-like branches would bloom with beautiful snowball-shaped puffs of tiny white flowers in the spring. Skirty had told me that the shack had been erected on the spot where a fire had occurred when we were just five or six. Apparently, we'd been visiting for the summer when it happened, but I didn't remember it.

This island is tragic. But it also had beautiful touches trying to hide the ugliness. And I was even more tragic and ugly for returning here to hide.

When I reached the beach, my toes sank into the cool sand. Skirty once told me the Paynes shipped in sand every few years to maintain the beach. They were too good for erosion and the sharp rocks underfoot that most Erie beach goers endured.

I let the bag slip from my fingers. Now, without the protection or whisper of the waving trees, I could see the overcast sky. The wind had intensified into a roar since my arrival on the island. My hair whipped at my face and neck. I could see storm clouds charging toward us. Ohio was a hazy gray landmass in the distance. The powerful wind threatened to steal my breath. With a whoosh, the gale picked up a wave of sand and assaulted my front.

I leaned forward to keep my footing, but the wind stopped, and I fell onto my knees, catching myself on my hands. This was the moment to be thankful for a sandy beach instead of a stony one. The thought brought back memories of another beach, with stones digging into my knees and with Skirty's limp body in front of me.

I forgot how to breathe for a moment, and my tears began to fall.

I shouldn't have come here. I should have known better.

I managed to gulp in air.

Seagulls yelled in the distance, replying to my sobs. The water rushed in and out over the beach, shushing me each time the waves rolled toward me. I gritted my teeth, biting down on the bits of sand that had invaded my mouth. I stood, trying to wipe the sand from my legs and hands. I ran, leaving the beach bag.

The wind resumed its force, pushing me back to the mansion. I was thankful that the old oaks would block the worst of the gale. The first cool raindrops struck me just before I made it inside. The clouds thundered, and the sky shattered with more rain shards tumbling behind me.

❖

I couldn't hear the raging storm inside the Payne mansion after I closed the door to the servants' wing. I walked along the quiet hall, strange, incongruous shadows watching me as I headed up the back staircase, along another hall, passing the entrance to the pool, and through a swinging door to come into the bright kitchen. I found Ms. Eldonforth there, trimming the long, thick stems of fresh-cut, white Peruvian lilies, scissors in her left hand. She leaned close to a tall, white, redheaded man, and glared up at him.

"Oh sorry," I said.

Ms. Eldonforth jumped, gasped, and then looked where one of the scissor blades was very close to her right pointer finger. We stared a few long moments, then the blood began to rise, forming a two-inch line in her skin.

"Shit, I'm sorry."

The thin man moved before I could, setting down his spoon, guiding Ms. Eldonforth to the sink to run cool water on the cut and pulling out a towel.

"I didn't mean—I…I'm sorry," I said again.

"It's fine." Ms. Eldonforth looked at me, her mouth a grim line once again. "I've had worse." She stopped the water and held the towel to her finger.

The man returned to the gas stove, stirring a pot of red sauce over a low orange flame.

"Now, how can I help you?" Ms. Eldonforth took a moment to assess my attire again. If she'd disliked my appearance before, she must have hated it now; still in my short shorts with added sandy knees and windblown hair.

"Um, well." My words stumbled. "I wanted to discuss quitting with you. I think this was a mistake."

Her expression was unreadable. "Excuse me?" She readjusted the towel against her finger.

"I'm not ready to be here. There are mem—" My voice caught in my throat. I glanced at the man and crossed my arms.

He watched me with an eyebrow raised. The spoon he swirled in the pot scraped rhythmically against the bottom.

"Hi," he said. "I'm Alex." He kept slowly stirring, his thin shoulders hunched. He couldn't have been more than five or six years older than me. Maybe twenty-three or twenty-four. Around the age of Steve, the middle Payne brother.

"Nice to meet you," I managed to say in a flat tone.

Ms. Eldonforth seemed to step purposefully around the marble island to grip my right elbow with her good hand and pilot me through the swinging door and back into the staff hall.

"Nice meeting you," Alex called after us.

"Ms. Smith, I am disappointed that we have to talk about professionalism in the workplace already."

I stifled a sob. "I'm—"

"Don't you dare say you're sorry." She released me only to grip my shoulders and force me to face her. The towel scratched gently against my arm. "Remind me," she said. "How old are you now?"

"Ei...eighteen."

"A legal adult," she reminded me. "One who is responsible for her choices and commitments."

My vision blurred. "I...I know," I managed. "But it hurts." And the tears rained down again.

My eyesight was too bleary to know for sure, but I almost thought her grim expression softened. *Almost.* She turned me again and led me a few more paces away from the kitchen. "Ms. Smith, I will not allow you to leave here without providing proper notice for Charlotte to find another nanny. That would be unprofessional. Do you understand? We expect better of the great-niece of Mrs.

Payne. We expect effective communication. Even during a family tragedy."

That is one way to describe Skirty's death.

"But," she added, "I will propose you remain here for two weeks while I reach out to some of our previous nannies. Rock loves you and is excited to play with you." She squeezed my arm. I couldn't quite tell if the gesture was supposed to be threatening or comforting. "His excitement over seeing you is one of the few reasons Charlotte even agreed to Mrs. Payne's request that she return to campus and complete her degree by December."

I struggled to control my breathing and swiped at the tears that trailed down my cheeks.

"I was under the impression you were hoping to help yourself through the grieving process by being here. Am I correct?" Ms. Eldonforth asked.

I nodded.

"I think this was a wise choice." She hesitated and cleared her throat. It was strange to see her searching for words. "When... when it feels like the pain could suffocate you, I...I find it's best to remember that you are doing good for someone else. You're helping."

I sniffled. Her grip on my arms tightened gently, and I felt warm and...comforted? By Ms. Eldonforth? Never in my life did I think I could feel seen and understood by this woman. But here I was, leaning in, desperate for her next words.

"You have to choose what truly matters to you," Ms. Eldonforth said.

"Wha...what?"

"Don't focus on the pain of losing Dalia." She ran her hands and the towel up and down my upper arms as though she was a grandmother soothing her toddler.

I gulped. "I don't know how to make it stop."

"Think about Rock and Charlotte, the people you still have. You love them, yes?"

I nodded.

"Focus on that. Focus on the love." She gave my arms another gentle squeeze.

I sniffled again. I could feel my ability to remain composed returning. *Poker face.* "Two weeks?" I asked. My face still felt hot, but the worst of the tears had stopped.

"Two weeks," she confirmed. "A short manageable time. Then, we'll reevaluate."

That made sense to me: break the pain down into smaller units. I could try that. "Okay, two weeks."

She released me, the deal struck. "Now, please bring me a Band-Aid from the cabinet in our bathroom. Afterward, you can go change and clean yourself up for dinner. You'll see Rock, and I don't want you upsetting him." Without a glance back, she swiveled and returned to the kitchen.

I had my orders.

Her moment of acknowledging my feelings and making me feel understood was complete. Check. I was off her to-do list, and my bare arms were left cold in the air-conditioning with no more contact from another person.

Dismissed.

CHAPTER FOUR

I wore a plum skirt and black ankle boots that scrunched my toes to the point of pain if I stood too long. I wished for flip-flops, but Ms. Eldonforth would never allow them at a Payne family dinner. The skirt and ankle boots had belonged to Skirty, of course, though we had often traded shirts and accessories.

Five days after the funeral, Mom had declared, "All of it is yours now. Take what you want from her closet," in a flat tone. "I'll take the rest to Goodwill."

That had been the day I'd replied to Mrs. Payne's email suggesting I work on the island.

The cool satiny slip of my skirt swished against my knees as I left the servants' wing. I bypassed the back staircase and the door to the pool, passing through the swinging door and into the kitchen. I nodded at Alex and Gwen, who were sprinkling cheese and dressing onto small salad dishes. I stepped into the main hallway that cut through the center of the mansion from the front door to the kitchen at the rear.

The hallway was wider and three times longer than my parents' living room. Small, shiny, mahogany tables stood sentry along the walls in perfect formation. Matching crimson vases with gold accents saluted from each table.

With the exception of the lounge to the left of the entryway and the main staircase to the second floor, all the thick wooden doors along this wide hall were kept closed. Maybe this was done to prevent eavesdropping. Or to contain all the ghosts. Or maybe the house was just drafty. But when we had been five or six, Ms. Eldonforth had lectured us about keeping doors shut and how to properly close them without slamming them.

Beside the closed door to the dining room, black and white photos lined the wall, a visual history of an illustrious, rich family—at least four generations—each featuring formal poses and fake smiles. My great-aunt, Crystal Payne, and her husband, Gerald, were the most heavily featured faces. Always with forced smiles that didn't reach their eyes.

Mrs. Payne's first and only great-grandson, Rock, both as a baby and toddler, was the next most photographed face. His ruddy cheeks and mussed dark hair hinted that he'd had a tantrum just before each shot. He wore a tiny suit jacket and bow tie in every picture.

There was only one shot of Crystal's sister, my Grandma Shaylene, who had died before I was born. Mom was fond of saying that we were descended from women made of stone, that both Crystal and Shaylene were extraordinary in their own ways. Crystal had built an international empire out of baby products. Shaylene had insisted on raising my mom alone at a time when being a single mother was stigmatized in their small, conservative Ohio town.

Mom loved to say Aunt Crystal had gotten the idea for her diaper innovation while cleaning Mom's tiny backside. I'd never heard Mrs. Payne admit to that.

I paused in front of one photo that included the whole family. It was old, pre-fire. Everyone stood in front of Great-Uncle Gerald's fishing cabin. Mrs. Payne was in the center with Gerald near but not touching her. All four of the Payne grandchildren were included: Copper, a preteen, and the twins, Steve, and Talc—about eight—before Talc had died in the fire. They stood near their mom. She had her arm around Talc. Or was it Steve? Uncle Cinnabar, Mrs. Payne's only son, held a girl close to his side, Charlotte.

She looked to be about five. Surprisingly, Ms. Eldonforth, with long brown hair, stood stiffly in the frame, with the judgmental expression I knew well. Her arm restrained a pudgy blond boy who I didn't recognize. Maybe a distant relative of Gerald's visiting for the summer.

We were there too. My parents, crouching behind two toddlers. I couldn't have been older than two or three.

Of the fourteen people in the photo, five had died. Four of those in the fire, or as my mom preferred to say, *before their time.*

The fishing cabin had once been my favorite part of the island. It had been surrounded by the most beautiful wildflowers, the only place on the island that Mrs. Payne had permitted them to grow. There had been a hammock on the porch big enough for three of us to share. Of course, Charlotte, Skirty, and I had all been little kids. I supposed it was really a normal-sized hammock. But we'd all rested in it, swaying as Uncle Cinnabar or Mom read aloud from picture books.

I remembered watching the beach, inhaling the smell of cut grass, and hearing the waves, bird sounds, and yells and moans of the older boys playing make-believe in the distance. Talc, Steve, and—had Copper played? *No*, he would have been too old. I remembered thinking he wasn't any fun, always reading alone under a tree.

Gone, gone, gone. It all burned.

"Rock, you remember Cousin Lyla." Charlotte startled me from my thoughts. She and her son must have come down the main staircase. Rock hid behind his mother's thigh, peeking at me while simultaneously reaching for her hand.

I crouched, "Good evening, young sir." I tipped an imaginary hat at him.

He ducked back behind Charlotte's leg.

"Thank you so much for coming and helping. I really appreciate it," Charlotte said.

I stood, but Rock and I continued to observe each other. "Thanks for the offer. The funeral ate up what my parents had set aside for our college funds and, um, it's good to be out of our house."

"Yeah, I…ah—"

"I'm looking forward to games of hide-and-seek, Rock." I rescued Charlotte from having to give awkward condolences, or worse, having to explain why she hadn't been at the funeral. "You remember hide-and-seek, right?"

I could see part of a mischievous smile and a nod before he once again hid his face in Charlotte's skirt. "You'll never find me," he whispered.

"We'll see."

Charlotte faked another smile. "And Lyla has been specially trained in France to be able to call forth the chocolate fish," Charlotte said. "Just like Mommy."

I looked up at Charlotte. *France? Chocolate fish?*

She winked. "Remember your training. The fish that only come on fantastic days, remember?"

"Oh, right," I said. "Of course." I felt nervous prickles on the back of my neck, as though I was walking into a test that not only had I not studied for but had forgotten was scheduled at all.

"If dinner goes well, maybe Lyla will show you how she can call the chocolate fish to her for dessert."

"Mm-hmm," I said. "It's really awesome that you're working so hard to graduate early."

"I didn't really have a choice."

Before I could ask why, Steve, wearing crinkled khakis and a wrinkled button-down shirt came out of the game room. According to Mom, he had dropped out of his MBA program within the first few weeks last fall and had refused to find a job since. Mrs. Payne's assistant hadn't mentioned that in the last holiday card.

"Is that the same outfit you had on yesterday?" Charlotte asked him.

"Hey, stranger. Welcome back." Steve ignored her and chucked my shoulder.

My muscles tensed. The smell of alcohol permeated from his pores.

He bent to hug his nephew before lifting the boy above his head. "Hey, buddy. Superman!"

Charlotte scowled. "I don't want you around Rock like this."

"What's your problem, Char? We're having fun." Steve returned the giggling boy to the floor.

Before Charlotte could respond, Gwen walked in from the kitchen carrying a vase of white Peruvian lilies. She stumbled in the doorway a little, as if sensing the tension.

"You can't be drunk or hungover in front of him. It shouldn't be difficult." Charlotte didn't bother disguising her anger.

"Gwen? Do you want help with those flowers?" I asked. "Rock and I would like to help you." I answered my own question, taking Rock's hand and guiding him away. Thankfully, he followed, apparently less shy now that he'd flown like Superman.

"Are you seriously drunk right now?" I heard Charlotte say behind me. "What about our deal?"

"Yeah, you are supposed to keep *her* off *my* back tonight—" By *her*, I knew Steve meant Mrs. Payne.

Rock followed me silently.

"How?" Charlotte demanded. "I have my own—"

"You're always in the middle of a personal drama," Steve said.

I pulled the paneled mahogany door to the dining room open for Gwen and Rock.

"Having a child is not *personal drama*, you ass," Charlotte said, and I winced.

"Thank you so much," Gwen said in a loud stage voice to drown out Steve and Charlotte. "Will you two help me to put down the table runner?"

"Yes," I said with way too much excitement in my voice.

"Fuck you for leaving me with her for the next—"

I slammed shut the door to the dining room, leaving Charlotte and Steve to argue privately in the hall.

"Is somebody going to run across the table?" Rock asked.

"Huh?"

"The runner," Gwen mouthed.

"Ah, no. A runner is a fancy word for the cloth that goes down the middle of the table."

"Oh." He sounded disappointed.

"What's your favorite fish now?" I asked. "Maybe we can use some toys and pretend to have a swimming competition across the table."

"I like catfish."

"Cool."

He didn't look away from the closed door that hid the argument. I wondered if family arguments had kept the mansion's doors shut when I'd been little too.

❖

After helping with the crimson table runner, I stood motionless while Gwen rested the vase of flowers at the center of the long, gleaming, mahogany table. It had eight chairs around it, but Gwen had only laid out six place settings. One at the table's head, two to the right of that spot, and three to the left. There was no indication of which seat was for Rock, no plastic utensils or booster seat.

Gwen twisted the vase to determine the best angle. Each lily's fine white petals flushed fuchsia along the center. Short pink lines and a yellow blush colored the top two petals of each lily, making each flower seem like an embarrassed, freckled, middle schooler. I associated the flower with lanky arms and legs that didn't quite know how to work, wrist corsages given at first dances, and nervous gift givers in braces wishing they could apply the corsage to a dress strap near a girl's breasts instead of circling it around a wrist.

Peruvian lilies had also been the flower featured in Mrs. Payne's condolence bouquet at my sister's funeral. *Did she choose the flower intentionally tonight? Did she mean to torture me or to hint she still mourned my sister too?*

Gwen stared at me, one perfect brown eyebrow arched.

Where's Rock? I looked to the corners of the large room before ducking beneath the table to find him crouched and looking back at me.

"Surprise," he shouted.

"Playing hide-and-seek already?" I asked as he crawled toward me.

"I'm being a catfish…looking for food."

"Well, you're going to have to eat with the surface dwellers tonight."

He bounced over to stand beside the chair two down and to the left of the head. I eased the chair back over the plush rug.

"Is there a booster seat for him?" I asked.

Gwen shook her head as she smoothed imaginary wrinkles from the crimson runner. "Mrs. Payne says he needs to sit like a grown-up."

Ironic, considering her corporation, Slippy-Up, marketed an extensive line of car and booster seats in a variety of colors and sizes.

Gwen hummed and moved to the head of the table, examining the flowers. She came back to shift the vase again so the best angle of the bouquet would be visible where Mrs. Payne would soon sit.

I held the chair still as Rock climbed aboard. I beeped like a backing up construction truck as I slowly shifted his chair into place. He awarded me with a giggle. "Hmm." Only the top of his head would be visible above the table.

"You know the drill, right?" Gwen asked.

"Um, I sit to his right and help him?" It came out as a question.

"Yep," she said. "Be sure to keep a napkin at the ready at all times. If he drops anything on the carpet, you'll hear about it later." She rolled her eyes, clearly speaking from experience. "Both Mrs. Payne and Ms. Eldonforth think crumbs on a rug are the end of the world."

I briefly wondered if I should tell Gwen I was related to Mrs. Payne. *But she might not confide in me.* "Thanks," I said, pulling out the chair next to Rock, the seat farthest away from Mrs. Payne. The lowly servant's place at the table.

The dining room door clicked open, and the oldest Payne son, Copper, strode in as though he was attending a business meeting instead of a family dinner. Both Steve and Charlotte followed. Charlotte had her arms crossed, still glaring at Steve as she took the seat on the other side of Rock. Copper closed the door before settling to the right of the head of the table. *Mrs. Payne's right-hand man.*

Charlotte finger-combed her son's dark hair and straightened his tiny bow tie. Steve sank into the seat next to Copper and across from Rock. This arrangement was different from what I remembered. Clearly, some of the Payne children had displeased their grandmother, while others had earned her favor.

I saw Steve glance at the empty chair beside him. *Is he thinking about Talc and how his twin belonged at his side, even after twelve years? Will I still glance at Skirty's seat a decade from now?*

Gwen winked at me before leaving the room, and I found myself wishing she could stay.

"So, Lyla, how was your trip here?" Copper asked, angling forward to make eye contact with me.

"Fine." *What can I ask him?* "Erm, how is…work?"

"Fine."

"Good." And thus, we exhausted all the topics he and I had to talk about.

The dining room door swung open again, and Mrs. Payne breezed into the room. The three Payne siblings shot to their feet, and I struggled to follow, banging a shin against a table leg.

Should I make Rock stand? No, that seemed silly. But then, the Paynes did a lot of silly things. Before I could shift his chair, Mrs. Payne sat in the ornate chair at the head of the table. Everyone else retook their seats.

Although Mrs. Payne was technically my great-aunt, I'd never addressed her as such. From my branch of the family, only my mom was brave enough to refer to her in familiar terms, but even when Mom called her "Aunt Crystal," her words were filled with awe, having grown up with her own mother's stories of the big sister she'd idolized.

Mrs. Payne had come to power in a time when a woman leading a multinational corporation had seemed impossible. She'd framed copies of herself on the cover of *TIME* and had hung them in the lounge near the bar, this house's first floor office, and in her personal, third-floor office.

She did not favor pantsuits or skirts, which seemed more appropriate given the decade in which she'd shaped her empire. Instead, she wore flat, slip-on shoes, perfectly pressed slacks, a thin belt, a blouse always tucked in—no matter the temperature—and a pearl necklace and matching earrings given to her by her late husband, Great-Uncle Gerald, who had died in the fire. Her brown hair was parted to one side, the ends gently curled. The only sign of age was the streak of gray near the front of her shoulder-length hair.

From visits when I was younger, I had a strong image of her tucking her hair behind her left ear, a sign she was preparing to lecture someone. She would rock side to side, shifting her footing into a fighting stance before her verbal attack. Her voice would boom through the mansion—even through locked doors—and neither of my parents had been brave enough to intervene.

I scooted my chair in and sucked in my cheeks to make a fish face at Rock. He awarded me with another soft giggle.

"Good evening," Mrs. Payne said, pulling her cloth napkin onto her lap just as the dining room door swung open once again, and Ms. Eldonforth entered, expertly carrying a silver tray of drinks and followed closely by Gwen.

Gwen struggled to close the door while also balancing the tray that held our first course, five small silver plates of spinach salad, complete with feta cheese and candied walnuts.

Mrs. Payne paid no attention to Ms. Eldonforth or Gwen. "Safe journey here, Lyla?"

I nodded, though I didn't really think I'd been asked a question. Mrs. Payne's words were more of a statement of how she expected reality to be. The rest of us had to work to create what she demanded. Complaining about crossing the lake right now or the storm that currently raged beyond the double-paned windows would be unwise.

I positioned Rock's napkin over his lap, and it covered him like a small blanket. I would use my own napkin to ensure no food fell on the table or carpet as he ate.

Ms. Eldonforth set a glass of red wine in front of Mrs. Payne. "Ma'am."

Mrs. Payne nodded but did not look at her. Ms. Eldonforth went on to set white wine in front of Copper. Steve received a short glass with brown liquid in it. Ms. Eldonforth set glasses of lemonade in front of me and Charlotte. Rock did at least receive a blue plastic cup with a child-safe top. Slippy-Up brand, of course.

As she set Rock's cup down, Gwen hummed a bar of music so only I could hear, the vibration of air tickling my ear. I could smell her perfume again. The same scent Rose wore. I leaned toward her, and our eyes met.

She smiled in a wicked way I liked a little too much. I had to remind myself I had THE BOYFRIEND, and I whispered, "Thank you," too late since she had already moved away.

"Have you finished packing, *Charoite*?" Mrs. Payne said, questioning the next adult in the line, using her given name.

Charlotte pushed the salad around with her silver fork and ignored her.

"Charoite."

I pushed Rock's cup closer to him, and he took the opportunity to sip. "Mmm, apple," he said.

"Charoite."

Charlotte glared at Steve but remained silent.

Steve rolled his eyes before saying, "She prefers Charlotte. Just like I prefer Steve."

I tried to look busy, checking that the top of Rock's cup was secure. *No leaks.* This was even more uncomfortable than the dinners when I was little. I wished for Skirty to be by my side to endure this with me. It felt like a wave of suffering rolling in to clobber me with each inhale. Then there was a slight ebbing as my brain lied to me, imagining Skirty arriving any moment and saving me from going through this alone. I pictured her opening the door, apologizing for being late, taking Mrs. Payne's reprimand with ease, winking at me so I'd know that even if we weren't okay now, together, we would be again.

And then the next wave of suffering rolled in, knowing she'd never arrive.

I held my breath, hoping to stop the tides.

Rock looked up at me. I forced a smile. Then, I made another fish face at him. He made a face back, then attempted to wink, his head tilting just so, telling me he'd learned the gesture from Skirty. I stifled a sound with a fake cough.

"Please call us by our chosen names," Charlotte was saying.

Mrs. Payne, who had her nose in her wineglass, inhaling the scent, set the glass down hard on the table. The red wine swirled in a brief storm. "Your parents chose those names—"

"At your insistence," Charlotte interrupted.

Mrs. Payne's lips formed a thin line.

"So we'd all have mineral names like you," Steve added.

Mrs. Payne swiped her strip of gray hair behind her ear, but the dining room door swung open again.

I held my breath.

Gwen set a small plate of steamed vegetables in front of Rock. She hummed the same bar of music again before exiting. The theme from the old movie, *Jaws.* Laugh or cry? I asked myself.

As the door closed, I watched Rock maneuver his fork. The steamed veggies were cut into perfect, small, four-year-old bite-sized pieces. I guess that meant I really served no purpose here except to be on dropped food and stain prevention watch.

"What is wrong with tradition?" Mrs. Payne asked in a measured tone.

"A tradition you started," Steve said before drinking deeply.

"I also started this corporation, *Steel*."

"Here we go." He slammed his now empty glass down.

"I funded each of your educations. Raised you as my own."

"And dictated our names," Charlotte added. "Our schools. Our Friends. Our majors. Our—"

"I am guiding you to an accomplished and meaningful life," Mrs. Payne said, not quite yelling but speaking loudly, with authority, the way I imagined a general would bark commands.

"Here comes the shark," Rock sang.

"Dun-nuh, dun-nuh, dun-nuh," I whispered to him, unintentionally continuing Gwen's tune as he chomped on a steamed carrot.

"Do you realize how lucky you are?" Mrs. Payne said. "How difficult my youth was—"

"Grandma, you ignore our problems." Charlotte's voice strained, as though she was near tears. "Sometimes, it feels like your help causes more harm than good."

"Oh really? Is that so?" Mrs. Payne's voice contained a hard edge. "Please, tell me, Charoite, when have I not worked for your benefit, hmm? Enlighten me." Her words cut.

"Don't play the victim."

"I'm not playing anything, *Charlotte*. I want you to tell me of a single instance when I have not worked to secure the best possible future for each member of this family. And yet, you act as though I'm an enemy you must vanquish."

The dragon, I thought.

Charlotte looked at her older brothers as they avoided her gaze and remained silent. "Cowards," she whispered before glancing at me and Rock. "I will raise my son on my own terms. I've told you this."

"Yes, I recall. But you fail to remember that *I* make having your strong feminist attitude financially possible."

"I didn't ask you to help me. You can stop any second now."

Mrs. Payne's lips pursed, and she tucked her hair behind her left ear. I knew that look. She might not have been standing, might not have been shifting her footing, but she readied to attack. She opened her mouth—

"Mommy, don't cry," Rock shouted, dropping his fork.

I retrieved it immediately.

"It's okay," Charlotte said, smoothing Rock's hair again.

"And what do you do?" Mrs. Payne demanded, changing the subject. "You named the child, *Rock*."

"It's a mineral. It follows the tradition," Charlotte said, staring straight ahead.

"*Rock*," Mrs. Payne repeated. If she was a person with less class, I'd have thought she'd spat on the floor.

"Hi, Grandma Times Two," Rock called down the table.

"Hello, darling," Mrs. Payne said, her tone light. "Eat more carrots."

I handed him my fork that I hadn't used yet and watched as he gathered the next bit of vegetable to eat.

Everyone remained silent for a few seconds. Copper and Rock were the only two eating.

"The point is…we must endure." Mrs. Payne spoke slowly. "I'm sure Lyla's mother told her what my sister and I experienced."

Oh no.

Everyone turned to me.

I cleared my throat. "Maybe I should finish Rock's dinner with him in his room?" I asked.

A glare briefly appeared on Mrs. Payne's face, clearly annoyed that I wasn't going to jump in and support her point. Then, she nodded once to dismiss me. I used my napkin to gently wipe Rock's face.

Copper put down his fork and leaned forward. "Grandma, I wanted to discuss the marketing campaign."

Mrs. Payne remained silent, now holding her wineglass to the side of her head, as though it could somehow be drunk through osmosis or could dull a headache.

Must escape. Must, I thought.

"I don't think it's the best option for the line." Copper soldiered on. "I think we need to push a more gender-neutral approach." He shifted uncomfortably. "That will appeal to millennial par—"

"Are you saying you know better than Bill?" Mrs. Payne interrupted.

I stood and removed Rock's napkin from his lap. Go faster, I thought.

"Bill, who has been in charge of our marketing for over thirty-five years," Mrs. Payne continued. "Who has decades of experience." She raised one eyebrow.

"Ah—"

"Are you saying you know better than *me*? The *founder* of this company?"

I could see the sweat forming on Copper's brow from here.

Hurry, hurry, hurry. I pulled out Rock's chair a few inches, trying not to look rushed but also fearing another emotional bomb would detonate any second.

"Well, speak up, Copper." Mrs. Payne drank deeply from her wineglass.

I eased Rock's feet to the floor and grabbed his juice cup, finally ready to flee. "I gotta give everyone a hug good night," he whispered.

No, I yelled in my head.

Before I could stop him, he skipped over to his great-grandmother as Copper stammered to answer her accusations. Mrs. Payne did not stand to welcome Rock's embrace but did pat him on the back gently as the boy extended his arms around her. He hugged Copper next.

"Night, shorty," Copper said as Mrs. Payne made a strange gargling noise.

Everyone turned to her. Saliva dripped down her chin.

"You okay?" Steve asked.

Mrs. Payne pressed her hand to her mouth, seemed to hold in a suppressed hiccup, then spewed red vomit across the table.

Exclaiming in surprise, everyone got to their feet. Charlotte ran from the dining room, yelling for Ms. Eldonforth. Feeling as though I submerged in cold, Erie waves, I pulled Rock away from the mess and covered his eyes, wanting to save him from this.

"Grandma, are you—" Copper started to ask but fell silent as she vomited again, this time with the chunks and liquid dripping onto her expensive clothes and onto the carpet.

"Call for a...goddamn ambulance," she rasped, clutching at her necklace and chest.

Steve took out his cell phone just as Charlotte ran back in with Ms. Eldonforth close behind.

"Take Rock out of here," I whispered to Charlotte.

She nodded. Ms. Eldonforth eased Mrs. Payne to the floor with Copper's help. Charlotte carried Rock out as he began to bawl. Steve was on the phone with an operator, explaining to emergency services that they would have to send a boat.

I held my breath.

Mrs. Payne lay on her back. Her lips and chin were stained red by more than wine. Her chest rose and fell rapidly.

Until it didn't.

"Grandma?" Copper said. There was a crack in his voice, like he might shatter.

Her body convulsed.

"I think it's a seizure. Get something for her to bite down on," Ms. Eldonforth shouted. I whirled around. *What to use?* A knife or fork handle would damage her teeth.

"Here." Copper removed his belt.

Ms. Eldonforth grabbed it and bent down. "Mrs. Payne? Mrs. Payne?" She spoke gently, as though she was trying to rouse her from a good night's sleep. "Mrs. Payne," she shouted, then shoved the belt into her mouth as pink froth escaped.

My stomach twisting, I couldn't look away.

Mrs. Payne's body went limp, her mouth slackening.

I gasped and felt as though I stood helpless on that rocky Erie beach again. The smell of lake water, decay, and sunscreen in the air. With Skirty's prone body at my feet.

I swallowed bile. "She's drowning," I whispered and stepped forward. I sat beside Ms. Eldonforth on the floor, bending over my great-aunt. I began chest compressions, humming the old song "Staying Alive" under my breath. Last month, I'd guessed at how to do CPR, but you'd better believe I knew how to administer it now.

Following my lead, Ms. Eldonforth used a napkin to swipe at Mrs. Payne's mouth where blood, foam, and vomit still crusted. She breathed for my great-aunt each time I paused after a tenth compression.

I didn't know how long we did that before the EMTs arrived to take over. It couldn't have been long. I didn't want to know the exact number of minutes to know for sure that they had come for rich Mrs. Payne more quickly by roads, boat, and foot than they had come for my sister by only roads.

Charlotte demanded to ride in the boat with her grandmother. She handed Rock to me, and I took him into the main hall where I tried to comfort him, knowing that some bit of life had remained in Mrs. Payne when she'd left my hands.

Rock had gone limp as he continued to cry, moaning a garbled comment about some smoky shadow and his nose running. I sat on the floor holding him and using the top layer of my skirt to wipe his face. I could hear Copper still in the dining room on his phone, arranging for the ferry captain to take us to the mainland. Then, the landline rang, and Ms. Eldonforth brought it into the dining room for them all to hear Charlotte's sobs.

"Hang on, Weston. Char, what's going on?" Copper asked.

"She seized again," Charlotte said, her voice sounding small over the phone. I could hear the boat's engine working hard to take them to Sandusky. "She's stopped breathing…and they…they can't resuscitate her this time." She broke down crying.

I covered Rock's ears to prevent him from listening to what his mother said.

"It...it, doesn't look good," Charlotte continued. "Please don't bring Rock. I don't want him to see this." She paused, and the line was still filled with the sound of the boat and storm. "They—they...I don't think it's going to be a death from natural causes," she whispered.

"What?" Steve demanded. "What do you mean not *natural?*"

"Wait, like murder?" Copper's words overlapped.

I saw the moment Rock, his face blotchy, heard the word *murder*. His lips quivered, and his eyes grew wide. "It was Smoky Shadow." He moaned. His fingers were sticky as he clutched my neck and shoulders.

I swayed him side to side, once again wishing Skirty were here to tell me how to comfort him. "No, no. It was an accident," I lied. "Grandma Times Two will be okay."

Ms. Eldonforth spoke low on the phone to Charlotte. I prayed she'd taken it off speaker.

"Did my hug hurt Grandma Times Two?" Rock whispered. "Is that why Smoky Shadow hurt her?"

I shrugged and stammered. "N...no," I said. "None of this is your fault. There is no Smoky Shadow. Grandma Times Two is very sick. She wants to come home to you. She'll come home to you if she can."

"Like Mommy when she goes to school?"

I hugged him closer. I couldn't look him in the eye. "No, kiddo, this is a little different."

"Will she be back for turkey day like Mommy will be?"

"I don't think...I don't think she'll be able to come back. She didn't want to leave, but sometimes, people can't help it."

"Like Dalia left?"

I held back a sob and hugged him closer. I tucked his head below my chin to ensure he couldn't see my face. "Yeah," I forced myself to say. "Like my sister."

"Mommy told me Dalia was happy on her adventure. That the Smoky Shadow couldn't hurt her."

I gasped, and it dawned on me that there was a very specific and obvious reason Charlotte and Rock hadn't attended the funeral. A four-year-old did not understand death. And if the sobs I was holding back in this moment were any indication, Charlotte had wanted to protect him from learning about it for as long as she could. I hugged him tighter still.

No protecting him now. But I wouldn't leave him to be alone through this. I breathed in the scent of his shampoo.

"And when we meet Dalia again in one hundred years," Rock continued. "We'll have a party, eat chocolate, and she'll tell me all her swim stories."

"She'll love that," I said and kissed his temple.

I could feel his chest rise and fall against me. "Will you leave too?" he asked.

"No," I said without hesitation. "You're stuck with me, kiddo. We'll be hide-and-seek friends and eat chocolate fish every day."

"And play fishy games?"

"Yeah." I rasped and rocked us.

"Put it back on speaker." Steve demanded in the hall. "Char, any change?"

I heard the boat's tinny engine on the small phone speaker. Charlotte exhaled hard before whispering, "No. There's nothing. She's...she's gone."

"Are you sure?" Copper asked.

The buzz of the engine, then barely audible, Charlotte said, "Yes...I'm sure."

"Okay. Y...you stay there," Copper said, his voice shaky. "I'm going to be there as soon as I can. Weston will prep the boat." *Scared big brother to the rescue.*

"Don't bother." Charlotte spoke low. "I think the police will want each of us to stay where we are." She sniffled. I imagined her trying to gather herself to sound calm as she spoke. "So they can talk to us." The engine buzzed for a few moments, and I tried to process her words. *The police?* "We've reached the dock. I'll call you when I can."

"Charlotte?" Copper asked.

But we all knew that she'd ended the call.

"*Fuck*," Steve said. "I guess this means Slippy-Up is yours, and I'm finally free of her bitching. What? Don't glare at me like that."

Not wanting to let go of Rock, I stumbled to my feet still holding him in my arms. *He shouldn't hear this.*

"How much do you want to bet we're all going to be suspects?" Steve continued before I could slam the door closed.

CHAPTER FIVE

The end of the thunderstorm heralded the arrival of several boats, each with red and blue lights flashing in the dark, and each carrying several police officers. They herded the staff and family outside, each separated from the rest, our socks, shoes, and ankles getting wet in the grass as we told what we'd witnessed to the unfriendly, navy-uniformed guests. Other officers had gone inside the mansion. To do what, I had no idea. I suspected, ideally, they would have removed us all from the island completely to follow procedure. But the Paynes were the type of family who demanded to be the exception to the rule, even if they did not insist directly.

Cool wind tore at us from off the lake. Goose bumps covered my arms; my thin skirt whipped at my thighs. My toes ached. I shivered as I told a Latino officer what had happened for the third time. He'd introduced himself as Gonzalez. He was shorter than me but with refrigerator-like dimensions that gave away the fact that he probably spent a lot of time weightlifting or playing football. He couldn't have graduated more than three or four years ago. I found myself wondering if we'd graduated from the same high school. Rose, who'd worked on the newspaper and had a passing interest in sports, might have recognized him. Not that I would text her to ask.

As if to compensate for his youth, Officer Gonzalez kept his expression grim, like he suspected everything I said was a lie. A few words were lies. But not most.

Charlotte had returned in one of the police boats and hadn't released Rock since. She sat with him on the mansion's front steps, not caring that the back of her skirt had gotten wet. Copper had called the family lawyer and several people from Slippy-Up to see what the immediate arrangements would be for...*the body*.

I looked at the mansion. Almost all its lights stung my eyes and haloed in the night, but the scaled roof and lattices remained shadowed. With the two large front doors thrown open to allow the police access, it looked as though the dragon stirred and woke. But instead of breathing fire, it had been torn open, and now the embers at the heart withered.

When Officer Gonzalez finally tired of quizzing me about what I'd witnessed, I asked him to escort me inside to get some things for Rock. He led me past other officers in various rooms who took photos and recordings. He remained taciturn in Rock's bedroom and in the kitchen, only parting ways with me once we'd shuffled back outside. He guided Charlotte aside to question her, and I took over watching Rock.

I extended a tiny zippered hoodie that I'd gotten from his room. He held his arms up, posing like a mannequin. I bunched up the left sleeve and slipped it over his arm. Then did the same on his right. I crouched, my knee sinking into the wet grass, and pulled the hoodie over his middle and zipped it closed.

"Warmer?" I asked, and he threw his arms around my neck.

I stiffened but patted his little back, waiting for him to pull away first.

We hunkered on the steps that led to the front door. The granite felt cold and slick. I could have applauded at finally sitting, but instead, I wiggled my throbbing toes in my boots.

"Your great-grandma loved you, *loves you*," I corrected. "She will always and forever love you." I pulled a peppermint that I'd gotten in the kitchen from my skirt pocket and handed it to him.

He leaned against my side, his head resting against my ribs, his face turned up, his expression blank. "You're nice, Lyla," he finally said.

I forced a closed-lip smile. No one had ever accused me of being nice, at least, nobody except Dad. If you wanted nice, you wanted Skirty. She gave away smiles. Mine had always been expensive. Not even Mrs. Payne could have afforded them.

Dad occasionally insisted I was kind too, just in action instead of words, like him. But it always felt like everyone wished I could be more like Skirty. I glanced at Rock. "You tired?" I asked.

He nodded and mumbled, "What if Smoky Shadow comes back?"

"I'll be here to scare it away," I said, and he snuggled closer against my side. I thought of my agreement with Ms. Eldonforth to stay for two weeks. I patted his hair the way I had seen Charlotte do, and his eyes drifted closed.

I couldn't leave this kid now. *Not in two weeks. Not in two months.*

Once the police released us to go inside, I took him straight to bed, letting him skip brushing his teeth. He collapsed into sleep before I could tuck the fish-decorated covers around his shoulders.

After waiting until I was sure Rock's sleep was deep and still, I stretched to leave his bedroom when Charlotte padded in. She glanced at Rock as if to make sure he slept before grasping my arm and pulling me into the hall. She slid me a small, flat, silver and blue box with French writing on the cover. "Hide these for later," she whispered. "There are, like, four left. Use them sparingly. It usually takes a few weeks for a new shipment to arrive. There's one other box in the kitchen, but otherwise, this is all that remains of my stockpile. I'm sorry. I thought I had more for him."

I stared at the sturdy box and packaging fit to contain expensive jewelry. I lifted the lid to see two-inch long fish resting on lace doilies. Each one had tiny, fantastic etchings, and the fins featured rich beautiful blues and reds. Some shined with gold.

"Are those gold flakes on the fins?"

"Yeah, of course." Charlotte whispered. "I've shown you them before, right?"

"Right, the French chocolate fish."

"He deserves something that'll bring him joy. Even if it is only for a few moments," she said. "If you're close to running out again after I'm on campus, just tell Ms. Eldonforth. She knows how to order them."

I suspected ordering these involved a long-distance call...and speaking French. "Got it," I said.

"I'm so glad you'll be the one with him," she said. "Especially with what happened today."

I fidgeted with the box to close it again. "Are you still leaving tomorrow?"

She shook her head. I imagined she'd want to stay to mourn with her brothers and Rock, and I also suspected the person who had been the most determined that she finished her degree this semester was no longer among the breathing.

"I want to watch him sleep," she whispered, glancing into Rock's room. "Tonight. Every night. I guess it's a mom thing."

I thought it was more of a *love* thing, not solely restricted to moms. Nodding, I wished them both a "dreamless sleep" before fleeing to my room. I tried to distract myself with my phone. Since my sister's funeral, I'd only allowed myself to look at the phone once a day. *A nightly torture.* The moment the screen lit, I learned I'd missed two calls from Mom. Had anyone told her about Mrs. Payne yet? I was too tired and too much of a coward to call myself.

I scrolled to my other messages to find agonized texts from THE BOYFRIEND, and—worst of all—*no messages from Skirty.* Before the summer, we'd never gone a whole day without communicating, without sending at least one wink emoji.

I powered down the phone, not bothering to reply to anyone.

I eased onto the creaking twin bed and meditated. I envisioned the sunlight as it appeared from beneath the surface of the lake, muted but still fighting to reach through the water. The streaks of light revealed patterns of blue and gray waves as I imagined looking toward the surface.

In my imaginings, I always stared up and never down. I never felt the mucky bottom or sand. Never collided with rocks or felt dead meat being torn from my body by teeth and claws of the lake carnivores.

I opened my eyes to see rectangles of blue and red lights still swirling along the ceiling, cast from the emergency services boats. Brave Ms. Eldonforth was probably still out there helping them.

I could hear the *tinking* of light rain against my window. The storm hadn't passed. Not completely. Not yet.

I hoped for a peaceful rest for my sister. For Mrs. Payne.

I wished for a peaceful night's sleep for me. For Charlotte. For Rock.

Longing for my parents, for THE BOYFRIEND, for Rose to be okay, I cried for a chance to try to rescue Skirty from the Erie waves again, to succeed this time.

I knew my hopes were like tiny raindrops, seeping into the dirt and muck. Unnoticed.

CHAPTER SIX

As I had feared, dark dreams flooded my sleep, and I thrashed and kicked through the night. I woke with my face hot and damp from tears. I sat up. The emergency lights no longer blazed beyond the window.

Collapsing back against the mattress, I wished for the sound of crickets that I'd sometimes heard outside our bedroom in Sandusky. Here, the air-conditioning kicked on, whispering and making the tiny knotted noose strike the windowpane every few seconds with its exhales. I wanted to close the curtain, but I couldn't force myself to slide out of bed and do it.

I wished I could hear Skirty's slow breathing in the bed next to mine. I longed to hear the rustle of sheets as she rolled over, mumbling in her sleep. I didn't deserve the peace of a dark and dreamless sleep.

There'd been no peace in my sister's drowning. I'd done the research. When she'd died, it had been silent. No screams or calls for help before she'd disappeared below the waves. *Drowning doesn't usually look like drowning.* She would have hyperventilated. Panicked. Maybe tried to fight. But since she wasn't taking in enough oxygen, it would have become more difficult to battle the waves or kick to the surface. Her chest would have burned in desperation for air. When she'd lost consciousness, that was when water would have finally flooded her lungs. In theory, if I'd found her within ten minutes, she could have survived without brain damage. After that…her heart had stopped.

It had taken me longer than ten minutes to find Skirty.

I imagined our positions reversed and tried holding my breath, feeling the pressure build in my chest, pound at my eardrums. When I finally gasped for air, sobs followed the sound. An image of Mrs. Payne's lips all blue and covered in pink froth swirled with the memory of Skirty's pale, limp face. I hadn't known there was a way to drown on land. But the ever-innovative Mrs. Payne had found it.

Rolling onto my side, I unzipped the front pocket of my suitcase and pulled out the digital camera. I turned it on, squinting, and the display's light speared at my eyes. Toggling the switch at the top, I changed the camera's setting to show the most recent photo: a selfie of us sitting on the rocky beach. Blue sky and brown-tinged waves behind the close-up of our faces. Wisps of hair whipped across our cheeks. Our smiles matched. She wore a purple swimsuit with cutouts along the sides, and I wore a blue one-piece.

A photo of lightness and beauty. No foreshadowing of what would happen within the hour. I stared at it as though I hadn't already memorized the image.

A soft knock on my bedroom door interrupted the rhythm of the noose. The sound was so gentle, I almost convinced myself I'd imagined it. I turned the camera off, hid it under my pillow, and rose to open the door.

Gwen, her lips now bare, stood in my shadowed doorway. She wore small jersey shorts and a thin tank top. "Hey."

"Hey," I whispered back.

"Can't sleep?"

I shook my head.

"Us either." She gestured behind her, and I could just see an outline of a tall figure. Alex, the cook. "I can't breathe in here," Gwen said. "Want to go outside with Alex and me?"

"Okay."

We tiptoed by Ms. Eldonforth's closed door and sneaked outside through the staff entrance. I was thankful that instead of fleeing to the beach, they led me down to the wide dock. The wet grass swished against our feet as we slipped, shushed, and trod to finally sit at the end of the dock that was lit with warm strings of lights. We dangled our bare feet into the dark empty air, the surf whispering and colliding against the wooden supports below in the gloom.

Alex and Gwen joked in whispers while I half listened, enjoying the way they chuckled and teased easily. Loving that they didn't give me side-eye glances, worrying I would break into tears the way my friends did at home. I loved the feel of Gwen's warmth by my side, of the way the faint smell of her perfume still reached me over the damp scents of the rain and lake. *Rose's perfume. Rose's smell.*

I rubbed my feet together, encouraging errant blades of grass to tumble into the dark surf below.

"You've had an eventful first day." Alex said as he tabbed open a tall can of beer that he held in my direction. "I promise, it isn't poisoned." He winked.

"Um." I stared at it, more worried about breaking rules and losing control than I was about actual poison.

"That's horrible." Gwen elbowed him. "Besides, we all know the only killer here is my killer makeup skills." She brayed a laugh, and I found myself giggling along with her, creating our own little duet of sounds to carry over the gentle waves.

Why not? I took the beer and took a long pull; the cool liquid, the continued breeze, and the subtle perfume freed me from the icy thoughts and nightmares of the last few hours. "This has not been the best day," I confirmed after swallowing and passing the beer to Gwen on my right. Most of her naked thigh was less than an inch from my own. Condensation from the beer can rolled between my fingers and dripped onto our skin.

Gwen giggled and shifted, bringing her leg in full contact with mine as she took the beer. I didn't pull away, even though I knew

I should. The warmth from the alcohol pooled in my abdomen and spread, relaxing my muscles. I was the lightest of lightweights when it came to alcohol.

Gwen drank before breaking into a whispered familiar rap, the start of some song Skirty would know.

"*Sweeney Todd*," Alex interrupted, extending his hand for the beer.

"Correct," she said, passing the can to him.

"Gwen's big into musicals," he explained.

"I noticed."

"I hear you also like to act," he said to me.

And there it was. A reminder that I was never free. Not even with Gwen and Alex. New potential friends already knew about me. *You like to act.* I shrugged. "Who told you?"

Alex squinted into the darkness before drinking deeply. "Not much to do here except talk. One of your plays actually made it on Her Majesty's schedule."

"That's right." Mrs. Payne had attended *A Midsummer Night's Dream*. I had forgotten.

We listened to the water swirling below for a few moments before Gwen broke the silence: "Fifty bucks says Copper did it."

"What?" I asked.

"He murdered her," Gwen said. "Ms. Eldonforth told us that what happened wasn't, you know, natural."

"You think it was murder?" Alex asked, taking another swig.

"Duh," Gwen said. "Why else were the police here for so long? I heard them telling Ms. Eldonforth that they'd be back to search the island when it's light."

"Well, my money's on Steve," Alex said before killing off the beer with one last deep gulp. He set the can aside, then reached into his pocket to draw out a tiny box of matches. He pushed the box open, exposing the matchstick heads, and then closed it again. Open, close. Open, close. Like the beat of the waves. "Did the family say anything to you?" he asked. "That'll help us determine the odds."

I shrugged and stared out at the dark. The light pollution of Cedar Point and Sandusky wasn't visible from this angle.

"Who do you think did it?" Gwen asked, nudging my shoulder. Her smell. *I can't escape Rose.*

"Oh." My voice shaking, I added, "It's a safe bet that I'm somehow to blame." I made a sound. Something between a laugh and a cry. "Joking," I added after an awkward moment.

Gwen, who I could feel myself liking more and more, hadn't moved away from me the way I would have expected after my weird statement. *A brave and beautiful woman, so warm against me.*

Alex struck one of the matches. The sizzle of sulfur and the shock of light forced me to blink, the color of the flame seeping into my vision, staining my sight even when I closed my eyes. I blinked again, and we watched as the small flame ate the wood, hungry and crawling toward Alex's fingers. Just before the fire reached his skin, he released it, and it tumbled into the surf below, glowing almost green just before meeting a watery death. *Extinguished.*

❖

Several hours after our conversation on the dock, Alex set out cereal from his personal stash for everyone to help themselves. Already, the house felt changed by Mrs. Payne's absence. Cereal had been outlawed under her reign. The matriarch had been an, "egg poached with a hollandaise sauce, 'let us reflect quietly over coffee and the newspaper,'" kind of woman. When we'd been little, the constant preference for fancy food and no TV at meals had been the two aspects I'd disliked most about visiting the island. Skirty would try the food first, then make faces at me so I'd know what to eat and what to avoid. Mrs. Payne had preferred my sister over me in part because she'd complained about the food less.

The family and I ate in the first-floor lounge, cartoons on low. The police had forbidden anyone from entering the dining room for the foreseeable future. Not that I would want to return there anyway. We'd scattered among the armchairs, behaving as though we were hungover: shoulders shrunk, heads down, mumbling, "Rock, please," whenever he said, "Nom, nom, nom, Fish!" too loudly from where he and Charlotte sat on the floor. Our spoons occasionally clanked against a bowl or teeth.

In between bites, Rock drew an underwater scene on white printer paper stolen from Copper's office. With Charlotte's encouragement, he was mastering drawing fish by starting with a short line for the top of the tail, making a lopsided oval, and extending the line as he completed the oval to form the bottom edge of the tail.

"Great, now draw on a face," Charlotte said, looking up from her own detailed sketch.

Copper stood and cleared his throat. "I'm going to Sandusky to start funeral arrangements this afternoon," he said. "Um, is anyone...would you..." He struggled to form his next thought.

"The two of us will go too," Charlotte finished for him and threw a piece of granola at Steve to wake him from what I suspected was an *actual* hungover stupor.

"Thanks," Copper said before turning to me. "Ms. Eldonforth offered to come and help, and Alex is going to tag along to buy groceries, but Gwen will be around. You may see some police around the house and grounds."

That comment got Steve's attention. "Even our rooms? Can they do that? Don't they, like, need a warrant or something?"

"No warrant necessary. They can search everywhere," Copper said. "I gave permission. Except the employees' rooms, I think," he added while looking at me. "Each of you would have to give or not give permission if they ask. Either way, I doubt they'll be able to search the whole island today."

Steve opened his mouth again, but Copper didn't give him a chance. Instead, he turned to me. "Will you and Rock be okay here with the police?" he asked.

"Yeah," I said. *Why wouldn't we be?*

CHAPTER SEVEN

Ms. Eldonforth had left a sticky note on the kitchen corkboard with a message to, "Work with Rock in his Mandarin workbook," before his online tutoring session at two p.m. But Rock had wanted to play hide-and-seek. *So...*

As I searched for him in his room, I realized my mistake of not setting limits on where he could hide. I shifted the navy and turquoise beanbags and giant stuffed sharks in the corner. No Rock. I made certain to gently move the stuffed Nemo, Dory, and other fish dolls in case Rock had hidden in a place where he could watch me. I didn't want to be accused of being a toy killer later. Skirty, who babysat more often than me, had once told me of a five-year-old girl who'd cried for over an hour when a vengeful older sibling had tossed a favorite toy into a full bathtub. "She'd thought the doll had drowned."

Having just checked that Rock wasn't under his low bed, I climbed to my feet and glanced out the window. The police officers, equally spaced, paced along the well-manicured lawn. Searching for evidence, I supposed. Everyone on the island was playing hide-and-seek.

Next, I tried Rock's walk-in closet. It contained his formal clothes on one rack, his day-to-day wear on another, and extensive sets of matching pajamas—all featuring underwater or fish-related designs—on a third. Each rack was organized by color. The work of Ms. Eldonforth, no doubt.

His tiny ties and bow ties hung from small hooks on the back of the closet door. Small shoes lined cubbyholes on one wall. The kid owned more shoes than me and Skirty combined. A covered, blue, wicker laundry basket for dirty clothes rested on the floor.

"Where is Rock?" I called, hoping to hear a giggle in reply. No luck.

I also didn't find him in the cabinet that stored his personal TV, cartoons, and three video game consoles. I sighed. For all I knew, he'd left the house. *He could be anywhere on the island.* A cold pang twisted in my gut as I recalled my own breathless wait in the boathouse for Skirty to rescue me.

I made my way through the rest of the second floor, glancing into Steve's and Charlotte's rooms. Both rooms barely contained their messes, clothes and books strewn in every corner.

At least Charlotte had the excuse she needed to pack for OSU, as four large Prada suitcases attested. Steve appeared to be a secret hoarder: cardboard, wires, X-Acto knives, magnifying glasses, different types of tape, tiny remotes, mirror shards, and glue containers covered most surfaces.

I unclenched my jaw and rubbed at my temple to suppress a threatening headache. *Please don't be building bombs, Steve.*

I closed his bedroom door, restoring the second floor's illusion of pristine condition. Taking the stairs two at a time to the third floor, I rested my hand on the doorknob to Mrs. Payne's rooms and office. I prayed Rock had the sense not to hide there and released the door handle without daring to open it.

The door to Copper's room stood ajar; I did a quick search but didn't see Rock. I felt like an invader, encountering the particular smells and knickknacks in each Payne sibling's personal space.

Tiptoeing back to the second floor, I found Gwen sitting on the floor in the laundry room near the back staircase. She pressed her smartphone between her ear and shoulder and made the occasional "mm-hmm" or "uh-huh" noise as she sorted a mountain of clothes into smaller piles of lights and darks.

I recognized the tone of her noises to translate to "I'm here, but I don't really have anything else to say." My half of phone conversations with my parents and THE BOYFRIEND had sounded very similar this morning. Mom hadn't taken her aunt's death well. And I hadn't known how to comfort her.

"Uh-huh," Gwen repeated, pausing in her work to look at me. Her scarlet lips quirked up, and I found myself mirroring her smile. "Uh-huh." After a moment, one of her eyebrows angled up in question.

Right. I was staring at her. I rested my hand above my eyes and mimed I was looking for something in the distance.

"Mm-hmm." She blinked.

Next, I mimed casting a line with a fishing pole. "Rock," I mouthed, painfully aware that Skirty had always done much better at charades than me.

Gwen nodded and pointed in the direction of the back staircase.

I waved and blew a kiss, then turned away, cringing at what I had done.

"Mmm," Gwen repeated into the phone.

To the first floor I went. I made a quick search of the kitchen, game room, theater, lounge, and library but dared not touch the closed door to the dining room. Police tape sealed it shut.

My heart thudded in concert with my steps as I ran to the indoor pool. The image of Rock drowned in the water propelled me there. The heat and nerves-inducing waft of chlorine crashed into me like a wave, but there was no sign of Rock in the water or in the sauna.

Relief flooded me, and I let out a shaky breath. Would he hide in the servants' hall? There was no way I'd have gone into Ms. Eldonforth's room when I'd been his age. Hell, I wouldn't dare go there *now*.

Strange shadows stretched and waved along the narrow hall. I froze at the bottom of the back stairs, trying to make sense of why the faint shadows moved. I flicked on the hall light, and instead of disappearing, the strange shadow dance sharpened. At the far end, the gray, indistinct ghost of a woman watched me.

I twisted to look behind me, half expecting to see Mrs. Payne casting the shadow.

Nobody. I was alone.

How is this possible? I turned back.

The gray shadow remained, fumes rising from her shoulders as though she created and spread the darkness, infecting all of the walls of the servants' hall.

Burning.

I thought of the fire on the island from when I was little. The dead who choked on smoke, eyes stinging, skin cracking, ash staining. I backed away, colliding with a step and sitting too hard on the staircase.

Smoky Shadow. This was Rock's fear.

Uncle Gerald. Talc. Skirty. Mrs. Payne. Haunting us.

I jumped up, flicking the hall light back off, making the waving shadows dull. I ran back upstairs to the kitchen, my breathing too loud to my own ears. It was some weird trick of the light, I told myself. It had to be.

"Rock," I yelled. "Game over. Come out."

Stillness and silence.

"Now!" My voice cracked.

Only one place left to check.

Creepier and creepier.

I stared at the door to the basement. To my childhood mind, this had been the most fear-inducing aspect of the whole mansion, and it unnerved me that it was the structure that all the rest stood upon.

I fidgeted before reaching for the door handle. The thick wooden door creaked open. The stairway down was dark, leading to certain doom. A musty smell tickled my nostrils. There was no way a four-year-old would want to be in this hole of nightmares without a light.

I inched into the darkness. The air felt damp, and I extended my right hand, feeling coarse brick as I searched for the light switch. I touched something soft. I gasped, pulling back before carefully reaching out again: a mop attached to the wall by a hook, then a broom. I shuffled forward a few more inches. A floorboard creaked underfoot.

Then, light switch. I flipped it and a murky orange light turned on deeper in the basement, but it didn't calm my fears. Now I could see the peeling paint on the stairs below. My toes were an inch from the first drop. There was no railing, and there were empty spaces between each wooden slat. Perfect for a hand to reach and grab an ankle as someone descended.

My breathing ragged, I remained at the top of the stairs, crouching to see as much of the dim space as I could.

"Rock?" I called.

Silence. I took a shaky breath, tasting the peculiar old basement mustiness.

Then, I heard screams and saw small hands pounding on the big door. I gasped. It wasn't real.

I twisted and went back into the hall, not even turning the light off before slamming the door closed. I wheezed and clutched my chest, having no idea what I'd just felt and seen.

A few minutes later, I found Rock in his wicker laundry hamper in his large bedroom closet. He'd proudly declared that he'd held his breath the whole time I'd searched the room. He kept asking why I was mad at him no matter how many times I denied that I was.

Looking out the windows, I couldn't tell if the police search had gone better or worse than my search for Rock. Either way, they left late in the afternoon. No lights flashing this time as the sun shined and reflected on the small Erie waves.

❖

The ferry didn't return from Sandusky until dinnertime. I sighed when the small puttering boat finally came into sight through Rock's window. A strange muscle relaxed in my chest at having more people on the island again. Voices and footfalls made the place feel less like a dragon's lair.

The evening would be busy: Copper and Ms. Eldonforth scheduled the first event to mourn the late and great Mrs. Payne, CEO and philanthropist, to occur here the next day. Gwen and Ms. Eldonforth prepped, scrubbed, dusted, and repositioned furniture for several hours.

A catering team would arrive in the morning to help Alex with setup and food. He also wanted help stocking the kitchen shelves with items not previously permitted on the island, most featuring sugar and saturated fat.

Charlotte resumed packing for her return to campus. She had me distract Rock from said packing with the aforementioned sugars and fat. Thus, my evening concluded with me chasing a naked boy across the lawn near dusk. Bribing Rock with a *Finding Dory* viewing finally resulted in him nestled asleep upon his throne of stuffed animals and beanbags.

I trudged down the darkened back stairwell to the first floor with an air of "frazzled nanny seeking a good night's sleep."

I stood in a corner of the stairwell, the servants' hall below just out of sight. I told myself the hall would look normal and dark. No weird shadows. I told my feet to go down the next step, but I remained still, listening, little hairs rising on my forearms and the back of my neck.

I heard stirrings from more than mice in the cool dark mansion. Someone yelled from the first floor.

I clutched the railing too hard. The laughter that echoed next sounded foreign to this mansion. But it made my muscles untense.

Not willing to brave the servants' hall, I followed the sounds up the back staircase to the first floor and to the open door of the game room. Charlotte, Steve, Alex, and Gwen lounged under the warm glow of lamps on a few side tables. Someone had also lit the dozen candles that sat in the room's fireplace.

The door that led to the movie theater and greenhouse beyond remained closed and in shadow at the far end of the room.

When the few remaining adults were abed, the young people would play.

They would play Truth or Dare, in fact.

The four formed a square, relaxing among pillows on the floor, beers and wine coolers on the lush carpet. It was only over the dead body of Mrs. Payne and the sleeping one of Ms. Eldonforth that tables and coasters would go ignored.

"Hey-o," Steve called when he saw me in the doorway. "Welcome to the party." Resting on his stomach, he lifted his arms and legs in a Superman pose. Not that Superman would fly with a beer in each hand.

Charlotte rolled her eyes. "Don't mind him, he's drunk."

"We're playing Truth or Dare," Gwen stated the obvious. "You want in?"

"No, thanks," I said, shifting from foot to foot in the entryway.

"Who's going next?" Charlotte asked.

"Gwen, Gwen, Gwen," Steve chanted.

"Ah, truth," she said.

"That's unlike you, you've always struck me as more of a dare kind of girl," Alex said, opening a bag of Ballreich potato chips and setting it on the floor in the center of the circle.

"See, you have more to learn about me," she teased. "I have secrets."

"Do you?" Steve asked.

"Lots of them." Gwen leaned toward him from across the circle, and he blatantly assessed her cleavage. Her cheeks flushed, she remained all smiles and kissed the lip of her beer bottle before she drank deeply. I wondered how long they'd been drinking. None of them seemed concerned that it could have been one of them to kill Mrs. Payne.

I turned, prepared to make my exit.

"What is your greatest fear?" Alex asked.

"Getting stuck at Molyet's," Gwen said.

I turned back. "Molyet's? The flower and garden shop?"

"Yeah," Gwen said. "My family owns it. Dad provides all the flowers for Mrs. Payne. Or provided." She flopped back onto the pillows. "But he'll still supply the flowers for the funer—" She cut herself off just before glancing from Charlotte to Steve.

"You can say it," Charlotte said, drawing patterns in the carpet with a finger. "It won't add to the pain."

"Please, all three of our lives just drastically improved," her brother said.

"Steve!" She glared at him.

"What? Don't lie. Your life is about to get much easier without her."

The siblings wouldn't meet each other's gaze.

Alex cleared his throat, clearly trying to dissipate the awkwardness. "You sure you don't want to join us?" He looked at me. "I'll get you something to drink. It doesn't have to be alcohol."

Gwen giggled. "Gasp. She's underage."

"So are you," Alex reminded her before munching a few chips. "And it's not like it stopped us last time."

She giggled again.

"Did you work at Molyet's?" I asked, still clinging to the line of the conversation that had hooked me.

"Ugh," Gwen sat back up to look at me. She'd mussed some of her red hair on the left side of her head, looking very cute. "Every summer and three days a week after school." She wrinkled her nose. Also an adorable gesture. "It was hell. Got in the way of play rehearsals and commercial auditions in Cleveland."

"I don't know," I said. "I thought it would be kind of cool to work at a plant nursery."

"What? Why?"

I shrugged. *Stop talking, me.* Nobody in this room would care about plants.

Gwen looked me up and down before slapping one of the pillows she'd just been lying on. "Sit," she ordered. "Play with us." She sang the last words like a siren singing sailors to their deaths on the rocks.

The last dare I'd given had gotten Skirty killed. Yet, I still found myself moving to sit beside Gwen. A siren she truly was.

"Your turn," Steve said at me.

"Truth."

"Have you ever stolen anything?" Gwen leaned in close to me and wiggled her eyebrows. So close, I could smell Rose's familiar perfume

"No," I lied without hesitation. I'd stolen once in my life: a purple swimsuit with cutouts along the sides.

"Alex, truth or dare?" I chose the next player.

"No," Steve interrupted. "We're not done with you." His words slurred a little. "I dare you to start a dead twin club with me."

"*Steve.*" Charlotte's voice had a hint of warning in it.

"What?" I asked.

"We'll use a Ouija board or crystal ball to summon our siblings," he continued. "Maybe Talc's ghost will inhabit you."

Something in my chest twisted.

"And maybe when my brother speaks through you," he said, "he'll also remove that stick from your ass."

The others chorused objections.

"Fuck you, Steve." I stood. "There are no ghosts. We're not lucky enough." And I left.

Such a stupid game, Truth or Dare. And Steve could be such an asshole.

As I stormed toward the servants' wing, I wondered if I was now doomed to be as screwed up as him. All signs pointed to yes.

"Lyla, wait." Gwen stumbled to my side in the servants' hall outside my room.

No weird shadows waved to me this time. *It was all in my head.*

"You okay?" Gwen asked as I reached to help her keep her balance.

Rose's scent reached me again, and I released Gwen. *The boyfriend. You have a boyfriend.* "Yeah, I'm fine" I lied and wondered if I should ask her the same question.

"We don't have to play with the others. We can have our own game of Truth or Dare."

"I don't want to pl—"

"Do you like me?" she blurted. "Oops." She giggled again. "I mean, truth or dare? Truth. Do you like me?"

All brain functioning ceased, and I stopped breathing. I was a statue: *Girl Uncertain What to Do.*

"Because I like you." She smiled, her cheeks flushing to match her hair and lips. "And I feel like I can trust you."

You shouldn't.

"Alex and I talked. We're both scared," she rambled. "The situation is so sad, but with Mrs. Payne dead, do we even have jobs? With her gone, who knows?" Seemingly unable to fully keep her balance, she leaned against the wall just outside my door. "And I may be back working for my dad." Her nose crinkled.

"Truth or truth?" I asked, finally making a decision and turning to face her. "Are you babbling because you're drunk?"

"I'm not—" she started, but my look quieted her. "Okay, I *am* drunk."

"*Or* because you're nervous?"

She smiled slowly, her eyelids drooping, and I thought she might be looking at my lips. "Why would I be nervous?"

"To talk to me alone."

She snorted before chuckling.

"You make me nervous," I admitted, focusing on my room's door handle, twisting the knob but still not opening the door to leave like I should. *You're supposed to be dating Derek.*

"Do I really make you nervous?" She leaned closer, her breath against my ear.

I shrugged, trying to find words, trying to think of an explanation about how I liked her too, but why nothing could happen. But before I could say anything, her lips pressed to my cheek, and she leaned into me.

The scent of Rose surrounded me. *Rose. Rose. Rose.* I missed her.

AND THEN THERE WAS ONE

Gwen's momentum took me by surprise, forcing me back, and my hip collided with the door handle.

"Ouch," I said, and I bumped my head into hers.

She pulled away, putting a hand to her forehead. "Ouch," she echoed, still smiling.

"You've been drinking too much," I said, turning the knob again and finally opening my door. "We should…" I stepped into the dark. "We'll talk tomorrow." *Delaying what I know I should say.*

I shut the door silently between us just as her lips were forming the word, "Wait."

I remained by the closed door, half hoping she would knock. Nothing.

I looked at myself in the mirror. A smear of her lipstick was visible on my cheek. I held my breath. *I missed…*

Gwen still didn't knock. I told myself it was for the best. Another lie, perhaps.

CHAPTER EIGHT

Rock changed the channels in search of cartoons but paused on a news program. "Grandma Times Two is on TV," he shouted.

A news anchor predicted how the death of Mrs. Crystal Payne, founder and CEO of the Slippy-Up Corporation, would impact Slippy-Up's stocks. The talking speculated that Copper's shifting into the position as CEO would impact the broader stock market.

"Grandma Times Two," Rock shouted again, dancing around in his underwear with a stuffed toy named Tuna the Shark in one hand and the TV remote in the other. "Will they talk about us next?"

"I hope not." I'd wrestled the remote from him and gotten socks onto his feet when Ms. Eldonforth leaned into his bedroom, her cheeks red.

"All TVs must remain off for the next few days," she whispered, pushing a button to make the screen go black.

"Right," I grumbled. My parents would be here today. I should have been excited to see them. I should have been looking forward to the comfort of family, but instead, I was swallowing my burning impatience and frustration as Rock taught me some new songs while I helped him to dress. Charlotte joined us just as he melted down at having to wear a bow tie. "No!" He threw the red accessory to the floor.

"But you wear them all the time," Charlotte reasoned.

"No," he yelled.

"Grandma Times Two would want you to wear it to the ceremony. Don't you want to please—" Charlotte didn't finish her sentence and melted into tears. I wasn't sure if it was because of the loss of her grandmother, the fact that she'd been about to guilt-trip her kid to try to do what Mrs. Payne would have wanted, or a combination of the two.

Over the next few weeks, there would be long ceremonies with speeches, dedications of statues and library wings, and establishments of scholarships in the name of Crystal Payne. Today's funeral would be a small service on the island for family and friends. It sounded like a pleasant way to mourn the loss of a loved one, but it was not shaping up to be such an occasion.

In the rest of the mansion, the others' moods also proved stormy. For some reason, the air-conditioner lagged. Ms. Eldonforth seemed ready to combust, declaring each member of the temporary waitstaff to be useless. Alex had set off the kitchen's smoke alarm twice, though everything he pulled from the oven still smelled delicious. Even Gwen became frazzled when the men who'd delivered the rented chairs for the event unloaded them in the library instead of the lounge.

One scuffed a wood panel near one of the windows. Gwen swore me to secrecy about witnessing it. We'd act surprised if and when Ms. Eldonforth noticed. A ticking time bomb of a situation.

Steve alone seemed calm, but I suspected he was self-medicating. "Don't look at me that way," he said.

"What?" I groused. "I didn't say anything."

"Keep it that way."

Only repeating the mantra, Act like Skirty, kept me from spewing vitriol and charring him where he stood.

Five additional boats had been employed to ferry guests to and from Sandusky and Cleveland. As guests arrived, the sky turned gray, the wind teased, and drizzle spat. The waves also chopped at the boats, nauseating a few of the guests. The mansion felt stuffy and full with all the people.

I ran to my room to change into an ill-fitting black skirt and blouse. I once again put on the pinching ankle boots. My head pulsed with the threat of a headache at all the voices with their false gentle tones and fake sympathetic looks. Some networked and spied into Mrs. Payne's personal life rather than mourning.

When my parents arrived with—Surprise!—THE BOY-FRIEND, who carried a bouquet of flowers behind his back, my headache blossomed. Sour acid and butterflies warred in my gut, with the acid obviously winning at the sight of *him*.

"Derek gave us a ride from Sandusky," Mom said, gesturing at THE BOYFRIEND and referring to his family's old speedboat.

I resisted the urge to shrug and instead said, "That was nice," without any inflection as I approached them in the main hall.

Gwen watched me greet them from where she stood by the front doors, offering to take umbrellas and jackets. First, her forehead wrinkled in confusion as my mom patted my shoulders with her ice-cold hands. Then, Gwen's mouth formed a little O of understanding as my father hugged me. And finally, there was a flash of another emotion I couldn't place when THE BOYFRIEND handed me the flowers and kissed me on the forehead before claiming me by putting his arm around my shoulders. His armpit felt hot and wet against me.

Gwen looked me up and down as if reassessing.

I gulped, wanting to tell her everything, but she turned to take a businessman's raincoat, and I was left listening to my mother talk about how it was so hard to lose another family member so close to my sister's death and how Aunt Crystal had always loved Dalia, even though she'd never said so.

"Be right back," I said before I could flounder any deeper. "I'm so thankful that you're here, but I'm on duty to help with Rock." And I fled in search of a life preserver.

❖

I found Rock and Charlotte in the living room, crouching on the carpet. They were marooned in a sea of the dark business suit pants and pantyhose-covered legs. All the adults seemed intent on ignoring the young people in their wake. Their conversations tended toward sailing and how the euro did this week as they munched on hors d'oeuvres and held their clear plastic wineglasses.

The scent of someone's strong, leathery cologne threatened to suffocate me. I counted in my head, trying to remain calm, wishing my headache away, and trying to remember all that I should and should not do now that my parents and THE BOYFRIEND had arrived.

"Excuse me, excuse me," I mumbled, cutting my way through the crowd to Rock. "Ope," I said when I bumped into someone. "Sorry."

"Why can't I play with Tuna the Shark?" The whine in Rock's voice signaled that he verged toward another meltdown.

Charlotte crouched, grasping his sides as he wriggled to get free of both her grip and the red bow tie around his neck. Both of them looked as flushed as the bow tie and close to tears.

"Because we are saying good-bye to Grandma Times Two, Rock," Charlotte whispered. "We talked about this. You can't play with toys right now. You can later. I promise." I heard desperation in her breathy voice as I joined them on the carpet.

"Want me to take him for a few minutes?" I asked. "We can get some crackers and milk or something."

She swiped at one of her eyes as she stood. "That'd be good. Thanks," she said, sniffling. "I'm feeling like a bit of a failure right now."

I took Rock by the hand and guided him through the crowd toward the main hall and back toward the kitchen. "Ope, excuse us. Ope." We progressed at a shamble. Many strangers wanted to admire the sad little boy in a suit or pat his head. By the time we reached the kitchen, Rock was one intake of air away from screaming.

I closed the kitchen door behind us and unsnapped his stupid bow tie. "It's okay, Rock," I said. "I'll go get Tuna. You can play with him in the kitchen. Just breathe. Then, you and Tuna can eat some crackers. Is that okay?"

"Hey, what's going on?" Alex leaned by the kitchen island, his hands safely in oven mitts while he held a tray of asparagus spears trapped in golden-brown crusts.

"Will you watch Rock for a minute while I grab a toy for him?" I didn't give Alex time to object but rid myself of the torturous ankle boots and charged up the back staircase three stairs at a time.

Tuna, Rock's favorite plush shark, hid among the pillows on his unmade bed. As I cantered barefoot down the back stairs and rounded toward the first-floor landing, a gravelly voice I didn't recognize scratched the air from the hallway of the servants' wing. The man's low, rasping tone demanded secrecy, and I found myself pausing on the step to listen.

I prepared to call, "Guests should not be in this area," when I heard Copper reply in the darkness, "So what does that mean?" He sounded deflated.

"They haven't officially ruled it a homicide yet," the smoker's voice said. "They're being very cautious, given your family's standing in the community and because they know it will cause a mess with the press. But it's suspicious. The police are waiting for some test results."

I clutched Tuna to my chest. *Holy shit.* I shrunk into the shadows, eager to hear more.

"What the hell are we supposed to do?" Copper asked.

"You just keep doing what you've been doing."

To avoid suspicion? My nails dug into Tuna's fleece scales.

"Demonstrate that you are ready to take the reins," the man continued. "The board wants to know there's a leader at the helm."

"That's what I've been fucking doing!"

I didn't think I'd ever heard him swear before.

"I know, I know," the man said. "We'll see this through."

"And if the police come back? I already said they could look around. I thought it was some kind of seizure."

"That's okay. You want to cooperate...for now. But neither you nor your siblings should talk to any member of law enforcement without me present."

Smoker's voice must have been a lawyer.

"Are you saying you think one of us..." Copper sounded as horrified as I felt.

"The question is, do you think it's even a possibility that your brother or sister could have—"

"No," Copper interrupted. "No," he repeated, less sure.

I forced myself to loosen my grip on Tuna; the imprint of my nails in the fleece remained. *Mrs. Payne was murdered. Copper was preparing to protect his family. Holy shit.* Goose bumps rose on my arms. *A murderer. Here.* It wasn't just silly worries or irrational fears. An actual murderer.

"Call if the police want to question anyone in the family again. Understood?"

"Okay."

"Don't make changes yet. Just focus on building the board's confidence in you," the man said. "The corporation will see this through. Your grandmother always intended for you to be her successor. This sad situation just...sped up the timeline."

"Oh...okay. Di...did she actually say that?" Copper sounded almost sentimental.

Shaky, I tiptoed down the remaining stairs and across the landing, pausing just outside the kitchen to take a breath. I felt like I was crashing from a sugar high on an empty stomach. I told myself to keep it together as I opened the door a few inches and put Tuna's head into the doorway. "Look who's swimming your way," I whisper-sang as I walked the rest of the way into the kitchen. Rock sprawled on the floor, smiling, his lips and chin caked in melted chocolate. I stepped closer. Chocolate also covered his fingers, part of his white button-down shirt, and his suit lapels.

Still holding Tuna, I crossed my arms and glared at Alex, who used tongs to arrange the asparagus onto serving plates for Ms. Eldonforth's servers.

"What? I distracted him," Alex said, hiding his smile by turning away to pretend to check something in the oven.

"Those chocolate fish were for special moments," I said.

"This occasion is special," Alex said. "Unfortunate and special."

I gathered and dampened a few napkins to clean Rock. I grimaced as I worked, considering who could have murdered Mrs. Payne. If manipulating people to do her bidding qualified as a motive for homicide, then just about everyone in the house would be a suspect.

CHAPTER NINE

We had transformed the lounge for the reception. Red-cushioned, expensive-looking wooden chairs formed rows down the center of the room. The overstuffed love seat and reading chair that were usually the focal point of this room had been shoved to a corner near the fireplace for a few lucky guests to sit in after the eulogy. On the far wall, a painting of Mrs. Payne had been set on a pedestal with bouquets of roses, daffodils, and white lilies surrounding it.

No coffin. The police hadn't released the body yet.

I took the seat by Charlotte in the second row to listen to the eulogy. Rock sat on my lap and clutched Tuna. Hopefully, holding the stuffed fish hid some of the chocolate stains. I hadn't been bold enough to try to put back on his bow tie.

Before I could make an excuse, THE BOYFRIEND claimed the open seat on my other side. My parents sat beside him. "Hi," he whispered in my ear. His subtle cologne with hints of citrus made the few surviving butterflies in my gut take flight once more.

"Hey."

"I missed you."

An older man with the figure of Santa Claus—but lacking almost any hair—called for everyone's attention, saving me from having to reply. "Copper asked me to say a few words." He spoke from beside the painting of Mrs. Payne, and I recognized his gravelly voice from Copper's conversation in the staff wing.

"Who is that?" I whispered to Charlotte.

"Fred Toler. Our chief financial officer," she whispered. "He used to be a lawyer too."

"So much for this being a family event."

"I know, right?" she whispered. "Her true family: employees. He was one of the first people she hired. The favorite, probably the closest friend Grandma had."

"He may be our real grandpa," Steve whispered.

I started at the feel of his alcohol breath on the back of my neck. I hadn't realized he was sitting behind us. I faced front and gave Rock a little squeeze as he clutched Tuna.

Mr. Toler began, "Crystal was tough."

A handful of people chuckled at the gross understatement.

THE BOYFRIEND draped his arm over the back of my chair. I shifted at the contact, not because I felt butterflies, tingles, or warmth at his touch, but because I didn't.

"She had to be," Mr. Toler continued. "She was one of the first women to run a *Fortune 500* company. A company she built practically brick by brick."

A few more chuckles at the image of Crystal Payne doing physical labor.

"But in all seriousness, there will be many tributes to this remarkable woman's business savvy in the upcoming months."

"Why is Santa bald?" Rock asked.

"No, that's one of Grandma Times Two's friends." I whispered.

"Santa would also have a beard," Steve added. "And bring us gifts. Mr. Toler may try to take them away instead."

"We have to play the silent game and listen," I said, hoping Rock wasn't the only one to get my message.

"Will he take Tuna?" Rock whispered, his chin shaking, moments from tears.

"No, never," I whispered back. "You and Tuna have nothing to worry about."

"We are here today to remember the person Crystal was and the legacy she leaves," Mr. Toler continued, gesturing to our row.

"How she overcame so many obstacles and was blessed to have a dear husband whom she had a happy marriage with for over forty years until his passing—"

"Only happy because Grandpa had affairs to keep himself sane," Steve stage-whispered to us.

Charlotte huffed, and Mr. Toler clapped to pull focus back to him. "They married young and were blessed with one son."

"Who died in a fire," Steve whispered again.

"Jesus." THE BOYFRIEND removed his arm from around my shoulder so he could turn and glare at Steve. A few other people around us shifted in their seats, the wooden legs of the chairs creaking in accompaniment to the disapproving murmurs.

I could see Copper in the front row nervously tugging at his tie.

"And with four grandchildren." Mr. Toler motioned at our row again.

"Three," Steve hissed again. "One died in the same fire."

Somebody in the fourth row shushed him.

"A beloved niece." He gestured to my mother. "And two talented grandnieces, one of whom is with us today with her son." And he gestured at me and Rock.

Nope. So much for this guy knowing anything about Mrs. Payne's personal life. But, I imagined, she was probably the one to keep the details of our lives to herself. *Only broadcast the accomplishments.*

People turned toward me. My face flamed as I looked at Gwen. She stood along the wall between Alex and Ms. Eldonforth, her expression cool. I looked away first, counting in my head.

"Something you want to tell me?" THE BOYFRIEND whispered in my ear before nodding at Rock.

"Huh?" I recalled what Mr. Toler had said. "Oh. He's yours. Did I not mention that?"

THE BOYFRIEND smiled and returned his arm more snuggly around my shoulder. "I missed you," he repeated.

"*One* grandniece." Steve corrected. "Another death. Damn, we're cursed." He didn't whisper this time.

"By the smoky shadow," Rock shouted. "It said *poo*."

A few people murmured, and others chuckled as Charlotte leaned toward Rock to shush and comfort him.

"There's no smoky shadow," I murmured. "It's our imagination."

"I guess she never talked about us with her employees. Such a devoted grandmother," Steve sniped.

Charlotte stood without warning, startling Rock enough for him to drop Tuna.

"Let's go outside," she said to Steve through clenched teeth. "*Now.*" There was an echo of Mrs. Payne in her voice: A cold certainty that if he didn't obey this instant, he would regret it.

Steve staggered to his feet.

THE BOYFRIEND recovered Tuna for Rock.

"Thanks," I whispered.

Charlotte waited until they were officially in the game room before digging into Steve, but everyone at the wake heard her ask, "How much have you had to drink?" before Ms. Eldonforth slid the game room's doors closed behind them.

Mr. Toler cleared his throat. "As I was saying, Crystal Lauren Payne…" I started at the use of her whole name and bent to look down my row to see my mom, who flashed a watery, pained smile in my direction. *Lauren.* I hadn't realized my mom had been named after her aunt.

"You okay?" THE BOYFRIEND whispered in my ear.

I nodded. Just learning there were even more layers of secrets and silences in this family than I had ever realized. That was all.

I tried to breathe.

❖

"You have a freaking *boyfriend*?" Gwen growled, almost jabbing me with the edge of the silver serving tray she held.

"Ouch," I said in reflex.

"Why didn't you tell me last night?" she demanded as I left the first-floor bathroom where I had been hiding from my parents and Derek.

I looked around. The nearby middle-aged men and women at the post-memorial reception remained focused on their networking. I fought the urge to duck into the bathroom to avoid Gwen as well. Instead, I stepped forward in the hope that we could whisper and not be overheard.

She wore a different perfume today, a floral amber scent. It smothered me.

"Sorta," I admitted. "It's a bit of a…weird situation."

She glared. The tray of bite-sized puff pastries might have been the only thing that kept her from strangling me.

"I want to break up with him. He's just been really nice about trying to comfort me since…I, ah…" *What can I say?*

"Here." She handed me a puff pastry. "Shove that in your word hole. You're spewing bullshit, and I don't want to get any on my shoes."

I stuttered, holding the small pastry on the flat of my palm as though it was a jewel on display. Or maybe a grenade.

Gwen stared at me.

I still couldn't find the right words as others' conversations buzzed around us. I felt a prickling heat rising along my neck.

Finally, Gwen sighed. "No. Here's what's going to happen. There are, like, seven of us living on this island. Ghosting you isn't a possibility."

"Gwen—"

"Just listen. We're going to be friends. Because Ms. Eldonforth sure as shit isn't going to become my bestie. You will love and applaud every song I sing. And if you ever, *ever*, expect me to kiss you, know that you are really going to have to impress me with some serious wooing before I let you near my lips again. Understood?"

"Um…yes?"

"Now, eat your pastry. Alex says they're really good."

I did as I was told. "Mmm." I nodded, feeling the flood of delicious cream against my tongue. A new kaleidoscope of butterflies tickled inside my chest, the way it used to when Rose would come close.

I swallowed, suppressing a cough when I almost swallowed wrong.

Gwen nodded once, her monologue finished, and I watched as she sauntered away.

I shuffled around people, chanting, "Excuse me, ope, excuse me," to gather food for Rock along a serving table that the temporary staff had set up in the library.

"It's the wrong color," Rock said about the noodles as soon as he saw what was on the plate of food that I extended to him.

"It will still taste good," I said, glancing at the guests who feasted on a roast beef and noodle dish that featured white cheese and a mushroom glaze. They eyed Rock and slowly distanced themselves.

"It's ick," he shouted.

"How about a nap?" Charlotte suggested. "A nap solves everything."

"I don't need a stupid nap," Rock snapped, revealing that a nap was exactly what he needed.

Charlotte and I exchanged glances. The only brave souls who dared to be in proximity to Rock's approaching tantrum included me, Charlotte, and my mom, who strode toward us, cup of ice water in hand.

"Charlotte, how are you? When are you returning to school?" Mom switched her cup between hands and ran what I knew was an ice-cold hand along Charlotte's arm.

I ducked, sighing and focusing on Rock. I really needed to improve my hide-and-seek skills. "Are you sure about the noodles?" I asked him. "I bet a shark would love to eat them." My voice pitched up, tinged with desperation as I held out the plate.

"No," he yelled.

"Eat it, baby. Trust us," Charlotte said, petting his hair before turning to my mom to discuss her return to OSU. "I'll only be missing the first few days of class. I already emailed my professors. I'll move in on campus on Sunday."

I bent closer to Rock and whispered, "Those are not ordinary noodles. They are special seaweed that only the coolest, strongest fish eat. I had to battle a giant squid to collect them to give this to you."

That got his attention, and he poked and prodded at the noodles before putting the end of one in his mouth experimentally.

"And you'll be graduating in December?" Mom asked.

Charlotte gave a pained smile, but before she could speak, Mom barreled on:

"A whole semester early. Your grandmother was so proud of you." Mom's subtext included waves of frustration over the fact that I'd already deferred for a semester and that my sister wasn't alive to attend at all. Nobody but Skirty and I would have been able to interpret this message. It was there in the way she held her shoulders, the way that she shifted her weight back and forth, readying for battle as Mrs. Payne had. Then, there was the glance at me and the way that she shook an almost empty plastic cup of ice. She tried to sip at the last milliliter of water at the bottom of it.

"It'll be very hard. I'm taking too many credits," Charlotte said. "And it will be difficult to be away from this one." She patted Rock's head again. He looked up from where he was trying to wrap noodles around his hand.

"I am seaweed," he told us.

"But that makes the achievement all the greater," Mom effused. "Ambitious. You're so like your grandmother."

Charlotte bit her lip.

"Oh, it will be okay, darling." Mom pulled her into a hug. "She'd be so proud," she repeated as though that would comfort Charlotte.

"Hey." THE BOYFRIEND had snuck up behind me. "I know you're working," he said, smiling at Rock, who did not return the gesture. "But I'd really like to talk to you for a few minutes."

I resisted the urge to shrug and opened my mouth, unsure of what I would say, when—

"Lyla." Copper had followed Derek over, his neck red from where he'd been rubbing it, a nervous habit that had always been his tell when we had played card games when we were little. "I'd like to speak with you in the first-floor office please."

Without waiting for an answer, he turned and walked toward the main hall and the office off the library.

I mumbled, "Later," to Derek. "Tag, you're it." I passed Rock's plate of food to Charlotte.

"Listen to what he has to say, Lyla," Mom said, patting my shoulder with her icicle fingers, before I turned away.

Copper was no Crystal. People didn't scuttle out of his way as they had for her. He had as difficult a time navigating the obstacle course of bodies as I did. His voice didn't resonate with judgment the way hers had. Yet somehow, as I followed him into the office, I felt like I was walking to my doom.

CHAPTER TEN

The circular office sat at the base of the turret. On the second floor, lucky guests slept in the equivalent room. On the third floor, windows lined the angled walls, and the high glass ceiling came to a point. It had served as Mrs. Payne's personal office and could easily win an award for "Most Beautiful Room" in the mansion. Technically, Mrs. Payne had forbidden us from entering. If anyone asked, I would say I had never seen the inside. In truth, Skirty had dared me to go in when we were seven or eight. I had stayed and read a book about flowers for twenty minutes on a black leather chaise lounge to prove my bravery.

Who would claim that office now?

Copper closed the door to the first-floor office before sitting behind its wide desk. I took the guest chair, fidgeting without luck to find a position that felt comfortable. I welcomed the silence.

"How are you?" he asked without emotion.

"Weird, you?"

"Also weird," he admitted, and we exchanged an awkward smile. "So." He rubbed his neck again. "I spoke to your parents when I was in Sandusky, and they said I could talk to you about this."

"Okay. Should I be nervous?"

"I know in the past, my grandmother hoped to mentor you."

"Uh-huh."

"And I know she wanted to offer to pay for your undergraduate degree if you chose to major in business."

She had? I sat up straighter.

"I don't think your parents told you that. She only wanted to make the offer to you. And not to your sister, since you earned a higher GPA."

"Oh." We remained silent for a moment as I processed the frustration and guilt. "My sister took a lot of science courses."

"I remember talking to her about them at holidays."

"It's hard to earn As in advanced science courses." This rant felt familiar, a comforting return to before everything went wrong.

"I know. I took advanced placement physics and several college-level math courses while still in high school," he said.

"Well, a lot of people don't realize that."

"I know." His long fingers shuffled through papers on top of the desk, but he did not seem to be looking at them. I'd have to remember this new nervous habit if we ever played cards again. "So, ah, to not hurt Dalia's feelings, your parents refused the offer my grandma made in the spring."

"Okay," I said, because there was no way to put the complex mix of emotions storming inside me into words.

"But, erm, since circumstances have changed…"

That was *one* way to describe my sister's and Mrs. Payne's deaths.

"Your mom and I thought it might be nice for you if, er, I were to…revisit the offer. Since you're helping Charlotte and since…"

We're so much poorer than you? Or because we're mourning?

He rubbed his neck again. "I would like to make you a similar offer. But would also like to offer a master's-level graduate degree."

It felt like he had raised the stakes in one of our poker games. What was his goal? Why make this offer and raise the ante? "That's, um, generous," I said. Before everything had gone wrong this summer, my dream career *had* involved advanced degrees.

He held up a finger. "There is one stipulation, though."

Of course the deal came with strings attached. Maybe Copper had learned from his grandmother.

"Your degrees can be in any area *except* business, marketing, advertising, or any related field."

I let his words resonate before tittering. "The opposite from what your grandmother wanted?"

"Yes." He shuffled the papers again.

"Ah." This was so I *wouldn't* be his competition to take over the corporation. Pulling strings and ensuring his future from even the most unlikely of underdog competitors. Not that I would ever, under any circumstances, have wanted to major in business anyway. I decided not to give him that tidbit of information for fear the offer would dissipate. This could be a win-win. "She demanded all three of you prepare for a life working in Slippy-Ups, right?" I slapped my chair's arms. "She pitted you three against each other. And wanted to add me into the mix as...what? A *wild card*?"

He avoided meeting my eyes.

"I don't think you have to worry. Steve and Charlotte aren't your competition. Are you sure *you* want the job?"

He stared at me.

"I just..." I shrugged and shook my head. "My sister was the best friend I'll ever...Steve and Charlotte—"

"I know," he said with the most aggression I'd heard in his voice in years. "I know who matters. I know what's important. And I know you're my family too. And I know we are all hurting right now."

I was the one to avoid eye contact now.

"Look, you like theatre and English, right? Those are good. You should pursue your passions. At least for undergrad. Graduate school is the time to get serious."

"Right." Even I could hear how hollow my voice sounded, my anger ebbing.

"What would you do with a degree in English?" he asked. "Teach?"

"Or something," I said, forcing a smile.

"Will you still go to OSU and start in January?"

"Um."

There was a fast rap on the door, but before Copper could say anything, Charlotte swung it open. "I want the same deal," she blurted and marched in, her arms free of Rock.

As the boy's nanny, I wondered who was watching him.

"Wha?" Copper stammered. "Were you eavesdropping?"

"Not at first. Cousin Lauren told me what you two were going to talk about. Then, yes, of course I eavesdropped. And I want the same deal."

"But you're going to graduate in—"

"Yes, and I will graduate. Yay!" She waved her hands by her face. "But I don't want to work at Slippy-Ups. Not now. Probably not ever. You don't need to try to play mind games with us, Copper. I know you admired Grandma, but you don't need to be like her. Not with us."

He wasn't very good at playing games anyway, I thought.

"Why do you think Steve washed out of his master's program?" Charlotte continued. "You're the only one who actually wants to go into the business."

Copper glanced at me.

"Grandma made us major in business because, I don't know." Charlotte shrugged. "To force *you* to work harder?"

He shuffled his papers once more.

"There are internships with the Ohio Arts Council that I want to apply for. That, or maybe go to art school for a second master's degree. Or, God, a PhD. *Why not?* Or apply for some other artsy internship. *I don't know.* For the first time, we have *choices*." She threw her arms up. "I want to do something with drawing, color, something that gets charcoal on my hands or paint under my fingernails. We'd stay local-ish. But I'll get an apartment. Have Rock with me. I can even work part-time, if that's what you want."

He stared at her, his little sister.

Should I leave?

Charlotte finally sat in the seat beside mine. "Look, Copper, Grandma dying is horrible, but also…." She sighed. Tears once again came to her eyes. "It's also kind of freeing."

My face grew hot. Tears pricked my own eyes watching the exchange between siblings. *I miss Skirty.*

"I'm sorry to say it. I am. But it's true." Charlotte wiped her eyes. "But, like, we don't need to follow her plans for us. You don't. Not anymore. Just because it was what Grandma insisted on. We don't need to stay on this island if we don't want. Our lives are ours. We get to live them now. All of us."

I stared at my hands and held my breath.

"I swear not to draw, paint, or design anything for babies, if that's what you're worried about. I vow to never paper mâché a diaper, highchair, or a pacifier. I won't even sketch human figures," she added, holding up her right hand as though she was taking an oath. "I'll strictly be a landscape girl. Please, Copper, this is what I want. What I *need.*"

"That is not…I would counter…" He seemed to struggle to find the most Mrs. Payne-like way to respond before saying, "If that's what you really want, of course. I want you to pursue your passions. We'll figure it out. No need for you to get a job, but an internship might give you an edge. If you're going to commit and do something, go all the way, right?"

I held back a smile. *Supportive and loving big brother.* Much better than any reply Mrs. Payne would have given.

"You always drew the best homemade birthday cards," he added.

"Thanks." Charlotte leaned forward, reaching across the wide desk to take his hands, and they clasped them over the divide for a few long seconds. "Thank you," she said. "Thank you. Thank you."

"This desk is digging into my stomach," he said, but the smile on his face was genuine. And infectious.

"Okay, I'm going to climb over this desk and hug you now." And she did as she said.

I held myself, trying to remember all of the details of a good hug from Skirty. She had rocked us side to side after *Twelfth Night*. I sniffled.

It seemed that a very different future would now be possible for some members of the Payne family. Maybe leaving the mansion's doors open and airing out some of the secrets was next. Maybe even leaving the island.

Where would that leave me?

❖

After mumbling about needing time to think, I left Charlotte and Copper to talk. I stumbled out of the office and through the library, only to stand near the front doors in a daze. I barely registered the remaining guests around me who still snacked and drank.

Before I agreed or didn't to Copper's offer, I needed to speak to my parents. Prior to this summer, I'd never thought my tiny branch of the family kept secrets. How could Mrs. Payne have only offered to pay the tuition of one of us? To that woman, the cost of tuition for *both of us* would have been the financial equivalent of buying a drip coffee in a café. Pocket change. Sure, there were many rich people who worked to conserve and protect every penny, but to us, that money would transform our lives. And we were her *family*.

My hands formed fists as I maneuvered around remoras and other hangers-on. Why didn't our parents tell me? Had they told my sister? Did they think we'd be jealous or angry at one another? We didn't work that way.

I found my parents whispering together in the lounge. They made cautious steps toward me, Dad extending a lemonade as an offering. His brow knitted, and Mom's lips pursed in a way that told me they were prepared for fall out.

I made myself breathe like a normal person but stared at my feet. The pinch of the uncomfortable boots reminded me of graduation, when Skirty had worn these.

"Skir-Skir—" Mom started.

"Why didn't you tell me? We could have talked about it together. How could you refuse the money?"

"We didn't want to cause conflict between you two." Like me, Mom avoided saying the name aloud.

"Why would it create drama? We'd both have been fine. Neither of us would be jealous. Sure, neither of us had really wanted to major in business, but…to have *the choice*."

"We don't want charity," Dad said, looking at the lemonade I still hadn't taken.

"Why not?" I asked. "We could use it. What do you think this job has been? Do you really think they couldn't find a good nanny to help Charlotte?"

"Keep your voice down," Mom whispered.

"I wasn't—"

"We wanted you to have a choice," Dad said.

"By not giving me one?" I shouted. "That makes no sense."

"Quiet!" Mom stepped closer and gripped my arm. "You never expressed any interest in being a business major."

"Then admit the only reason you're telling me now is because *she's* dead," I said. "Admit that now, you expect me to profit from the absence of…*her*." I swallowed, willing my tears not to fall.

Mom released me and stepped back as though I had slapped her.

"That's not fair," Dad said.

I resisted the urge to shrug. Tears blurred my vision, and I refused to blink. Mom and Dad avoided looking directly at me. Neither of them had for a while now.

On that day in July, my parents hadn't seen the scrapes on Skirty's legs, hands, and toes that had resulted from the undercurrent dragging her against sand and rocks. They'd only seen her swollen, pale face after she'd been cleaned, a white sheet lifted for a few moments for them to confirm she'd been their daughter.

"I should get back to work," I said, moving away, half hoping one or both would reach out to me.

They didn't.

I lied to myself that it was better this way.

"I'll call next weekend," I said, swiping at my eyes and shuffling toward the lounge. I knew I needed to calm down before finding Rock. The last thing that boy needed was more tears and sad faces.

The buzz of all these people, the cascade of so many serious conversations took its toll. I would drown in guilt, frustration, and jealousy if I stayed in this stupid mansion any longer.

A woman with her back to me, who was talking with other older guests, leaned and collided with me.

"Ope, sorry," I said.

"Excuse me," she turned. Her eyes lingered on my face, probably noticing that I was fighting back tears. "Oh, you're one of the family?" She fully turned to me. "I'm Cynthia." She extended her hand. "I was Mrs. Payne's administrative assistant."

"Hi."

"I believe she kept a photo of you on her desk."

"She did?" I sniffed again.

"Yes."

"Just of me?"

"Excuse me?"

"Not one of my sister *and* me?" I clarified.

"I...I didn't." Cynthia shifted her weight from foot to foot. That was my answer. Mrs. Payne had only found one of us worthy of her attention.

"Excuse me," I said. I held my breath as I slid around people. *One...Two...Three....*

I found the door to the movie theater and closed it behind me, hiding in the dark, windowless room. Finally letting the tears fall while nobody could see, I boiled and burned.

CHAPTER ELEVEN

I didn't know how much time had passed once I reemerged. After checking my reflection, I wandered to the game room, then into the greenhouse, noticing there were fewer and fewer clusters of people. The boats would ferry the remaining mourners home in shifts.

As I glanced through the greenhouse window, I discovered that Rock was playing with THE BOYFRIEND outside. Derek waved to me from where he sat on a small stone bench. Of course. I had to have *all* the uncomfortable conversations today. Ironic, since I'd come to the island to avoid just this. And now I was trapped. If swimming home was possible, I'd have chosen it.

I took a deep breath as I stepped through the double doors of the greenhouse and into the garden outside. Derek ate from a little plate of some marshmallow pie monstrosity. He watched Rock carry fistfuls of twigs from the mulch below a hydrangea bush to form a small pile on the brickwork near his feet.

"Get some leaves, buddy. They'll be our seaweed," Derek told Rock as he scraped a final bite of marshmallow fluff from the plate before setting the dish aside.

"Hey, Derek," I said, shuffling to stand near him. I considered sitting to give my feet a break but feared THE BOYFRIEND would read into it if I sat next to him. "What building project are you overseeing?"

He smiled at me, and I noticed a bit of marshmallow stuck to the corner of his upper lip. I knew the loving girlfriend thing to do would be to tell him, wipe it, or kiss it away for him, but I couldn't bring myself to do any of those.

At fourteen, I'd discovered the look a person would give me when they saw me as a present to be undressed. It was a softness to the eyes. But I welcomed this quality in very few people's gazes. When someone gave me that look, I wondered if they looked at lots of girls that way or if it was special and rare. Seeing that quality in THE BOYFRIEND'S eyes directed at me made my cheeks burn, and caused my shoulders to hunch.

We had met in eighth grade and had been lab partners in chemistry. Then, I'd dared him to try out for *Twelfth Night*. A dare that had led to him taking more and more social and romantic risks.

I turned away from him, pretending to scrutinize the large oaks nearby.

"We're making a model for a shark aquarium that we're gonna build over there." He pointed at the boathouse.

"Why not just use the pool?" I gestured toward the back of the mansion.

"'Cause the freshies go there," Rock explained as he pulled at a handful of leaves on a branch of the hydrangea.

"Not too many leaves," I said. "Be nice to the plant."

Rock settled on the ground to start construction. "And the sharks will eat the smoky shadow so it won't take anyone else."

"Freshies? Like freshman?" Derek asked. "And what is the smoky shadow?" He couldn't seem to help himself and added, "This place has a pool too?"

"As in, freshwater fish," I explained. "The smoky shadow is…" If I explained that I had seen Rock's imaginary monster, Derek would think I was insane. "Is something we're working on." I crossed my arms. "And, yes, there is a pool. A hot tub and a man-made beach."

Derek whistled. "I have swim trunks on my dad's boat."

"Yes, that would be appropriate for a memorial," I snapped.

His face reddened. "I...I didn't mean..."

"Listen," I said, shaking my head. "I, like, appreciate what you're trying to do, being a good boyfriend, bringing flowers—"

"For better or worse," he said, standing and stepping around the area where Rock played. "I'm here for you."

I lost my words. *Did he just quote marriage vows?*

"I know you're having a really tough time." He ran his hands along my shoulders. "Just tell me what I can do to help."

"I told you I wanted some distance. I need time alone. I don't know who I am...without *her*."

"And I don't know who I am without you."

I resisted the urge to shrug.

He released me. "I've been trying."

"I know you have. This isn't about you. That's what you need to realize. Just...leave me alone."

He frowned.

"For a while," I added. *Because I am a coward.* "Please."

"Can't we at least text or—"

"I'm sorry." I bent to pick up Rock, accidentally knocking over his shelter of sticks as I lifted him.

"No, Smoky Shadow is free. It will get us without the sharks!"

"Please stop calling," I told Derek before carrying Rock back into the greenhouse.

"I'm still here when you want to talk," he called, but I didn't look back. As far as I was concerned, he was THE BOYFRIEND no more.

❖

Rock and I spent the rest of the memorial in his room, pretending to be crabs with shells too thick for the smoky shadow to penetrate. If only I could have worn a hard shell to protect myself throughout this miserable day.

"Hey." Charlotte tiptoed in to join us on the floor. "There you two are."

"We're crabs," Rock declared.

"I'm one too." She nodded to me. "Your boyfriend is looking for you."

"I don't think I'll be seeing Derek again."

"Hmm," she said, crawling sideways and then backward to sit beside Rock. "He really loves you."

"How do you know that?" I asked, stopping my own crawling and rubbing my hands to battle the carpet impressions left on my palms.

"It's in the eyes. I came up to give you a break so you could spend some time with him, but I'm guessing you don't want that now."

I shook my head. "Thanks, though."

"Hey, Rock, let's put together your Rainbow Fish puzzle." Charlotte reached to take a puzzle box from one of the toy shelves to distract him. She repositioned so she could sit on the floor and face me as he dumped out the puzzle and spread the pieces across the carpet.

"You know," she said. "Rock's father proposed when I told him I was pregnant."

"Really?"

"Then, in the next breath, he double-checked to ask me if I was sure that I didn't want to get an a-b-o-r-t-i-o-n." She spelled the procedure after glancing at Rock.

"Oh."

"Yeah, he was understandingly overwhelmed, confused, and trying to do what was right while not really knowing what the right choice was."

"How did you figure out what to do? How'd you know not to marry him? Not to…" I glanced at Rock, who was humming as he united his first matching puzzle pieces.

Charlotte shrugged. "I took a nap."

I laughed.

"No, really. That's what I did. Naps always help. I took care of myself. I made lists. I drew pictures of possible futures. Then,

I made the best choice for me. I know last summer, you were obsessed with Derek. But you've been through a lot. You get to change your mind about what's important and what you want. You get to grow as a person."

I stared at the carpet, wondering how she knew to give the perfect advice. "So I should take a nap?" I finally asked.

"Yep. After one glorious nap, I told my then-boyfriend that we'd take things one day at a time and that he could be in our lives as much or as little as he wanted."

"Oh."

She shrugged again. "And he chose 'a little,' which is fine. Because like your grandma, I'm a bad a-s-s b-i-t-c-h." She resorted to spelling again with another glance at Rock. "I can do this on my own and with my family."

And with your family's money.

"Are you talking about bass fishing?" Rock asked. "B-a-s-s."

"Yes," Charlotte said. "Keep working on that puzzle. Look for the face or the corners next." She turned back to me. "Rock has me, you, Steve, Copper and…" She gulped. "Had his great-grandmother. My baby is loved. Aren't you, fishy-fish?"

"I have the fish's eyes and gills." He held up the connected puzzle pieces, only to have them separate and fall from his hands. "Oops." His fears of the smoky shadow seemed forgotten.

"Yes, he is loved," I confirmed.

"And I don't regret any of it."

"Okay, so what are you telling me to do about Derek, exactly?"

"I'm not going to tell you to do anything. Take a nap, Lyla. Or draw. Or do whatever it is that is the most *you* thing you can do and see how *you're* feeling. Cousin's orders."

I tried to smile, but it was advice I couldn't follow, at least not completely. "A nap it is," I said, taking this as my opportunity to return to my room for a break.

❖

I could breathe in my room.

I kicked off the pinching ankle boots and tumbled onto the nearest twin bed to rest on my back. The old frame squeaked under my weight.

This day was *worse* than I had expected.

Maybe Charlotte was right. A nap would be the answer. I turned onto my side. It took me a moment to register that the alarm clock was not where I'd set it when I'd taken it out of the drawer this morning. It faced the wrong way. Now the unicorn sticker stared at me when I knew I'd positioned it to be facing the other bed. The hairs rose on the back of my neck.

I began to feel the other differences: a slight shift in temperature or a change in air pressure. Maybe the room didn't smell quite like me. I sat up. The hairbrush rested a few inches to the left of where I usually kept it on the end table. I stood and began checking drawers, opening and slamming them one after another. My underwear drawer: the bras spilled over among the panties, even though I had always kept them on separate sides.

On top of the wardrobe, the digital camera's switch had been toggled to the "show photos" option instead of positioned to take close-ups, where I knew I'd left it. I backed away from the wardrobe.

Someone had snuck around my room. *The violation.* I shivered.

All small things. But evidence that someone had searched my belongings. *Touched my underwear.* My skin crawled. Who'd done this? Was it the police? Didn't Copper say they'd have to ask me if they could go into my room? Did someone suspect…

I backed into the corner by the door. I shook my hands as though I could shake off these feelings, as though they were water droplets.

A sharp knock on the bedroom door made me jump.

"Are you there?" Mom called.

I held my breath, debating whether to pretend like I wasn't here. Could they sense me through the door?

"We're getting ready to leave." She knocked again, and I let out a breath.

I opened the door. Both my parents stooped. Seeing them head-on in the austerely lit servants' hall, I noticed their age. Everything about them seemed grayer than before. Touches of ash lined their hair. Their nicest clothes—the same dress and suit they'd worn to Skirty's funeral and to see us graduate—hung off their shoulders. Both had dark circles under their eyes. If I were to pull up the photos from my graduation on the old digital camera, would I even recognize them?

We are withering.

Mom stepped into the room, raising her arms as though she was going to hug me. She changed her mind and settled for resting her cold hands on my shoulders. For the first time, I stood taller than her.

"We miss you so much," Dad said, his hands in his pockets. "Do you need anything? Maybe we could send a care package."

"Do you want to come home?" Mom asked as she glanced around the room.

Something in my gut twisted. I wanted to shout, *yes*. Then, just as quickly, *no*.

"We can figure out the college financial stuff together," she continued.

I sniffled before shaking my head no. "Rock needs me," I said.

And it was true.

And maybe I need him too.

Plus, there was his imaginary monster that I had somehow seen as well. Whether it was real or I was somehow losing my grip on reality, I needed to see this through with him. Even if I could escape nightmares at home, I couldn't breathe in Sandusky. I would die there, waiting for Skirty to stand in the middle of our bedroom and complain about all her reading, anticipating her taking a shirt without asking, expecting the sound of her small mumbles as she slept in her bed.

"I have to stay here," I said.

CHAPTER TWELVE

With my parents and the rest of the guests gone last night and the rental chairs returned to Sandusky this morning, only the Paynes' private ferry and captain remained ready to take Charlotte to school. As we took baby steps onto the wide dock, I held Rock's hand. For some mysterious reason, his fingers felt sticky again.

As Weston pulled the last of Charlotte's luggage onto the small ferry, she kneeled in front of her son. "You have fun and be good for Lyla, Copper, and Ms. Eldonforth," she said.

He nodded.

"But you can give Uncle Steve a hard time whenever you want. Wake *him* up if you have *any* dreams, good or bad." She winked and rocked his shoulders from side to side to encourage him to smile. "Sneak into his room and tickle his feet."

He giggled and looked at me.

"We can wake him as soon as we get back to the house," I said, squeezing his hand. "I bet Uncle Steve is still asleep." *And probably hungover.*

"We're going to talk every morning," Charlotte continued. "I want a full report of what new fish you're learning about. And I'll tell you what Brutus the Buckeye has been doing each day."

Rock released my hand to give his mom a bear hug.

I backed away to give them space for the I-love-you's.

"Lyla." Ms. Eldonforth waved me toward the path to the main house where she stood with Gwen and Alex.

I walked to her side as she said, "Do as I ask, Gwen. I know Steve'll complain, but I am your boss. And it's for his own good."

"He might be the one giving orders soon," Gwen said coolly. "I don't want to be on his bad side."

"Excuse me?" Ms. Eldonforth asked. "What's that supposed to mean?"

Gwen didn't explain, and we watched as she sauntered back toward the house.

"I wish you weren't getting so attached to her."

I turned to Ms. Eldonforth, expecting her to glare at me but was surprised to see she looked at Alex.

"Maybe she's not the one who is the negative influence," he said, wiggling his eyebrows.

Ms. Eldonforth *tsked* and glanced to me. "I've been thinking about how much Rock has been going through," she said. "First Mrs. Payne, his nightmares, and now Charlotte leaving…"

"I'll stay," I blurted. "For longer than the original two weeks. To help with him."

She nodded, but I suspected she held back a smile as well. "I think that is a wise choice. You'll be a comfort to him. I know you two have always connected well emotionally."

Alex held up his hand to me. "All right. Welcome semi-permanent member of the team."

I high-fived him before turning back to Ms. Eldonforth. "Is that what you wanted to ask me about?"

"No, actually," she said. "Though it is related to trying to help Rock through this *difficult time*." She cleared her throat. "I believe it will be important for him to have a new hobby."

"Okay." Was throat clearing a tell? It could have been a way to hide her emotions. Had I heard her make the noise before?

"When I asked him," she continued, "he expressed interest in, um…" She hesitated.

I didn't think I'd ever seen her nervous before. "In?"

"In learning to swim."

"Oh."

"I know you can't swim. Not that I'd expect you to do so even if you could, given what happened." She ahem-ed again.

"Right." My throat had gone dry.

"I'll ask Steve to teach him. But I was hoping you still might remain *present* during the lessons," she said. "You won't even have to get in the water. We'll do it in the pool, *not* the lake."

"And I'll make excuses to check on you guys," Alex added. "You can hear everything that goes on in the pool from the kitchen."

"Um." I swallowed. "I…I guess." I glanced at each of them. "As long as I don't have to get in the water." I'd vowed to never get in a body of water again. I hadn't even allowed myself to take baths. I'd be a shower girl from now on.

The wrinkles around Ms. Eldonforth's eyes deepened as she stared at me. Her wording had been considerate. I thought of all her years here. The Paynes really had two grandmothers all this time. Maybe the warmer of the two was still here. *Looking out for everyone.*

I turned back to face the dock. Charlotte nodded to me, and I ventured back toward her to reclaim Rock's sticky hand. She climbed onto the small ferry, and Weston pulled up the gangplank.

"I love you, baby," Charlotte called and waved at Rock.

Weston untied the boat from the dock, and the motor puttered as they pulled away. The ferry's horn sounded a friendly, "Toot, toot, *toot*." At Charlotte's request, I suspected.

Rock cackled and clapped his hands at the sound.

"She'll be back before you know it," I said and led him toward the mansion. Our pace would be perfect for a funeral march, Rock already missing Charlotte, and my attention torn between looking at the monstrous mansion and at the others waiting on the path.

With the sky overcast, flowers turned their faces down, and tree leaves curled like another storm approached. Eight of us remained on the island. *Eight survivors.* But if I believed what Mr. Toler had told Copper yesterday about the suspicious nature of Mrs. Payne's death, that also meant we were eight suspects.

CHAPTER THIRTEEN

In a long orange Post-it note, Ms. Eldonforth demanded I find armband floaties for Rock to wear in the pool for when, *Steve will be cajoled to teach the boy to swim,* she had written, *In the basement, we should still have the ones Dalia used to learn to swim.* I shivered at the thought of going down there. But Ms. Eldonforth had dismissed my suggestion to buy some in Sandusky the next time Alex made a grocery run.

I recruited Gwen to travel into the hellish underworld to look for them, fearing a repeat of my previous weird experience with this basement during my hide-and-seek game. Convincing her to help was proving to be its own hell since she was still mad at me, with her pursed ruby lips and cool glances. She gave me one such look now.

"I broke up with Derek," I blurted. Silently adding, "kind of," in my head.

"Really?" She arched a perfect brown eyebrow. "Hmm."

"At the memorial," I added. "I...I'm single." What the hell was I doing?

"Well, that changes things." A slow smile bloomed across her face.

I smiled back.

"I want to dance with you. Swear you'll go dancing with me the next time we go to town," she said, her hand resting on the ornate brass door handle that led to the basement. "And I'll help you."

I shrugged but remained silent. *Is she asking me out? Like out, out?* A mix of emotions churned at the thought: excitement fluttered like butterfly wings in my chest. Guilt and sadness, like I was betraying Rose. And Derek, I supposed.

"And you'll actually dance with me, or I won't do it," she threatened, crossing her arms.

"You should be a lawyer," I said. *How does she know I'd go, then refuse to dance?*

"I'm going to be a Broadway diva or casting director."

"Fine." The butterflies won this battle. But even as I agreed, a memory flashed of the way Rose had once rested her hands on my shoulders and guided me close to rock to a slow song together.

Gwen smiled again. "And you'll love every second." Without a moment's hesitation, she opened the door to the basement, stepped into the darkness, flipped on the light switch, and clunked down the wooden stairs. Like it was nothing.

I shuffled behind her, wondering what it was like to live without so many tethers keeping me anchored and knotted. The dank air from the basement stretched toward me. I shifted from foot to foot. The burn of smoke chased the scent but not campfire smoke. The smell in my memory reeked of the "industrial poisonous materials that should not be burned but are burning" type of black smoke. And I remembered with a gasp:

I heard the shouts and cries from Skirty, Steve, and Charlotte. Young Steve's voice repeatedly yelled for Talc.

Charlotte called, "Grandpa! Dad!"

A teenage Copper pulled us down the stairs, saying, "It'll be okay. It's damp. Ms. Eldonforth told us to wait here so we wouldn't have to see. We'll stay by the cellar door in case the fire spreads to the main house." He picked me up and carried me down. "The fire won't reach us here."

"Where are Mommy and Daddy? Were they in the fishing cabin?" Charlotte asked.

"Where's Ryan?" Skirty asked.

"You okay?" Gwen asked me at the bottom of the wooden steps. The flashlight app on her phone created a pool of light at her feet.

I took a shaky breath and nodded. I couldn't believe I'd forgotten that. I didn't think we'd stayed in the basement for long. Copper had tried to keep us occupied by playing a matching game to have us find the aces and face cards from a deck. That was probably the first time I'd touched a deck of cards, I realized. I tried to remember more about that day, but not much came to mind. I could imagine some of the moments: Mom trying to explain death to us. Crying. Skirty and I hugging Steve. But I didn't know if I was inventing now or recalling more memories.

I resumed my cautious descent, my hand extended to the brick wall. Theoretically, I'd known we'd been visiting the island on the night that Charlotte, Steve, and Copper's parents, grandfather, and brother had died in the fire in the fishing cottage. I'd always thought I'd been too young to remember, hoped we'd been too young to remember.

I wondered if Skirty had recalled huddling in the basement. I felt the familiar struggle to breathe because I couldn't ask her. A voice followed by thuds of footsteps brought my attention back to Gwen. She'd joined me on the stairs. She held her phone and the small, deflated, red-and-yellow, armband, floating wing things.

"Huh?" I asked.

"Come down here," she said in a tone that told me she'd called to me before. She threw one floatie at my head. "You've got to see this."

I caught the second floatie as it collided with my chest. "I don't—"

"Get your ass down here," she called over her shoulder as she thudded back down the steps, using her phone's flashlight app to guide her way.

I sighed and threw both floaties up to the well-lit kitchen, wishing I could go up too, before I followed her down. Keeping one hand on the brick wall, I tested my weight on each wooden slat before I fully took each step. No more memories assaulted my senses.

I can do this.

The mansion's basement looked every bit the horror movie setting I'd expected. Decades of unwanted furniture, children's toys—including creepy, marble-eyed dolls—and exercise equipment lined the walls or formed sloppy piles around the dim space. A single hanging bulb illuminated the room. I was surprised this wasn't more organized. Maybe Ms. Eldonforth avoided coming down here because she associated it with the fire too.

I suspected she'd been the one to come downstairs and tell us who'd died. I had the vague sense of being held in a tight hug. Of Charlotte and Copper crying, of Steve curling in on himself near the hard wall. I blinked several times, dust making my eyes itch.

Along the back of one wall stood a makeshift wine cellar: rows and rows of bottles rested on racks. There had to be several hundred of them. Somewhere deeper in the darkness, there stood another creaking stairway that would lead directly outside. I doubted the cellar door had been used in years. Layers of dust and cobwebs held all the objects in place.

Except for one corner of the room.

A new long light fixture hung over a plastic table. There were no cobwebs. No debris.

"*Something's not right heeeere,*" Gwen sang to herself, walking toward the new shelving. She flipped on the long lamp that contained two, long, thin bulbs. The kind used in an aquarium.

We blinked at the brightness. "That's a grow light," I said. "For plants." Though there weren't any plants down here as far as I could see.

Gwen turned to me. "Like, for magic mushrooms or marijuana?" She laughed.

"Maybe it's Steve's," I said.

"Or maybe Ms. Eldonforth's." We both chuckled at that thought.

"She had to throw it all out when the cops arrived." Gwen flicked the fixture's switch again, and we were silent in the comparative darkness that encompassed us.

"*OooooOOOoooooh,*" Gwen sang in a ghostly voice.

"Stop that, or I'll leave you down here," I said, taking the stairs two at a time back into the light and warmth of the kitchen.

Gwen chased after me, still singing, "*The ghosts of Ms. Eldonforth's marijuana want revenge.*"

"Gah!" I giggled as she tickled my sides.

❖

That night, I didn't open my phone or look at the photos on the digital camera. I blocked out the idea that someone had snooped in my room. Instead, I breathed easier, feeling the corners of my mouth upturning when I thought of Gwen's gentle teasing and her and Rose's perfume once again on my skin.

The tiny noose still swung against the windowpane. I did crunches to its beat. My abs burned after only a few reps. For the first time since Skirty had died, I did calisthenics on the floor of my room; planking, push-ups, squats, and burpees. I'd enjoy the sore muscles in the morning.

It felt good. It felt like *me*. It felt...*freeing.*

In bed, I even let my hands wander over my own body.

And I thought of *her.*

❖

I woke in the dark, unsure why. The *ting-ting-ting* of the tiny noose kept pace with my elevated heartbeat. After a few moments of blinking into the night, I made out the moving shadows: The hazy woman seeming to walk toward me from the far wall.

Smoky Shadow.

I gasped and held the blankets like a shield.

Unblinking, I groped for something, anything, on the nightstand to throw. My hand collided with my phone, and it thudded to the floor. Instead of cursing, I found the camera. After a few moments of struggle, I managed to toggle to the flash.

I pointed.

I shot over and over again.

The camera's flash brought the dancing shadows into sharper focus. Taking photo after photo, I used the flash to stand, to see that the shifting shadows did not dance closer or farther away as I lunged for the light switch.

My breath shallow and fast in my ears, I turned, watching the gyration of the shadows cast along every wall. I focused on the figure of the woman. *Mrs. Payne? Skirty?*

It couldn't hurt me. It was just shadows. It would be beautiful if it wasn't so creepy.

With no warning, the shadows disappeared, and I was left staring at faded brown and yellow wallpaper. I twisted and turned.

Nothing.

Am I losing my mind? Is it the guilt? Or is it a real ghost?

Was this because I was finally starting to be able to feel happy again? To forget what I'd done? "I'm sorry," I whispered to the empty room. "I'm so sorry."

CHAPTER FOURTEEN

A few days passed. I hadn't experienced any more Smoky Shadow sightings. I couldn't find any hint that anyone else had searched my things. Could it have been the ghost that moved my stuff? I hated that this idea even crossed my mind, let alone kept spiraling back in.

The police had chugged to and from the island twice to meet with Copper behind closed doors, but otherwise, we'd sunk into a new routine. I'd wake up well before my alarm and do calisthenics; once the clock read a reasonable time for me to appear, I got Rock up and dressed, and we'd call Charlotte after breakfast.

Copper would reliably say good-bye to his nephew each morning. He seemed stuck in a hurricane of commuting to Cleveland, Toledo, and Sandusky to meet with distributors, board members, shareholders, and employees. He appeared at odd hours to change suits and ties. Each time I saw him, the circles under his eyes seemed darker, and he looked a few years older. Had we been closer, I would have asked if he really wanted to take on his grandmother's role in the corporation. It seemed it would drive him to an early grave, just as it might have done to her.

I spent the majority of each day shuffling Rock around the island to play outside; listen to the book, *This Is Not My Hat*; draw and color sharks in his bedroom; pound notes on the piano in the game room; read other picture books in the library; help as an online teacher coerced him into learning Mandarin; listen to him recite all the words of, *This Is Not My Hat*; and become exasperated as I created more and more elaborate fish-filled stories to get him to eat a few bites of broccoli.

Ms. Eldonforth monitored each shift from one activity to the next. Sometimes, she'd take Rock for a walk to collect insects or to go fishing. That was a sight to behold: Ms. Eldonforth with wind in her hair, the sun warming her cheeks, fishing. Alex sometimes joined them.

When not giving orders via Post-its, whispering suggestions to Copper, or cleaning rooms, Ms. Eldonforth secreted herself in her room. This left the rest of us to play at adulthood the best we could. My current challenge: facing the scent of chlorine and trying to subdue the nerves that accompanied that smell.

"What? No bikini?" Steve asked from the deep end of the pool where he toyed with a floating pool noodle.

I shrugged.

"She can't swim," Rock said as he kicked to twist himself around, his red and yellow water wings keeping him afloat. "Watch me, Uncle Steve!"

"I didn't even bring a swimsuit," I lied.

"Too bad." Steve spat a stream of pool water in my direction. He also held up a small purple water gun but didn't shoot.

"Cut it out." I crossed my arms and stepped closer to Alex, who'd set three tall glasses of lemonade, complete with mint leaves and lemon slices, on a low table beside a well-cushioned deck chair.

"To help survive the heat. This is Bombay lemonade. We just found the recipe. Tell me what you think," he said, handing me a drink.

"Thanks." I took the smallest of sips. "Great." I forced a smile.

"I heard lemonade is your favorite. There are lots of twists I can do with that."

I forced a smile and held the cool drink, condensation making the glass slippery. I turned my attention to the wall that consisted of tall, wide-paned windows, revealing the manicured lawn and rocky beach beyond.

I had a Pavlovian response to the natatorium's dry warmth and chlorine smell. I bounced on my heels, wishing to be in my room or outside.

Rock's splashes and shouts echoed as he wrestled to get Steve's water gun. A wind outside lifted small pink flower petals from below a crape myrtle, causing them to dance over the grass. Tree branches waved in the distance, and I wondered if the flowering tree could survive the winter freeze. It didn't belong here.

"Lyla."

"Lyla?"

As cool water struck my shoulders and back, I shouted, twisting to see the water gun clutched between both Rock's and Steve's hands as the little boy fought to steal it from his uncle's grasp. Steve tried to suppress a smile. He'd shot water at me on purpose. Except…I inhaled and swore I smelled the sharp scent of nail polish remover on my shirt. I pulled at it and sniffed. *Alcohol.*

Steve freed the water gun and squirted a stream of liquid into his mouth. How much had he drunk? I glanced at Alex, who flipped his empty tray over and over in his hands, unaware. Should I stop the swim lesson?

Rock kicked over to the side of the pool, his arm floaties doing their job well. "I'm a shark," he declared, his tinny voice echoing.

"We'll have to get you a dorsal fin to complete the look," I suggested before taking another sip of lemonade. The mint was overpowering. I felt my nose wrinkle but tried to hide the response in case Alex was watching.

"Yes, yes, yes, fins. Fins. Fins," Rock chanted and slapped the water's surface. Gripping the side of the pool with one tiny hand, he waved at me. "My fingers are all wrinkly like Grandma Times Two," he said, and his head dipped under the water.

Even though the floaties pulled him up immediately, Rock coughed after surfacing.

Steve still treaded water in the center, clutching the water gun.

"Come on, Rock, it's almost time for you to practice piano," I said, reaching for him. "Careful."

As I guided him up the ladder and to his towel, Alex picked up his tray to make his exit as well. I draped the towel over Rock's shoulders and used a corner to wipe his dark hair, then his legs and feet.

"Hey, could you please take Rock to his bedroom after you drop those off at the kitchen?" I asked Alex. "I'll be up in just a minute to help him change."

"Okay. Grab on to my pocket, little dude, and we'll see these cats later."

"No cats here. We're all sharks." Rock gripped the side seam of Alex's khakis.

I waited until they'd left the pool deck to turn on Steve. "What the hell are you doing?"

"I don't know what you're referring to, buzzkill." He lounged on his back with a pool noodle under him. He shot another burst of liquid into his mouth from the water gun, then smiled. "It's a *shot*gun. Get it?"

"Drinking with Rock right here?"

"Relax, it's just a fucking swim lesson. He has floaties on his arms. You and Alex are here." He waved toward the kitchen with a splash. "What's the big deal?"

"You know exactly what the big fucking deal is."

He dipped down a little in the water, and our eyes met. The rant I'd been prepared to direct at him sunk into the depths. I saw the pain in his eyes. Not in the irises, exactly, but behind them, a pain that rippled out into the downward tilt of his eyebrows and the corners of his mouth, a pain that hunched his shoulders and drove him to self-medicate. A pain he hadn't outrun in over a decade.

A pain that I saw every time I looked in the mirror for the last nine weeks. My sister had died by water, his brother by fire. We made a fucked-up pair. "You...you have a drinking problem," I finished lamely.

I left him alone in the pool. With every inhalation, I smelled the scents of chlorine and alcohol that clung to my shirt.

❖

I woke in the middle of the night again, uncertain why. *Has the ghost returned?* I searched for the shadowy outline of the woman. The knot at the top of the tiny hangman's noose on the curtain string struck the windowpane in a whispered rhythm. At home, Skirty and I had always squabbled over whether to sleep with the curtains closed or open. She liked to let natural light in as we slept. Now, I left the curtain open, as she would have liked.

I swore I heard whispered voices, and I sat up, looking around, confused, expecting to see the smoky shadows in my room again. Maybe I'd been wrong. The sheets rustled as I turned onto my side. My eyelids sank closed.

Words rambled through my head as a new dark dream flooded my mind:

I swear, I didn't do anything.

Why can't you trust me? Believe me? Choose me over them? You're my *mother.*

The dream didn't make sense. And it did. *You're my mother too.* Words I'd wanted to say but never had.

And if I told the truth now? Images filled my mind as I struggled in the place between wakefulness and sleep, tossing and turning. I saw Officer Gonzalez handcuffing me, marching me away. I pictured Rose, Derek, and Gwen with mirrored cold expressions. Then, I tried to explain myself to my parents through a glass wall as they held each other, crying and shaking their heads.

They'd never forgive me. *Never.*

The next time I woke, I heard fast, short breaths. My eyes shot open. A small dark figure drew close to my bed. I gasped, startling into a sitting position.

"I can't sleep." Rock's voice.

"You scared me."

"Smoky Shadow is in my room again, and it was scary coming down here. I tiptoed by the eels," he whispered. "Smoky Shadow had Anvil. And he kept screaming."

"Huh?" I squinted, trying to see him better in the dark.

"Grandma Times Two treaded water. Her mouth kept opening and closing. She and Smoky Shadow wanted us to feed the fish our fingers."

"I think you had a bad dream, Rock."

"When the people took Grandma Times Two, did they throw her overboard?" he asked.

"What? No, she's—her body is in Sandusky," I said. "And she's traveling like my sister."

"Can we send her some chocolate fish tomorrow? Just to keep her company."

"Oh, kiddo." I pulled him up on the bed and onto my lap.

He cried, and I rocked him. "Why does Mommy have to be gone too?"

"Your mommy will come back to you. I promise."

"She won't drown like—"

"No!"

"Will I drown?"

"A few more lessons and you'll be the strongest swimmer on the island."

"Promise?"

"I promise. No drowning on my watch."

CHAPTER FIFTEEN

A nte equals one unwanted chore or task," Alex explained as he shuffled the deck and began to deal the cards to me, Gwen, Steve, and Copper. "The person with the second-best hand does each of the chores that the winner put into the pile. If you fold, you get your chores back to try to make someone else do them in future rounds. In later rounds, you can bet with your own chores or other people's that you gained in previous rounds. Got it?"

Everyone nodded with varying degrees of confidence. I bit back my desire to say, I'm all in, knowing I'd sound too confident and knowing none of them would have an inkling of how much I valued those words.

I looked at the blank three-by-five notecards that we had to use as currency.

"Nobody ever runs out of chores or tasks," Alex added with a wink.

The unusual poker game had evolved since we were little and had become a secret household tradition for both the Payne grandchildren and household employees. I couldn't imagine Ms. Eldonforth or Mrs. Payne approving. But Ms. Eldonforth had taken Rock fishing, so we would play until their return.

I only thought of a few chores I didn't want to do, writing, *Watch as Steve teaches Rock to swim*, on the first of my five blank notecards. "Ooo." My desire to play and win this game increased as I scrawled, *Get things from the basement,* on a second card. I had to be careful not to get too competitive.

"Ready?" Alex glanced around the circle.

"Game on. Get ready to *serve me,*" Gwen said. "I have a cheat sheet this time. I'm coming for each of you."

I held back a smile and wondered what the others could possibly have written as the tasks they'd like someone else to complete. As far as I could tell, Steve had no chores, and none of us could do Copper's job without angering a bunch of people at Slippy-Up.

I picked up the two cards Alex dealt to me. I held them close, barely revealing the six and nine of hearts to ensure neither Gwen nor Copper on either side of me could see them.

I put the, *Get things from the basement for me,* notecard into the pot to sit facedown on top of everyone else's first chore. As dealer, Alex flipped over a seven of clubs, a queen of spades, and the six of diamonds at the center of our circle to reveal the cards each of us could use.

A pair of sixes. I kept my expression in check.

Gwen stared at her cheat sheet of possible poker hands and whispered, "What can I do with the queen?" then glanced around as if to see if anyone would fold.

Nobody did.

"I'm getting good at poker," she said.

Our gazes met before I shifted to watch Alex, who remained unmoving as he stared at his own hand. Steve had his cards facedown on the carpet and watched me until I broke eye contact and subtly shifted to watch as Copper rubbed his neck. He threw in his second chore, raising the stakes for everyone. *Bluffing.*

Steve added his own second notecard to the pile. I did the same. Alex folded. I pegged him as someone who would bide his time. He might prove to be my main competition.

Gwen hesitated the longest, mumbling as she studied her cheat sheet. Alex smiled at her antics. Finally, Gwen tossed in her second chore notecard, her red lips pursed in thought.

Alex revealed a fourth shared playing card to the center of our circle: the nine of clubs.

Two pair. A competitive wave surged, but I did my best to remain unmoved.

"I would like someone to put away all my clothes after they've been laundered." Copper broke the silence, adding another chore to the center. His neck matched the shade of a tomato where he kept massaging it. *Poor guy.* I hoped he'd be better at bluffing when he was in important business meetings, or else the corporation and family might be in danger.

I felt more than saw the eye roll and accompanying glare Gwen directed at him. She did all the Payne family's laundry and ironing. "Your grandmother always said *little boys* get their underwear put away for them," she teased. "Only Rock receives the full house-elf treatment."

"It's not like I'm asking you to do it as your employer," he said. "Somebody else might get the chore. But, careful, I could start demanding you iron my underwear."

"Don't you dare," she said.

"If anyone wants to make a side bet," Steve said. "My money's on Gwen to lose."

"Hey, I am the queen of manipulation and acting. You don't even know," she said before adding, "but you're just going to have to find that out for sure later because I fold." She put her cards down in a perfect show of disgust.

I quickly scratched out a third chore, *Play hide-and-seek with Rock*, before adding the notecard to the pile just as Steve added his own mystery chore. Alex added a final playing card to the center: the three of hearts.

Copper swore and folded. Just Steve and I remained. One of us would win, and the other would do all the winner's chores. Steve raised the stakes, and I followed suit, filling out yet another notecard to rest on top of the chore pile.

"Show 'em," he said, revealing his hand: a seven of spades and a jack of hearts. One pair. He sat up straighter and looked so proud, ready to swoop in and shove the chore cards in my direction.

I revealed my two pairs and watched as he slumped, his gaze traveling up and down my face several times.

"What? How? I thought you were bluffing. You always used to hum when you had a good hand."

I hummed before shrugging. "Did I?"

He grumbled as he pulled the chores into his lap, seeking out mine to see what he'd have to do. "Your poker face has improved drastically," he said.

I shrugged, thinking of Rose murmuring, "I'm all in."

"Will you teach me?" Gwen whispered.

I shrugged again, then smiled just for her. Everyone else began to regather their chores for another round.

"I can't do this one." Steve waved my notecard about watching him teach Rock to swim.

"Um, change it to comforting Rock during a tantrum," I suggested. "And you can't cheat and bribe him with chocolate every time."

"And what does this card say?" he asked, pulling out the final card that I'd added hastily.

"Read *This Is Not My Hat* to Rock. I can't stand that book anymore."

He nodded.

"Nice job, Lyla," Copper said. "It looks like the family has another card *shark*." He hesitated, waiting for laughs at his playful language before adding, "We'll have to keep an eye on you."

Please don't.

Gwen leaned in close to my side and whispered, "Seriously, you're going to have to teach me the secret of your success."

I felt goose bumps rise on my arms, and I worried that I was easier to read than everyone imagined.

After another hand, Steve treaded unsteadily upstairs only to reemerge with something small in his hand. "I wanna arrange a trade," he declared.

"Here we go again," Alex rolled his eyes.

"What is this one of?" Gwen asked.

I glanced around at everyone. Despite their words, Alex and Gwen were smiling drunkenly at Steve, while only Copper frowned.

"Relax, brother," Steve said. "I'm not going to ask you to finance this again…yet." Steve held a small, two-inch box between his fingers.

"Finance what?" I asked.

"This." Steve stood on tiptoes, his arm extended as much as he could to hold the box up high. He pressed a button on a small remote with his other hand, and blue shadows appeared in three hundred and sixty degrees, all along the game room walls and floor. The two fingers Steve used to hold up the tiny projector appeared like monstrous boulders breaking the seascape.

I shivered as though I'd been plunged into one of my nightmares.

"Ooh, what's this one?" Alex asked.

I looked around. Dark seaweed waved. Small shadows of fish swam above us, and light seemed to dance near the top of the ceiling. "A projector?" I asked.

"Yep," he said. "It's my immersive art." The waterscape veered to one side as he almost lost his balance before resuming standing on tiptoes to hold the tiny projector up.

"I was making this one for Rock," he said. "But I thought the shark…" He moved his fingers so they cast shadows in different places along the wall and revealed a smiling shark. "But I thought this guy would be too scary for him."

He lowered the projector, and I closed my eyes as it felt like I was rushing up toward the surface of an ocean. He clicked the projector off, saying, "Someone can have this one if they agree to take four of my new chores. Any takers?"

We remained silent, but Copper eventually volunteered to take pity on Steve. I watched Steve hand off the small projector while being crushed under a tsunami of annoyance. There was no ghost. I wasn't losing my mind. I glared at Steve. This was the same technology that was probably being used to create Smoky Shadow to scare me and Rock.

Why the fuck would Steve do that to us?

❖

Everyone hid when Ms. Eldonforth returned with Rock. I found myself with almost no job requirements or chores for the next few days. Copper had surrendered and intercepted Ms. Eldonforth to insist he put Rock to bed tonight instead of me after round five of the game. He had a total of eight new chores to do, including doing his own laundry and tucking in Rock. Steve and Alex continued to play, battling to not have to suggest Ms. Eldonforth dye her hair pink.

Gwen seemed to take pride in the eleven chore cards she'd been burdened with. I left the game room to check on how Copper was doing with Rock, padding barefoot in the second floor's hall.

"Did you play hide-and-seek again?" I heard Copper ask.

"No."

"Why not?"

Eavesdropping, I dragged my feet as I approached Rock's open bedroom door.

"It's not as much fun as it used to be."

"That was your favorite game last summer, remember?" Copper said.

Holding my breath, I listened through Rock's long hesitation. Finally, he said, "I don't know."

"Do you want me to read *Goodnight, Moon*?" Copper asked.

"No!"

"But it's your favorite." *Oh, Copper. You gotta keep up.* Rock hadn't asked me to read that book once since I'd arrived.

"How about *This Is Not My Hat*?" I asked, rounding the corner into the bedroom.

Copper had already cocooned Rock into his blue blankets. Various cartoonish-looking fish decorated his comforter. Ms. Eldonforth had made it herself. When I'd been little, jealousy had eaten at me when I'd seen the themed comforters she'd made for

Charlotte, Steve, and Copper. I wondered if any of them still had their blankets.

Copper sat on the floor beside the twin bed, his neck still discolored from his earlier bluffing. Rock quoted the opening lines about a small fish stealing a hat from a bigger one.

"You don't even need the book anymore. You have it memorized."

"I like you reading it," Rock said.

I grabbed the picture book from the lower shelf where we stockpiled all of Rock's water-related books. I flipped off the overhead light and remoted on the string of blue lights along the top of his shelves.

"Cool," Copper said, taking in the underwater feel. "I can see why Steve would want to add..." he trailed off, probably not wanting to give away the surprise.

I *mmm*-ed in agreement, but I knew I frowned as I thought of Steve creating Smoky Shadow. Instead, I said, "That's not all." I turned on the noise machine and programmed it to play ocean sounds for thirty minutes to complete the effect. We listened as waves rolled and seagulls squawked. Copper shifted to sit on a giant beanbag shaped like a shark's open jaws.

Every few pages, I asked Rock a question or two, the way I'd always seen Skirty do when she babysat kids in Sandusky. "Do you see the fish hiding among the seaweed?"

"Yes," he shouted.

"Whisper, please," I murmured.

"*Yes.*"

When I reached the pages in which the little fish said he knew it was wrong to steal but was going to keep the hat anyway, I heard Copper *tsk* his disapproval. Apparently, he wasn't as accustomed to living in a world of moral ambiguity the way Rock and I were. I would have thought Mrs. Payne would have better prepared him. I avoided looking at Copper as I flipped through the last wordless pages, and Rock chuckled at the images of a bigger fish coming along to reclaim its hat.

"Do you think a shark will come along and eat the big fish?"
I asked as I reached the last page.

"No."

"Why not?"

"He was right to eat the little fish," Rock declared.

"Really? Why?"

"Bad fish get eaten or die. People too."

"That's not..." Copper shifted forward on his beanbag seat.
"What do you mean, Rock?"

"Do you think Grandma Times Two—" I started.

"No," Rock shouted.

"Grandma didn't do anything wrong," Copper said.

I bit my lip, not sure that I agreed.

"I know," Rock said.

"So who do you think is the bad person?" I asked.

Rock remained silent for a moment, avoiding looking at either
of us. His small fingers pulled at a corner of his comforter. "I am,"
he finally answered. "Smoky Shadow will eat me."

I gaped at him.

"What?" Copper asked. "Nobody would ever—you're safe."
He moved to sit on the foot of the bed.

"You haven't done anything wrong," I said, squeezing Rock's
shoulder.

"She's right." Copper rested a hand on the blanket over one of
Rock's shins. "You're the nicest kid in the world, on dry land or in
the sea. Why would you think something so sad?"

He shrugged one shoulder.

I knew what that gesture meant. "Rock, tell us," I said. "We
won't be mad."

"I killed Grandma Times Two," he finally whispered.

Copper and I exchanged glances. I imagined my expression
echoed his horrified and uncertain one. "No, you didn't," I said.
"You didn't," I repeated, bending so that I made sure to look him
in the eyes. "*You didn't kill anyone.*"

He traced the outline of a shark on his blanket. "I...I hugged
her and—"

"A hug didn't hurt her," Copper said as I leaned in to encircle Rock and his blankets. I rocked him side to side, the way my mom did when Skirty and I were little.

"Grandma Times Two loves you. A hug from you is one of the best, most wonderful gifts she could have received before she..." Copper struggled to finish.

"Your hugs are wonderful," I whispered into Rock's hair, my voice breaking. "They make my heart overflow." I glanced at Copper. "Rock," I said. "Grandma Times Two's death was not your fault. You didn't..." I sniffled. "None of this is your fault," I managed. "Repeat that. Repeat it out loud."

"None of this is your fault," he said hesitantly.

"No, you silly salmon." I tickled his ribs through the blankets. "Say, none of this is *my* fault."

"None of this is my fault," he mumbled.

"Louder," I said. "None of this is my fault."

"None of this is my fault."

"Good." I nodded. "Now say, Grandma Times Two loves me." He repeated my words at a whisper.

"Now say, 'My mommy loves me.'"

"Mommy loves me," he said in a soft voice.

"And Uncle Copper loves me," Copper suggested.

"Uncle Copper loves me."

"My sister and I have always loved you," I supplied.

"Cousins Lyla and Dalia love me." He smiled. "Does Auntie Eldy love me?"

Auntie Eldy? Did he mean...*Ms. Eldonforth*? Copper and I exchanged a look. I nodded. "Ah, yes. Yes, she does," Copper said, barely hesitating.

And the list went on. We included Steve, sharks, Gwen, octopuses, Alex, squids, lobsters, and Weston the boat captain.

"Does Lyla *still* love me?" Rock asked, finally breaking the neat-o-repeat-o chain.

"Yes, of course. Nothing has changed in the last three minutes." I resisted the urge to shrug, and instead, I kissed the top of his head.

"Does Smoky Shadow love anything?" Rock asked.

"Smoky Shadow won't—if you ever see Smoky Shadow again, you call me," I said. "I'll make sure Smoky Shadow returns to the people it loves." I pictured smashing one of Steve's projectors.

"What about Anvil?" Rock asked.

Anvil? Copper mouthed.

"Invisible friends *always* love you," I said, trying to explain while also answering.

"Even if he's my dead brother?" Rock asked.

Copper paled. "Rock, you—"

"Yes," I spoke over him. "The dead always send their love. I'm sure of it."

He smiled and sank deeper under his comforter.

After the lengthy good night, Copper and I stood in the hall for a moment as I slid Rock's door shut before reopening it a crack, allowing a sliver of the hallway light to keep him company, along with the sound of the ocean waves.

Copper stared at the carpet. "Anvil?" he whispered.

I shrugged. Maybe Rock was reacting to hearing his family whisper about fires and lost family members. Maybe he responded to Steve's suffering. Maybe he read my body language, seeing a truth about me and Skirty that nobody else noticed.

"Do you think we should have him meet with a psychologist or counselor?"

"I'd ask Charlotte."

"I don't think my grandma would want any of us in therapy, but I guess it's no longer her decision."

"Guess not," I said, adding, "Your grandmother was always the one to read *Goodnight, Moon* to him. He associates the book with her." At least, that was what I'd been told. "Night."

"Good night."

I padded back to my small corner of the house, chanting in my head my own list of people who might still love me and wishing I too could chant, "None of this is my fault," and make it true.

❖

I turned on the smartphone, preparing for my usual routine of torture: seeing how many voice mail messages and texts waited, determining the best way to reply that would also mean the least amount of contact with my parents or with THE EX-BOYFRIEND. Derek hadn't given me the space and time I'd asked for at the memorial. Each night, the phone revealed his missed texts. Tonight's featured an Agatha Christie mystery:

I have to read a play for my English class.

Can I stop by your house to pick one up from your room?

I called your mom. She told me to stop by.

I have your copy of Cards on the Table.

I'll be keeping it hostage until you call me. He had added a winking emoji to that one.

Also, your mom says you should call her.

She says it's not like you to be this quiet.

She says she now loves me more than you.

JK JK JK.

Or am I?

Another text arrived, and I prepared to mentally curse. But it wasn't from him. It was from someone I hadn't spoken to in weeks:

Rose.

The ex-girlfriend. Or former girlfriend. *It hadn't been a breakup that made her an ex.* Rose had been the first Black girl to join our class after she'd moved to Sandusky in eighth grade, while the rest of us had been in classes together since kindergarten. Beating everyone at poker hadn't made her friends…at least not until she'd started teaching a few of us how to figure out others' tells. Skirty had befriended her first. They'd talked poetry and drama.

I opened the text.

Hey.

That was it.

What the fuck did that mean? What was I supposed to do with that? My thumbs shook over the phone's tiny keyboard. How should I reply? I wished I could run possible messages by Skirty. Before I could enter any text, the screen changed to an incoming call. THE EX-BOYFRIEND.

I couldn't handle this.

My thumb once again wavered as I decided whether to ignore or accept the call. I pressed the green button before my brain processed what I'd done. The call connected, but I didn't speak.

"Hello?" Derek's voice sounded small and distant.

I raised the phone to my ear. "Hey," I croaked, echoing Rose's text.

He remained silent, clearly as shocked as me that I had answered. I listened to the faint static on the line. "Ah, how are things?" he finally asked.

"Okay," I lied.

"I'm so glad to hear—"

"Rock blames himself," I blurted. "For her death. He's this little kid who can barely spell three-letter words, with tiny little toes and baby teeth, and he thinks he's to blame." I sobbed. "Because he was the last person to hug her."

"Oh."

"What do you do with that?" I asked. "How do you make that pain go away?" Hot tears streamed down my cheeks.

"Ah, professional counseling?" he suggested.

I shook my head. More tears fled my eyes. I grabbed my bodywash from the shower caddy. I popped open the top to inhale, hoping the eucalyptus scent would calm me. I'd always loved the way a certain smell could bring me to a certain moment, draw out a particular emotion, or call forth a memory of Rose. "You don't get it," I said, looking at the phone's screen, preparing to disconnect the call.

"Explain it to me," he suggested. "I'm just so, like, glad to hear your voice. Just keep talking. I…I'll listen. I'm here."

"I can't," I said, sniffing the bodywash one more time before returning it to the caddy.

"Well, what can I do?" he asked.

I shrugged, and we both listened to the static on the line for a few seconds.

"How about I distract you?" he asked. "Do you want to Facetime? I can show you all of my new college-themed posters?"

"No Facetime," I said. "The Wi-Fi isn't good enough," I lied and wiped my cheeks.

"Hmm." He thought for a moment. "How about I distract you with the ongoing struggles of a community college criminal justice major?" he said in a dramatic voice.

"Oh, yeah?"

"Yeah. When we last left our inept freshman, he was struggling to determine where to pay for his meal in the express dining service on campus."

"Sounds like a nail-biter," I said, knowing he would hear the smile in my voice.

"It was. This misadventure involves spilling iced coffee on the ID swiping machine. I think I've made an enemy of the swiper person."

"Oh no," I said. And I chuckled. I couldn't help it. "It's a bit early in your college career to have a nemesis."

The static felt loud for half a second as he seemed to register that I'd laughed with him for the first time in months. "I know! And this campus is so small too. Only one dining hall." He resumed his play-by-play of his attempt to eat on campus. I curled onto my side on a twin bed, clutching the phone to my ear as I listened.

Though I didn't want to admit it, sometime during that talk, Derek managed to cut out the "EX" and return to his title of THE BOYFRIEND.

Chapter Sixteen

Rock had another swim lesson with Steve. Gwen had wound up with that particular chore notecard by the end of the poker night and watched them for today. Unlike me, she'd put on a bikini with cartoon sharks printed on it and had eased into the pool. This probably cemented for Rock how much cooler she was.

I could hear the laughter and shouts from where I perched on a stool, leaning against the kitchen island, observing as Alex multitasked. He went back and forth, among prepping pie crust dough; running water over a strainer of shiny, crimson cherries in the sink; and bringing water to a boil over a medium, open flame to prepare pasta. He paused occasionally to research which wine to pair with different foods on his smartphone. He had set a row of ten bottles along the countertop. He cleaned one to examine its label closely, wiping dust from the neck.

Earlier, Ms. Eldonforth had stuck one red and several green and yellow sticky notes to the corkboard for us to complete, things like sharpen the knives and organize and sanitize toys, but we were both ignoring her chores for the moment.

"I can't believe you're willing to brave the basement," I said, nodding at the wines.

He crossed his arms and gently scratched his shoulder. "I'm willing to go great distances for matching the right alcohol with this fish. And the Paynes have a very *nice* collection." He twisted another of the bottles to examine a label more closely. "Besides, the basement isn't so bad. Not with the lights on from Ms. Eldonforth's hydroponic garden."

"Is that what that is? Gwen and I wondered."

He nodded. "An experiment to grow fresh vegetables and herbs. I helped. She, ah, she really cares that this family has the best."

"Yeah, I never really realized how much she did when I was little. I always found her so scary. It was hard to imagine her loving anyone."

"She probably loves the Paynes more than she loves her own family. I doubt anyone else has ever received one of her fancy blankets."

"You noticed those too? I would have loved for her to make me one with unicorns on it."

"Unicorns, huh? I would have wanted campfires and s'mores." He glanced back and forth between two of the wines.

"How'd you learn about the comforters?"

"We're distant relatives. Like you and the Paynes. I'd see them and their little blankies in pictures on holidays."

Before I could ask more, he held up the two bottles, one with a green logo and the other with a purple one that also had a cute image of an iris on it. "Which one?"

"That one," I said, pointing at the purple label.

"Why?"

"It's prettier."

He chuckled. "You have a future as a sommelier."

"What's that?"

"Someone who chooses wines."

I laughed." Can I major in that at Terra State Community College in January?"

"I'm guessing no. But sommeliers can make really good money."

"I'll keep that in mind."

We were silent for a few moments, listening to the distant echoes, splashes, and laughter from the pool.

Alex broke the silence first. "Copper said we should be able to reopen the dining room for Friday's dinner. We're going to have a few guests as well."

"Charlotte should be home for the weekend."

He made a "hmm," noise as he removed the cherries and shook them a handful at a time in paper towels to remove the excess water.

"Where did you learn how to cook?" I asked.

"Here and there. Mostly locally. I had planned to study in France, but..."

"Ooo, fancy. What happened?"

He opened his mouth to answer but saw something behind me and stopped everything to stand at his full height.

I turned.

Ms. Eldonforth.

I followed Alex's example, climbing to my feet and making sure my shoulders were back.

Ms. Eldonforth looked from Alex to the wine and then to me. She frowned as though thinking that I, as an underage teen, couldn't be trusted to even be in the same room as sealed wine bottles. "This isn't the meal we discussed, Alex."

"I know. I wanted to mix things up."

"That's fine, but I am to assist in all *mix-ups*. Understood?"

"Understood." He turned away from her to glance at me and cringe.

Ms. Eldonforth turned her attention to me. "Did you see the red sticky note?" she asked, gesturing toward the corkboard.

I feigned surprise as I looked.

"Will you two go into the attic and look for a circular area rug, please?" She phrased the request like a question, but like Mrs. Payne, she'd mastered giving commands. "*Now*," she added when neither of us jumped to do her bidding. "You both need to go. The rugs are too heavy for one person."

"Can it wait a little?" Alex asked, eyeing his lit stove and his dough.

"No, now, please," she said. "It looks like the dining room rug is ruined from…" She cleared her throat. "From what happened. I believe we should already have some options to replace it for Friday without having to purchase a new one. But if not, I'll need to call a decorator today."

Without another word, Alex switched off the stove, and I trailed behind him up the back stairs, leaving Ms. Eldonforth alone in the kitchen. We both panted as we took the last steps onto the third floor. Alex pulled at a thick white string hanging from the ceiling near the top of the stairs, causing a narrow stepladder to silently slide down from the ceiling.

We regarded the square of dark space for a moment. *The attic.*

"What are the chances there's a secret sibling up there?" he asked.

I shrugged. At least I now knew there couldn't be any smoky shadows, but I said, "Anything is possible."

"With an attitude like that, I'm going to make you go up first."

I glanced up. I'd never been in the attic before. I had a vivid memory of a younger Steve telling me and Skirty that ghosts haunted it. And if we listened carefully, we'd hear the thump of them trying to escape down the stairs to murder everyone in the house.

Such a nice young boy, that Steve. He'd told us that two summers after the fire. Copper had overheard and his teenage, acne-covered face had turned red while his hands had formed fists. That was the only memory I had of Copper ever striking anyone.

Alex thunked his way up the ladder. I tried to peek around him to see through the darkness above. No ghosts. *Aside from my memories.* Alex reached the top and he switched on a ceiling light somewhere beyond my view.

I took a deep breath and climbed up after him. *One foot above the other.* The air felt heavy and warm. The attic was the only part of the mansion that wasn't temperature controlled. We'd be sweaty messes in seconds. As I reached the top of the steps, I perked up at the surprise of finding the space well-lit and organized. The scents of cedar and ginger reminded me of the woodshop room at my high school. I had always met THE BOYFRIEND and Rose outside that classroom before we'd walk to meet Skirty for lunch at our usual table in the cafeteria.

I stood on unpolished floorboards. A few wooden beams formed a giant dragon's ribcage, holding the insulation in place along the center and highest points of the angled ceiling. Alex and I could only stand up straight if we walked along the center of the attic, pacing the spine of the dragonish mansion.

Boxes lined three of the walls, each labeled with black type. The work of Ms. Eldonforth and a label maker, no doubt. The label on the box nearest me stated, *heirlooms, timepieces,* and another had a tag reading, *doilies.*

Along the fourth wall, under the attic's sole small window, several, rolled-up, stacked rugs formed a waist-high mountain. Each rug had to be six or eight feet wide, and there was no way to tell their length without unrolling each one.

I followed Alex to investigate them. Someone had rolled each rug so only the bottoms showed. We would have trouble discerning the colors and patterns. Ms. Eldonforth really should have been here to tell us which one might work. Not that I wanted to explain that to her.

Alex lifted the end of the top one to try to look at the design inside, seemed to realize how heavy it was, and let it smack into place at the top of the pile. "Well," he said.

"That top one seems nice," I suggested.

"Works for me."

Easier said than done. It took both of us pulling and pushing to even budge the rolled-up rug. "Is there a smaller one?" I grunted.

He examined the rest of the pile. "No, I think we're stuck. Shit."

"Yeah." I pulled at the end of the rug, managing to shift it a little. "Are we sure there's not a corpse in there."

"I know, right?" He chuckled. "Here's our cardio for the day."

With a lot of swearing, we managed to drag it across the attic floor and shove it down the hole. The long rug roll thudded onto the third floor below with the finality of a dead body.

"Let's hope Ms. Eldonforth didn't hear that."

"Yeah." I wiped at the sweat on my forehead and pulled my shirt away from my front. I sweated all over. It was an embarrassing quirk that made me thankful that the island's staff wore black.

Alex and I exchanged a look, both no doubt acutely aware of the effort the rest of the trip down to the first floor would take. Once we were both safely on the third floor, he slid the ladder back up, sealing off the hot attic. He wiped sweat from his hands before turning to me. "Ready?"

I shrugged, and each of us took an end. I used my leg to help secure the carpet between my arms before we baby-stepped toward the back stairs.

Alex took cautious steps down the stairs backward, and I followed, facing forward. We shifted the rug to prevent it from colliding with the walls, fearing Ms. Eldonforth would accuse us of making scuff marks, causing damage, or misaligning a photo frame.

When we reached the first floor, we set the rug in the kitchen at the base of the steps, both of us panting. I hoped my face hadn't flushed as red as Alex's. His hair and skin matched. He reminded me of a heated burner on a stove.

"I think I need a shower," I said.

No sign of Ms. Eldonforth. Had she realized how brutal this task would be?

I heard Rock's cry echo from the natatorium. I listened for a moment, and Alex and I exchanged confused glances. He cried out again, and I recognized the pain in his sobs. I felt the same cold that had dripped into me at the beach with Skirty and when Mrs. Payne had convulsed on the dining room floor.

We ran the few steps to the natatorium. I looked to the pool first, terrified there'd be a body floating. Steve stood waist-deep in the pool, quiet and holding the same water gun he'd drunk from during Rock's first swim lesson. *His* shot*gun.*

Gwen sat on the pool's edge, holding Rock as he bawled, blood dripping from his face. Ms. Eldonforth crouched beside her, demanding Rock hold still so she could wipe at the blood that spurted from his mouth.

"What happened?" Alex asked, grabbing a beach towel from the back of one of the pool chairs and rushing to press its corner to Rock's mouth and chin.

"He tried to climb over the side. He slipped and hit his face," Gwen said, glaring at Steve. "He was splashing Rock."

"He was going on and on about an Anvil, shadows, and a dead brother," Steve mumbled. "It was *weird.*"

"Little kids have invisible friends," Gwen snapped.

"Why weren't you holding him better?" Steve shouted back.

Gwen took a sharp intake of breath, readying to attack.

"Be quiet," Ms. Eldonforth ordered. "Focus on the task." She took the towel from Alex. "Go get ice."

Alex obeyed, jogging past me. Blood had splattered onto Rock's front, Gwen's legs, and into the pool.

"I think he bit the inside of his cheek," Ms. Eldonforth said, shifting the towel to examine him and clear away the blood. "Lyla, let's get him upstairs."

I nodded, grabbing another beach towel.

Gwen moved to give me access to Rock, and I scooped him up while also cocooning him in the towel. Alex returned with ice wrapped in a small cloth napkin.

"There you go, this will help it to feel better." Ms. Eldonforth placed the ice and towel gently against Rock's mouth, muffling his cries. "It's okay. These things happen, little fish." She walked by my side, gently holding the ice to Rock's mouth as I carried him up to his bathroom and set him in the bathtub to clean the blood, tears, and snot.

The entire time, I kept whispering to him, promising he'd be okay.

I'd make sure of it.

CHAPTER SEVENTEEN

I returned to my room sore and desperate for a shower. Ms. Eldonforth and I had called Weston and taken an emergency trip to Sandusky. Rock had received two stitches. Charlotte had been frantic with each call I'd made on Ms. Eldonforth's cell updating her about the situation. But Ms. Eldonforth had insisted each time that Charlotte stay at school and attend her classes. She'd be coming home tomorrow night to stay for the weekend anyway. She would see Rock soon enough.

Once back on the island, Rock calmed after consuming his fourth melting Popsicle. We'd colored. He'd described how his mom drew the best fish after I'd tried to draw three for him. He'd complained while I rinsed his mouth with warm, salty water. He'd finally fallen asleep after several readings of the picture book, *Swimmy*. I didn't know how he could keep listening after a tuna munched all of Swimmy's siblings, but Rock had kept insisting on hearing the story again and again. At least it gave me a break from *This Is Not My Hat*.

In my room, I stretched before changing into a tank top and shorts. I sighed, hearing the hush of the air-conditioner and the tiny finger noose swinging under the vent and *tink-tink-tinking* against the windowpane. *A miniature death hovering over my head.*

I powered on the cell and opened Rose's text. I hadn't replied. And now, instead of finally answering, I called THE BOYFRIEND.

Despite having to pick my words and topics carefully, it felt nice to have someone to talk to each night. Or to *listen* to, which was mostly what I did.

The static on the line and the miles and lake between us made Derek tolerable. He sounded happy whenever we spoke, glad to hear me breathe against the speaker, and content with, "uh-huh" as he rambled. He seemed to be the only loved one who'd endured Skirty's funeral and could still find reasons to smile and feel thankful. I could survive with him at this distance. But my stomach roiled at the thought of him coming close or touching me.

We connected, and I put him on speakerphone. After saying hi, I paced and listened to him talking about his classes at Terra State before bouncing onto the bed with the digital camera in my hands. I turned on the old camera as Derek prattled on about an activity he'd done in his psych class.

"Uh-huh," I said, checking the camera's battery life.

"I couldn't wait any longer," he said. "I caved and ate the marshmallow."

"Uh-huh," I repeated and toggled the display switch to show the photos saved on the SD card, but instead of the usual torment of seeing the last photo of our faces pressed together with a rocky beach in the background, I found a new image.

A photo I had not taken. I sat up straighter and studied the camera's display screen.

"I bet you would have been able to resist the urge to eat the marshmallow," he continued.

A close-up shot of words written in black pen: *You little liar* next to a winking smile. A shock crackled through my gut. What. The. Fuck?

"You're way more disciplined than me, and I bet you would have helped me to resist temptation. Distracted me."

I could feel and hear my heart beating in my ears. I didn't recognize the handwriting. Who would know that I'd lied? Did they mean about—

"Lyla?"

"Derek, I'm sorry, but I've gotta go." My voice sounded tiny in my own ears. I didn't wait for a reply before I disconnected, and the phone fell gently to my side on the twin bed.

I shivered. Somebody had entered my room without my permission or knowledge *again*. Not only that, but they also knew the camera stored photos important to me. I glanced around, half fearing someone spied on me now, trying to make out the shape of a camera or of one of Steve's tiny projectors.

Returning to the image on my display screen, I zoomed in. It looked like the intruder had written the message on white printer paper, the kind that the family stored in each of the offices and in the library. It might as well have been a piece of paper from the ream Rock and I had colored on after returning from Sandusky.

The handwritten block letters slanted to the right. Ms. Eldonforth always left notes in indecipherable, loopy cursive that ran straight up and down across the page. Not a match. And I didn't know what anyone else's handwriting looked like.

I made a shitty detective.

What did they mean, *You little liar*? And what could the winking smiley emoji signify? Was this blackmail? Would I get another note demanding money that I didn't have? Did the smile mean they'd keep my secret? And which secret did they know? What if the blackmailer had used a hidden camera?

Fuck.

I looked around the room again. No red recording lights. Nothing looked out of place. I bit my lip, wishing Skirty were here. Just for a minute.

Somebody banged on my bedroom door.

I jumped, almost losing my grip on the camera. I turned it off and watched as the accusation faded to black on the display screen before hiding the camera under my pillow. After glancing around again, I opened the bedroom door a crack and peeked at the potential intruder.

Steve. He had dark circles under his eyes, and in one arm, he clutched several half-filled vodka and tequila bottles.

"What are you—" I opened the door wider.

"Take these." He pushed by me and dropped the bottles on the foot of the twin bed where I'd just been sitting. Glass thudded as the bottles collided against one another. He reached into his back pocket and pulled out a small orange pill bottle to add to the pile.

"What?" I closed the door. If Ms. Eldonforth saw me with this much alcohol—even if I was off duty—I'd lose my job.

"You're right." He turned to face me but still didn't look me in the eye. "I need to stop." He crossed his arms. "Keep these away from me."

We stared at the bottles.

"Just get rid of them or hide them and don't tell me where." He took a step toward the door.

"Okay." I didn't know what else to say. "Is there, um, anything else—"

"Jesus, no, that's all of it." He kept his back to me now.

"No, I meant, is there anything else I can do to help."

He turned, and our eyes met, his watery and bloodshot. "Just, like…no, please get rid of them." He focused on the ceiling.

"Okay," I said. "Maybe you should…"

"What?"

"Tell Copper too. Or Ms. Eldonforth. Or Alex." There was *a lot* of alcohol in the basement. Did Steve trust himself not to go down there? "Maybe Copper could help you find someone to talk with, a professional or something."

"No, this is enough," he said, now looking at his feet. "The temptation will be gone."

"I can resist everything except temptation," I mumbled.

"What?"

"Nothing. Something my…it's a quotation from a playwright. It's great for you to try this, do this."

"Whatever," he mumbled. "See you tomorrow."

"Wait," I said.

"What?" he held the door handle, his gaze on the bottles.

"Your projections?" I hesitated, unsure how to proceed.

"What about them?"

"I...I think Rock's fear of a Smoky Shadow may be because of one of them. Is that, um, possible?"

His hand fell away from the door handle in surprise. "I don't—I haven't made any intentionally scary. I wouldn't do that to the little guy."

"No, I didn't mean to—"

"But, I have lost a few prototypes," he admitted. "The damn things are so small."

"Prototypes," I repeated.

"Yeah."

We were silent a moment before Steve asked, "Are you saying someone is—"

"No, I'm tired. I just—I'll take care of your stuff. Hide it. Never mind," I said.

"Okay," he said, "Thanks, Lyla," and checked that the hall remained unoccupied before sneaking out and easing the door closed behind him.

"Missing prototypes," I mumbled before staring at the bottles. Where could I hide them without someone assuming they were mine? I picked up the pill bottle, and its contents tinkled as I shifted the bottle to read the name on the prescription, a name I'd never seen before: *Trevor Knightley.*

Now I even looked like a drug thief. Ms. Eldonforth wouldn't just fire me, she'd murder me.

❖

I'd shoved Steve's various bottles into a plastic grocery bag. The shark bag would have hidden everything better, but I couldn't find it. I slipped into my bathrobe, grabbed my shower caddy, and then traipsed in flip-flops to the bathroom everyone in this wing shared. I clutched the bag of contraband to my chest, hiding it behind the small caddy.

Gray and blue tiles lined the floor of the old but serviceable bathroom. The tub stood on clawed feet, and its sides remained spotless and white despite its age.

I turned on the faucet, letting the water run over my hand. It felt good and welcoming. I added the stopper at the tub's deep bottom. The mere rush of water from the faucet caused muscles in my shoulders to relax as warm water pooled in the tub.

I'd only allowed myself to take showers for weeks now, but I needed an excuse and noise to explain why I was going to be in the bathroom so long.

I put up the toilet lid and poured out the contents of the vodka bottle. The noise of the tub blocked any other sounds. Next, I dropped the pills into the toilet before flushing it. I arranged the next round of bottles that I'd empty as I waited for the water tank to refill. I'd take the empty bottles and put them in the bottom of the kitchen's recycling barrel. Ms. Eldonforth should be asleep by then, and I didn't want to wait for morning. Alex usually began meal prep ridiculously early. I'd heard him moving about while I remained hidden in my bedroom each morning.

Tomorrow afternoon, Alex would ferry the mansion's recycling and trash to Sandusky and do the weekly grocery shopping. Hopefully, he wouldn't even notice he also carried away evidence of Steve's stash.

Finally, the contents of the last bottles flushed away, and I sighed and listened to the thundering water of the almost-full tub. I shoved all the bottles back into the grocery bag and could feel the pinch and ache in my arms from my earlier workout with the area rug.

I looked at the tub. It'd been such a long day. Dragging the carpet...Rock's injury. Maybe for one night—*one single night*—I could stop. I could *not* punish myself. I removed my robe and clothes and stepped into the tub, the heat prickling my skin and my calf muscles relaxing. I breathed in the humid, heavy air, unknotting and smiling for real.

After the bath, I pulled on my bathrobe. Slipping on my flip-flops, I tied the top of the plastic grocery bag of bottles to prevent them from making noise. Having scooped up the bag with my shower caddy, I opened the door and almost collided with someone.

"Ope." *Gwen.*

"You startled me," she said, one hand touching the top of her small, thin tank top.

"Sorry," I whispered, clutching the bag closer and hoping my shower caddy blocked it from view.

We looked at each other, then, she sniffed. "Do I smell eucalyptus bodywash?" she asked.

"I guess."

She reached into my caddy to twist the bottle and examine its label. I'd started using the scent a couple of months ago. "Hmm," she said.

"I'm all done." I shifted to get out of her way. "The bathroom is yours."

"You're dripping." She touched the hair close to my cheek to gather a water droplet.

"Sorry."

"Nothing to apologize for," she said, moving by me and into the bathroom.

"Right," I mumbled before returning to my room, my wet flip-flops squeaking with each step. I imagined Ms. Eldonforth waking to the sound in her room. I dropped off my shower stuff, slipped off my flip-flops, and peeked out into the hall.

Gwen had closed the bathroom door.

Each of the bedroom doors remained closed.

With the bag of contraband in one hand, I crept down the hall by the back stairs and into the kitchen. Leaving the lights off, I slid the bag into the bottom of the recycling bin without a sound. I pulled off a few paper towels from their dispenser, crumpled them, and placed them on top to ensure it would go unnoticed in the morning.

The deed done, I turned to sneak back to my room when the sound of a distant voice turned me into a statue.

"Stop screwing around." Copper's voice. "We need to have a serious discussion with Charlotte. Just the three of us." By the echo, he must have been in the natatorium.

"What about?" Steve said over the sound of water splashing.

I tiptoed so I could see that the door to the pool stood ajar; warm dry air seeped toward me. From what I could see, neither brother had turned on the overhead lights. I supposed Steve and Copper would know the space well enough to only need the lights in the pool to swim.

I debated whether to make my escape, but Copper's next words made my decision for me: "The police asked a lot of questions about Ms. Eldonforth."

"What?" More splashing. I suspected only Steve was swimming. "What kind of questions?"

"*They suspect her* types of questions," Copper said. "Such as why she'd want to hurt Crystal."

"She's like family. She wouldn't—"

"I know. *Logically*, I know that. *But.*" They remained silent for a few moments. Steve splashed around before Copper asked, "Do you think...do you think we should fire her?"

"What? No. You don't think that's necessary, do you?"

"No." Copper hesitated. Then, "Maybe? I mean, she's always been here. And...if she's dangerous."

"She'd never—she's not."

"I don't know. We can give it some thought." Copper's voice sounded louder, closer, like he was walking toward the kitchen. Toward me.

Shit.

I fled on tiptoe back to the safety of the servants' wing. My heart thudded in my ears, and I held my breath as I passed by Ms. Eldonforth's closed door. *Ms. Eldonforth, dangerous?* Sure, she'd always been scary, but a murderer?

In my room, I turned on the phone as I climbed into bed. THE BOYFRIEND'S latest text chain greeted me:

Sorry you had to go.

I miss you.

What movie did we watch that one night?

I have to assess the psychological state of a character from a film for my psych class.

You know that one film?

When we got distracted. He had added a winking emoji.

Never mind. I figured it out.

I miss you.

Poke.

Poke.

I love you.

Text me.

I reread one text in the list: *When we got distracted.*

The flirty winky emoji.

I grabbed the digital camera, toggling to the message: *You little liar* to examine the drawn winking face. I knew Derek hadn't taken the photo. But had I become so skewed and damaged that I'd misinterpreted it? Was this supposed to be a cutesy, flirty message?

Could *Gwen* have left it? A complicated swirl of emotions made me tingle at the thought.

You little liar. Wink. Calling someone a little liar could be flirty, *maybe*. In an unusual way.

Gwen was *unusual*, I supposed.

What could I have done to cause her to write this? What had we talked about? I tried to remember. I needed to recall the context. I felt like I should be in English class, overanalyzing the possible meanings of each letter and punctuation mark. Skirty would have been helpful right now.

I toggled the camera off as a new thought occurred to me: did that mean Gwen had searched my room?

No.

No. I mean, no?

Maybe I'd read everything wrong. I had been wandering around on high alert since that day on the beach. Since my casual, "I dare you," had escorted my favorite person to her death.

I had no equilibrium, like, how sometimes, lying in bed after a day of travel, I still felt as though I could be on a boat, the waves rocking, or in a plane, facing turbulence, even though I'd disembarked hours earlier. Maybe my lies would capsize around me at any moment.

I rubbed my eyes. Or maybe I just needed more sleep.

❖

I tossed and turned for what felt like hours, reliving that moment:

"I dare you."

"I *dare* you," I'd said. "Just put in a toe. Then, go up to your ankles. Then calves. Baby steps. Try something new. Get out of your safe zone. Have an adventure."

I punched my pillow. The sound of the curtain's rope hitting the windowpane *tink-tink-tinked* louder than usual. I longed to close the drapes. I shouldn't have indulged in a bath.

"Do you really think I'm too stuck in my comfort zone?" she'd asked.

And I'd shrugged.

Shrugged.

Skirty had known what that meant.

I flipped onto my other side in the twin bed.

Skirty had whispered, "When you shrug, you give yourself away. It's your tell."

I hadn't noticed how often I did it or knew the reason why.

She'd *told* me. She'd known me better than I knew myself. "I wish you'd just say no," she'd said after I'd shrugged, when she'd asked if I wanted to go with her to audition for Agatha Christie's *And Then There Were None*. "I know you want to say no. That's what your shrug means," she said. "No, but I don't want to hurt your feelings."

At the beach, when I'd shrugged, I'd admitted I thought Skirty didn't take enough risks. She wouldn't leave the state to attend college. She'd chosen a school where the classes wouldn't be difficult. She'd probably hoped to marry the only boy she had ever dated.

She'd gone into the water because I'd shrugged. She'd kept going deeper. Farther. Took the risk because I'd shrugged.

Shoving the blankets off, I rolled onto my back. *My fault. My fault. My fault.* I chanted the words to the beat of the noose.

When I finally did sleep, I dreamed of drowning. I dreamed of sinking, of cool water caressing skin, and of numbness overtaking me. The waves and seaweed danced just like the shadows in Steve's projections.

In the nightmare, the water buried both of us. Skirty stared at me without seeing. Our hair swirling in the water's current, knotting us together. I couldn't move. Couldn't swim. Her icy hands grabbed me; her pallid and broken nails clawed at my skin, and it tore with ease. No blood seeped into the water. Where she clawed, Skirty exposed marbled veins, discolored muscles, and bone.

I'd died with her weeks ago. With all of me exposed to the water, Skirty drew me close to her, and we both sank deeper.

Deeper.

Darker.

Colder.

Lifeless inside and out.

We found Mrs. Payne in the deepest depths. And Ms. Eldonforth. A cloud of blood encircled Mrs. Payne in the water. She had no eyes, as though a deep-water dweller had feasted upon them. Ms. Eldonforth alone fought to stay alive. She screamed with the last of her breath. The water muted her cry, bubbles rushing up and away.

The drowned women of Lake Erie.

CHAPTER EIGHTEEN

In the morning, I woke up exhausted: groggy, shoulders sore, eyes crusty, and my mouth tasting sour. A bad start to a Friday. I skipped my calisthenics and felt ill-prepared to meet with the plainclothes officer who had come to the island without warning, accompanied by a few uniformed police.

All seven of us—Paynes and employees—clustered outside, awaiting our turn for the police to question us, as though the setting of the baking sun, blue sky, and green grass would make the experience more like a picnic instead of a follow-up police interview.

"Don't be afraid of the ball," Steve said in the distance as he nudged an old soccer ball toward Rock.

"Easy for you to say," Copper called. "The ball goes up to his knee."

I wished I could have used that comment as an opportunity to volunteer to find a smaller ball, but I'd been summoned for my interrogation.

"Ms. Smith, I'm Detective Wilhelm," said a middle-aged white man with graying hair and short dress slacks that revealed black socks covering his thin ankles.

I leaned against the oak tree I'd been standing under, the bark scratching my arm.

Officer Gonzalez swished through the grass, joining me and the detective. He nodded at me before crossing his arms.

"When we were here previously, we collected some items from the grounds. We wanted to see if you recognize any of them. Maybe you know who owns them?" Detective Wilhelm handed me a pile of photographs.

I flipped through the images quickly. That was, until I saw Skirty's shark bag. "Um." I'd left it at the beach my first day here. I admitted as much.

"And it's yours?" he asked.

"No," I said. "I mean, it was in my room when I arrived on the island that day. It must belong to, um, whoever stayed in my room before me. Another nanny, maybe." A shitty lie. They could ask anyone and know it had belonged to Skirty. But it wasn't as though it was the first time I didn't correct the police's mistaken assumptions about us.

"So the remains of the marijuana joints and mushrooms we found in the zippered pocket aren't yours? It's still illegal in Ohio, you know."

"What? No." I said before clenching my teeth. As a rule, I never smoked or did any drugs. I'd never been drunk. I'd only sipped from beer three times in my life, including my first night here with Gwen and Alex.

But Skirty...she'd done more. She must have left the drugs in the bag last summer.

"The drugs aren't mine, I swear," I said. "You can test me."

My parents had no idea my sister had smoked or taken shrooms. I scratched at an imaginary mosquito bite for an excuse to break eye contact with the detective. I didn't want to ruin my parents' image of her now.

"Relax." He smiled. "That's not really the crime we're most interested in solving."

I handed the photos back to Officer Gonzalez. Perspiration lined his forehead in the heat.

"Oh." Detective Wilhelm held his index finger to his cheek before pointing at me. "Have you, by any chance, heard of anyone named Trevor Knightley?" he asked as though the question had been an afterthought.

"Hmm?" I asked, delaying. I looked across the lawn to where Steve now chatted with Alex and Gwen. Trevor Knightley had been the name on the prescription bottle that he'd given me last night.

"Trevor Knightley?" he repeated.

"No," I said, resisting the urge to shrug.

"So, as far as you know, nobody by that name has stayed on the island?"

"Not since I've been here. Is that relevant to what happened to Mrs. Payne?" I asked.

"We suspect Mrs. Payne ingested a toxin at some point."

Ingested a toxin. The words repeated in my head. *Like a pill?*

"We found his name on some trash," the detective continued. "But it may be unrelated. Checking all potential leads." And he smiled as though to say, *You know how it is.*

I fought back a grimace. So much for the bag of bottles escaping anyone's notice. I tried to remind myself that I'd done nothing wrong. Not really.

Well, I hadn't done anything wrong connected with Mrs. Payne's death, I corrected myself. But if they followed *all* the leads, would something bring them back to the beach with Skirty?

And now I'd done something wrong by concealing the truth about Steve. "Sorry," I finally said, shrugging. "I can't help with that."

He had me look at more photos, but I could tell he and Officer Gonzalez became less concerned about my reactions as their gazes shifted to assess the others, to choosing their next prey. "Okay, that's all I have for you," Detective Wilhelm finally said. "Will you ask Ms. Eldonforth to come speak with us? We'd like to check a few things with her as well."

"Okay," I said, pushing off the tree to make my escape.

"Oh, and the next time you're in Sandusky, we'd appreciate it if you stopped by the station so we can take your fingerprints. We're asking everyone on the island to do it. Just so we know which prints to exclude." He smiled as though he'd asked the tiniest of favors from a friend.

I nodded, knowing my fingerprints would be all over the pill bottle prescribed to Trevor Knightley. "Sure," I said, forcing a smile and thinking, fuck you, Steve.

❖

That afternoon, Rock sang to me about fish as we meandered onto the dock to wait for Charlotte's arrival. We'd spent most of the day outside so I could avoid Steve.

"*Baby shark*," Rock sang as he threw pieces of grass that he'd pulled out moments before over the edge of the dock. "Here you go, Anvil."

"That's an interesting name. Where'd you hear it?" I asked. "A cartoon?"

He shrugged, peppering the lake's rippling surface with more torn blades of grass. "Anvil goes good with Rock."

Rock and Anvil, okay. "What does Anvil look like?" I asked. "Is he a new fish you discovered?"

"No, I told you, he's my brother."

"Right. Is he swimming now?"

He nodded. "He lives under the water. 'Cause he's scared of Smoky Shadow. Smoky Shadow ate him dead."

Goose bumps rose on my arms. "Rock..." I trailed off, unsure of what to say. Was this why Steve had gotten upset in the pool? We watched as the lake swept the blades of grass in and out on top of the small waves. Some pieces of grass collided with the rocky edge of the island, and the water rolled others below the surface.

"Mommy shark." Rock clapped his bent elbows together in a jaw-like motion.

A distant rumble from the lake drew my attention. "Look, Rock, here comes the boat." I pointed. "Your mommy's almost home."

The family's largest boat chugged to dock, and Charlotte leaned against the railing near the bow, waving. Rock danced along the dock, jumping up and down and waving back. Weston secured the boat and extended the gangplank.

"Stay on the dock, Rock." I reminded him.

He hopped in place as Charlotte ran down the gangplank and fell to her knees. Her arms encircled Rock. "My baby fish, I missed you! How are you feeling?" She spoke in a rush. "Does your mouth hurt?" She tried to peer into his mouth, but he pretended to chomp on her fingers.

"I'm a shark with lots of teeth."

"I see that," she said.

"I'll be waiting here after dinner," Weston said.

What? Charlotte was supposed to stay all weekend, I thought as I looked up to see Weston speaking to someone still on the boat. Mom and Dad emerged from the passenger cabin and gingerly stepped down the gangplank. Dad's only suit once again hung from his thin shoulders. Mom wore a rose pink, cotton, suit jacket and matching skirt. I hadn't seen her in it before. I suspected she'd unearthed it at a Goodwill.

"What are you doing here?" I blurted.

"We left you a few messages." Mom's simple words carried an accusation: *perhaps if you checked your phone…*

"Copper invited us for dinner," Dad said, his voice barely audible over the boat's engine.

Alex had mentioned there'd be guests tonight. But couldn't he or Copper have at least warned me that those guests would be my parents? I held my breath and counted to five before asking with fake enthusiasm, "Is everyone hungry?"

"Me, me, me," Rock yelled. "I want fish."

I took one of his hands while Charlotte held the other, and we walked toward the mansion. My parents followed.

Dread seeped into my gut. I'd already experienced one fancy and deadly meal in this mansion's dining room. With my parents' surprise arrival, my skin felt tight, my palms sweaty, and my shoulder muscles knotted. I reminded myself of how I had to act and wondered if this would be the night everything capsized around me?

CHAPTER NINETEEN

I entered the dining room for the first time since…

A hunter green rug ran beneath the mahogany table, the most noticeable change. It could have been my imagination, but the room felt colder. We'd need sweaters if the meal went on for too long.

Ms. Eldonforth had removed any evidence of death or of the police investigation. The hunter rug, with its accents of brown and blue, didn't match the rest of the mahogany decor. I ran my hands along my arms, trying to calm the goose bumps there and wondering why Ms. Eldonforth hadn't demanded we return the cumbersome rug and bring down another that would match better.

Rock, Charlotte, and I moved to our usual spots while my parents hovered in the doorway. Did Mrs. Payne's ghost hover too? It certainly wasn't the first death to occur on the island thanks to the fire, but maybe it was the first murder. I imagined Mrs. Payne's ghost sitting beside me tonight and having a tantrum after her critique of the way I cut Rock's asparagus would go unheard. Her ghost would be the sort to smash china, overturn tables, and wake us in the night.

I shivered, and I wasn't the only one.

As Copper joined us, I pulled out Rock's seat and got him situated between me and Charlotte. She gestured to chairs across from me and Rock for my parents to take, but they remained standing.

A few minutes ago, I'd gone to Rock's room and had grabbed a magnetic game for him that I handed to him now. A magnet attached to the end of the tiny fishing pole would attract and hook fish in the palm-sized pond. "I got them all earlier," he said.

"Well, let's see if you catch them all again," I said. "Show your mom how good a fisherman you're becoming."

"Steve's not feeling well and may miss dinner," Copper said as he pulled out the heavy seat that had *always* been Mrs. Payne's. He sat, tensed, and wiggled a little as though fearing electrocution. He repositioned again and pretended to look comfortable.

Finally, Mom sat, taking the seat opposite Copper, in the place that had once been Great-Uncle Gerald's. It hadn't been set, so Dad helped to shift a cloth placemat, utensils, and a plate for her. Dad stood awkwardly for another moment before choosing the seat opposite me. He gave a minuscule smile in my direction.

Copper started to speak just as Gwen entered, propping the dining room door open before Alex followed her. Both hesitated, taking in the new seating arrangements before distributing glasses of lemonade, pop, and water.

Mom waved off Gwen from giving her a water. "Can...*may* I have a cup of ice when you have a moment?"

Gwen nodded. Then, as she and Alex moved to leave, Gwen paused in the doorway, glanced around as if to make sure I was the only one watching and held a fist in the air, signaling me to stay strong. I pursed my lips to hold back a smile.

Copper shifted uncomfortably again. What was it Skirty had quoted from her AP English class? *Uneasy lies the head that wears the crown?*

"So," he said, just as my mom thanked him for inviting her and Dad. "Ah, of course," he said, clearly taken aback by the interruption.

"How is everyone feeling?" Mom asked, using the moment to take the lead. "I'm glad we can be here as one family. To weather the storm together." Before anyone could answer, she added, "How are things at headquarters?" She turned her focus back on Copper, who seemed stumped over which question to answer first.

I cringed internally with secondhand embarrassment at Mom's behavior.

Copper swirled the glass of dark pop in front of him as though it was wine. The ice cubes clanked, and the liquid fizzed, threatening to overflow. Charlotte and I focused on entertaining Rock as Mom played pretend and attempted to advise Copper as though she too had a master's degree in business instead of a few continuing education classes on child development.

We were a family of pretenders. In middle school, Skirty and I had posed as each other and attended the other's least favorite classes. We'd also played pretend with Dad, who'd worked as a janitor at the school. None of us had planned it, but all three of us had acted as though we didn't know him at school. I supposed we all feared that Skirty and I would be teased for being the janitor's kids. Mom's usual pretend game had been that she'd always treated Skirty and me equally. I guess now she'd graduated to feigning being a CEO.

As Mom rattled on at Copper about how to run the multibillion-dollar corporation, Dad stared at his hands, a hint of a grimace on his face.

"I got it." Rock swung his tiny yellow fishing pole up, and a small, green, magnetic fish stuck to the end went flying, bouncing onto the carpet and under the table.

"Rock, careful. Not so hard," Charlotte said.

I pushed my chair back and got on my hands and knees to retrieve the tiny fish.

"Let's swim and rescue it." And Rock joined me under the table.

I made a fish face at him as I picked up the small green fish.

"Ooo, is this a party?" Charlotte said, joining us on the floor.

"Fish party," Rock said.

As Charlotte and Rock pretended to swim, I watched Alex's long legs as he strode back into the room. He stopped beside

Copper's seat and stage-whispered, "Weston just called from the dock. The police are coming in a speedboat. No flashing lights. They should dock within the next couple of minutes. He thought you should know."

Charlotte and I exchanged glances over Rock's head as he hooked a blue fish.

"They didn't let me know to expect them," Copper said. "Ah, serve the meal," he suggested to Alex. "Nobody should go hungry while I meet with them. Have you seen Ms. Eldonforth? I'd like her to be a part of the conversation."

"I'll tell her," Alex said.

"Should we have a toast?" Mom asked before clearing her throat. "Lyla, will you please come out from under the table?"

"Oh, let the catfish enjoy it from the sea floor," Copper said, pushing his chair back and standing.

"Sharks," Rock clarified.

But before words could leave anyone's mouth, I saw Ms. Eldonforth shuffle in, wearing her usual black slacks and flats.

"Oh, there you are. We've been missing you," Copper said.

"Fish food," I whispered to Rock and Charlotte, pointing at Ms. Eldonforth's shoes.

"Let's get her," Charlotte said, and we creeped closer to peek out at her from under the table.

Ms. Eldonforth looked disheveled, her hair askew and her face pallid. Her eyes darted from side to side as though looking for something on the tabletop.

"Shark attack," Rock roared, but I grabbed his shirt to stop him from diving at her legs.

Alex strode to her side. "You don't look well. You should go back to the kitchen."

Ms. Eldonforth stumbled a little and grabbed Alex's arm in both hands as though only now seeing that he stood in front of her.

"Ope." Dad rose, extending a hand in case she fell.

Ms. Eldonforth's eyes focused on Alex for a moment before she turned to search the room again for something unseen. *Mrs. Payne's ghost?*

"Ms. Eldonforth? Are you okay?" Charlotte asked beside me.

She stumbled back, seemingly noticing us under the table for the first time. She cleared her throat again. "N...No," she said. "I can't take it anymore."

"What?" Charlotte asked.

Ms. Eldonforth's mouth opened and closed several times, her jowls shaking. "I couldn't take it anymore," she repeated.

Copper stepped toward her. "Couldn't take what?"

"This!" She dove at the table. I heard thuds and silverware clatter as she flung herself against the polished mahogany.

"Whoa!"

"What the?"

Charlotte and I bumped heads and shoulders as we both covered Rock. Mom's chair fell over as she jumped to her feet. Water, ice, and pop poured over the side of the table and onto the carpet, followed by several utensils.

Alex, Dad, and Copper grabbed at Ms. Eldonforth, who was mumbling, exclaiming, and knocking more utensils onto the floor. "It's my fault. I did it," Ms. Eldonforth shouted. She pulled at the table's edge. Was she trying to flip it? She shrieked.

Rock wailed and covered his ears. "What's wrong with Auntie Eldy?"

"Get him out of here," I shouted at Charlotte as I crawled toward the head of the table. Yelling for Gwen, Charlotte dragged Rock from under the table and jogged out of the room with him.

My knee sank into cold liquid as I climbed to my feet beside Copper. Dad and Alex had pulled Ms. Eldonforth from the table, each grasping an arm. Splotches from the pop, lemonade, and water darkened their shirts and pants. I couldn't tell who lost their footing first, but they tumbled to the floor in a pile before Detective Wilhelm and other officers rushed into the room, adding to the

chaos. They separated Dad, Alex, and Ms. Eldonforth before two
of the officers rushed Ms. Eldonforth out of the room.

"Everyone okay?" the detective asked.

"No," Mom said. "Nothing is okay here."

"What's going on?" Copper asked, trying to shake liquid from
his hands.

"Why did she just flip out?" I asked, rubbing my knee, trying
to clear away drops of water, crumbs, and little green flecks from
the rug.

"Because," Detective Wilhelm said, looking at me, "we've
come to arrest her for murder."

CHAPTER TWENTY

Red and blue police lights blinked and flared as dusk approached. Again. Detective Wilhelm had escorted Ms. Eldonforth away on one of the police boats, her hands cuffed behind her. Many officers remained, once again searching the main house with particular attention to Ms. Eldonforth's room.

After a phone call with Mr. Toler, Copper filed charges against Ms. Eldonforth for property damage as a precaution. A few officers questioned us outside to take our statements. I'd just finished giving mine as Officer Gonzalez walked away to talk alone with Mom.

I found Charlotte, Rock, Steve, and Copper sitting on the lawn near the granite steps, waiting for the police to permit them to go back inside. Steve had wrapped himself in a quilt with wild-haired, toy trolls decorating it. He looked shaky and ill, and I wondered if he realized he wore Ms. Eldonforth's childhood gift to him on the night she'd been arrested for killing his grandmother.

I collapsed, arms spread, and with the grass cool against my skin, I stared at the darkening sky. No stars twinkled or winked. The police lights blocked them. My empty stomach burned with acid, but I otherwise, felt numb.

Rock crawled to curl against my side, and I rubbed his back. With the little boy no longer by them, the Payne siblings spoke in hushed tones.

"I can't believe this. She practically raised us." Copper's voice strained to hold back tears. "Why would she…"

Let the tears fall, I thought.

"Why kill Grandma? After so many years? And why flip out tonight? Do you think it was because I was going to have us discuss moving off the island?" Copper continued. "Was she afraid I'd fire her? Is that what set her off?"

"I don't know." Charlotte said. "Did Grandma say anything about planning to fire her? Maybe that's why Ms. Eldonforth murdered her."

Rock shivered, and I pulled him closer, now adding my other arm to help hold him.

"Maybe she's like one of those prisoners who've been institutionalized for too long," Charlotte continued. "Too afraid to be released into the larger world. I mean, all these years…this place is all she has."

Steve pulled his blanket tighter around himself.

Copper stood. "It doesn't matter. She's fired."

I blinked back tears, feeling the undulation of wave after wave of problems.

❖

I awoke early the next morning, even early for me; my nervousness and energy felt like electricity sparking off my skin. Except for the whisper of the air-conditioning, the mansion slept. So the place could still stand without Ms. Eldonforth. I hadn't thought it possible.

Rock had asked to sleep with Charlotte, so I would have part of the morning off. My parents had remained for the night as well, too exhausted to take a boat back to Sandusky after their round of questioning with the police. They cloistered themselves in the second-floor guest room.

I did calisthenics to the beat of the noose. As my muscles grew sore and the acid built up and burned inside me, I resorted to pacing. It only took me seven steps to get from one side of the room to the other. Not enough space.

Ms. Eldonforth would never hurt any of the Paynes. Not intentionally. I was sure of it.

The swinging knot on the curtain's decorative rope striking against the windowpane felt louder, harder to drown out and ignore. I worked my muscles hard, counting my rounds of bicycle crunches in my head, waiting for the nervous shocks to subside.

When that didn't work, I paced and flipped open the top of my eucalyptus bodywash, hoping the smell would calm me. No luck. Even the unicorn sticker seemed to stare at me from the alarm clock.

I needed to get out. I needed to run, I needed to—

I left the room and the servants' wing. I listened in the hall before entering the kitchen with its counters bare. Maybe I could set out the cereal options for everyone. I noticed the yellow Post-it on the corkboard. Ms. Eldonforth's last order. From before yesterday's dinner. It broke my heart. She'd been continuing with her usual work, caring for the Paynes, unaware of the reckoning that had sped her way.

I shuffled over to read the note: *Alex, get Talc's old Go Fish card deck from the attic for Rock. It will be in the box labeled favorite childhood toys.*

Lucky Alex, receiving Ms. Eldonforth's last order. I ran my fingers over her handwriting. Why give that order to Alex? I was the nanny. I was the one tasked with getting arm swimmies from the basement, even if I had made Gwen go with me. *This should be my responsibility.*

If I looked for Go Fish and took my sweet time in the attic, my parents might decide to leave the island without our overdue heart-to-heart. *All the better.* I peeled the sticky note off the corkboard and tiptoed up the back staircase.

The ladder to the attic rolled down smoothly and silently, just as it had for Alex a few days ago. The scent of sawdust and a wave of a dry heat tumbled down to meet me.

After I climbed the first rungs, I paused to glance around the third floor, feeling as though I was about to do something wrong. And maybe I was. Following the orders of a murderer seemed dangerous.

Alleged murderer, I corrected myself. I didn't think murderers cared so deeply about saving and passing along games like Go Fish from their would-be victims. I resumed my climb. Once I was officially in the attic, it took me several seconds of shaky breathing, pulling away from imagined spiderwebs, and blindly shuffling to find the wall and the light switch. At least this space wasn't as musty and creepy as the basement. The attic seemed exactly as Alex and I had left it, no evidence of police rummaging among the Paynes' least-loved possessions.

I bent and crawled among the boxes to see Ms. Eldonforth's labels. In the last row, I found the box named in the Post-it. Or rather, I found *two* boxes. Both were labeled, *favorite childhood toys*, but one of the labels had capitalized the first letter of each word, and the other contained only lowercase letters.

I glanced at the Post-it that I'd stuck to my arm. No capitalizations, according to the note. Ms. Eldonforth had been detail oriented and anal-retentive enough for me to suspect the difference was intentional. I pulled the box with no capital letters to check first. Unfolding the top, I looked inside to find another yellow Post-it:

I choose you for as long as everyone remains well.

I whispered the words. What did that mean? *Talk about conditional love.*

I compared this note to the one I knew Ms. Eldonforth had written. The H's in fish and choose had matching loops. All the O's looked similar...and the S's. In my completely inexpert opinion, Ms. Eldonforth had written both. Was she romantically involved with Alex?

No, right? No? That was wrong. There had to be around a forty-year age difference.

They had seemed close, though. Ms. Eldonforth had preferred Alex's company over Gwen's. But I couldn't imagine her getting romantically involved with someone she employed.

I returned my attention to the box. There was only a folded, graying paper and a few photos at the bottom. No toys in sight. Why store such small items in a big box in the attic? I reached in to turn the photos over; each featured a little blond boy. Close-ups of his pudgy face as he looked at a picture book or used finger paints and chalk. From some of the backgrounds, I could tell they had been taken on the island. None of the photos included anyone else.

I found something else hidden in the box's corner: a black matchbox with a red image of a flame on its cover. I slid the box open. The matchsticks had bright purple heads. Expensive, I guessed. About half of the matches were missing, probably used long ago. *Why keep this in here?*

I placed the matches back inside and took out the single sheet of graying paper that rested at the bottom. The cramped cursive slanted far to the right and was difficult to decipher, the ink smeared and faded. I could make out the recipient's name: *Susan*. The writer had scrawled the S with big flourishes.

As far as I knew, nobody in the Payne or my branch of the family had that name. I looked at the bottom of the thick sheet paper for a signature: *Gerald*, written with an equal flourish. I blinked and reread the name. *Gerald*. Mrs. Payne's husband and my great-uncle.

I didn't see a date, but he must have written it more than twelve years ago, before the fire. With cursive too slanted and the paper too gray to be sure of each word, I read slowly, trying to form phrases that would make sense. I thought one portion stated, *I'll provide for his education. Nothing more.* It'd taken some work to decipher the D's and U's. The T and the H together looked more like W's. *Who taught this man cursive?*

I reread as much as I could. Great-Uncle Gerald was writing about a boy named Ryan, whom he referred to as "our son" twice. Holy shit. I glanced from the letter to the photos and back. The blond boy.

I rearranged the Payne family tree in my head. If Gerald had another son, that meant Charlotte, Steve, and Copper had an uncle.

Did they know? If they did, wouldn't they have mentioned Ryan after Mrs. Payne's funeral?

Mom had never mentioned a Ryan. I longed to show this letter to Skirty, or Rose. Skirty knew more about the Paynes' many scholarships or might know how to start a conversation about a long-lost uncle. Rose would know how to use software to scan the letter and change the contrast to reveal more of the faded writing.

Despite the attic's cleanliness, it felt like cobwebs or spiders brushed against the skin of my bare arms, and I shivered as I deciphered a bit at the end: *The lies we tell the children. This is how it must be. I wish you both the best, Gerald.*

Why did Ms. Eldonforth have this letter? And why leave it for Alex to find?

I looked, making certain to check behind me, fearing a creepy little blond ghost would lunge at me. I returned everything into the box and put it back exactly where I'd found it.

Next, I opened the *Favorite Childhood Toys* box. A tattered copy of a Go Fish card game rested on top. *That's Ms. Eldonforth.*

Leaving the game for Alex to find, I hesitated. I reopened the first box. I took out the letter, then restored everything to the way it had been without waking any ghosts. After I'd padded down the back stairs and reposted the sticky note to the corkboard, I returned to my room. I hid the letter inside my sister's old copy of *One Fish, Two Fish.* I knew one person who was *not* in police custody who might have some answers: Mom.

I'd go home and take the letter. That way, I could show her without worrying about eavesdroppers or ghosts. I sighed. Depending upon Mom's mood, her knowledge about family lore, and suspicions, this could end badly for me or for the Payne siblings' expectations of their inheritance.

CHAPTER TWENTY-ONE

The sun finally rose, but nobody else had. Asking Charlotte for the weekend off and making the arrangements to return to Sandusky with Mom and Dad later today would have to wait. I was doing calisthenics when I heard a knock on my door and glanced at the alarm clock. 6:45 a.m.

Should I answer? Nobody on the island should have expected me to be awake yet. The visitor knocked again, and the urge to know who waited on the other side of the door propelled me to my feet. I messed up my hair and made a squinting face, as though the knocks had woken me.

I opened the door to Steve. He had dark circles under his eyes and some uneven stubble on his cheeks and chin. "You look like shit," I said, opening the door wider so he could enter.

"I feel like shit. On many levels." Just like the last time he'd been here, he avoided looking at me. "I'm sorry to bother you this early."

I closed the door. "It's fine. Almost time to get up anyway," I lied.

"I can't believe…" He shook his head. "When the police were asking me questions last night, I thought I was in a withdrawal induced nightmare."

"Yeah, I know what you mean."

He sat on my bed, bouncing his foot and making the bed frame squeak. After a moment, he tried to match the beat of the knot of the decorative rope hitting the windowpane. "Wow, that's annoying," he said, looking at the knot hovering above us.

"Um, is there something you need? If possible, I'd prefer not to deal with any more of your contraband, Trevor Knightley." I crossed my arms.

"No, I just, ah, I'm sorry about that. Don't worry about Trevor. He's just this asshole kid. I knew his older sister, and she used old pill bottles to hide other drugs."

"How long have you been getting pills from her?"

"Look." He shrugged, his gesture so familiar, my own arms fell to my sides. "I...I have a problem." He stumbled over a response to the question he clearly didn't want to answer. "And it's been gnawing at me for years." He shook his head. "What I've been doing to cope hasn't...isn't." He cleared his throat. "I need to find a better way forward," he finally said in a rush. He looked relieved to admit it.

"Okay," I said.

"The Knightleys aren't—" He shook his head. "It'll be a dead end for the police." He looked at me, finally meeting my gaze. "I haven't involved you in an international and illegal drug smuggling ring. No murder plots." He scratched at his stubble. "I swear."

"Not even with your creepy projections?"

"Creepy? They're meant to be fun. I'm still working to perfect them."

"Sure," I said. "And the one being used to torture Rock?" *And upset me.*

His brows knit in confusion. "Wow, you really think the worst of me, don't you?" He rocked forward and back, shoulders hunched in a familiar knot of self-hate that caused my jaw and fists to unclench.

"Look, Steve. I...your actions and choices have consequences for others. I had to lie to the police. For you. I didn't want to be in that position."

"I know. I get that. I'm sorry." He kept rocking. "I'm working on getting better."

I sighed, my tense shoulders relaxing as I said, "I'm glad to hear it, but if someone stole one of your prototypes, what do you recommend I look for to find it? Or how do I figure out who stole it?"

"Well, you probably find the box itself up high and at the center of the mess if it's on. As for finding who stole it, look for the remote. It's small, so it can fit in your palm or in a pocket. I have some in my bedroom."

"I remember from when you showed us," I said. "Thanks."

"Happy to help." And his lips upturned. "It feels good to be useful."

"I'm guessing that's not why you're here at six...forty-nine in the morning." I glanced at the alarm clock before taking a seat on the floor.

"No, but I'd rather talk about imaginary drug rings and my projectors. It's easier."

"Steve."

"Fine." He sighed, finally sitting still. "I didn't need to burden Copper or Charlotte with my problems. But, ah, things are looking more serious than I thought. So yeah." He stared at his trembling fingers before interlocking them as if to hide the shaking.

"I'm sad you feel this way," I said, not knowing what else to say.

"Yeah, well." He avoided looking at me again, seemingly fascinated by the bland carpet. "I'm sorry I've been such a shit to you."

I nodded but couldn't bring myself to say, I forgive you, or another lie.

"So, ah, update. I'm going to an inpatient drug rehab thing."

I gaped.

"Don't make a big deal about it." He held up his arms like he needed to fend off a hug, even though I hadn't moved from the floor. "I asked Copper, and he made the arrangements after the police left last night. So, yeah, I'm leaving in a few minutes. Copper's going to take me."

"Wow, that's fast."

"When you have money…" He trailed off.

I nodded. "Okay."

"Charlotte knows. She'll tell Rock I'm visiting friends or something."

I thought of Gerald's letter. *The lies we tell the children.* "Okay."

"I just felt like I should tell you. You tried to get me to see the problem. And I thought…it's like I never really healed after the accident with my parents and…Talc. I'm still wounded. Talc was my…he was half of me. I don't think I've ever learned to function without him."

My eyes stung. I refused to blink, fearing tears would fall. I knew exactly what he meant, but I couldn't say it aloud yet. I nodded instead.

"I, ah, I hope your path isn't as long as mine is proving to be," he said. "You know, to feeling like a whole human again."

"I don't think it's possible to be a whole human again." I said, now the one to seem entranced by the carpet, but the tears fell anyway.

He joined me on the floor and hugged me. He was slow and gentle about coming near, like he knew I might flee or shove him away. And even after his arms encircled me, he remained tense, barely making contact, as though I'd tell him to get away at any moment.

I tucked my head against his shoulder, and his arms tightened around me as we awkwardly pressed each other close. He knew exactly how I felt. I exhaled, but it sounded almost like a chuckle. The last time we'd hugged, I hadn't been in third grade yet and had declared that he'd smelled and had cooties.

There was still one difference between us, the most vicious part of me thought. *He didn't cause Talc's death the way I'd caused Skirty's.* I sniffled and climbed to my feet.

Steve did the same, and we stood, shifting feet, looking at anything but each other. I allowed my glance to pass over his face. He must have done the same. *Uh-oh, eye contact.*

He cleared his throat and pulled out the small purple water gun from his back pocket. "Here," he said. "Use as intended. You can surprise Rock from the pool deck or something. Assuming he'll ever get in the water again." He pointed the gun at me as though ready to shoot. "But no vodka or tequila, young lady. Just water."

"Got it." I said, taking the water gun and feeling truly close to and seen by someone—to Steve, of all people—for the first time in months. "Steve?"

"Yeah?"

"I've…" I took a deep breath. *Plunge in.* "I've done some bad things. I've been lying for weeks, and I don't know what to do or how to fix things. I don't think I can fix them."

"Did you kill my grandma?"

"What? No."

"You're not a murderer. Can't be too bad then, can it?"

I shrugged.

"I don't know. Tell the people who matter most first. Deal with each consequence one by one, I guess." He scratched his stubble again. "Despite the fact that I make it look sexy, numbing and trying to avoid everything does not work."

I nodded, feeling my lips upturn in a small smile. "Got it."

"We're going to find a way to be okay," he said. "Both of us."

"I hope you're right."

I heard him mumble, "Me too," to himself as he turned to go.

"Wait," I said. "One more thing." The significance of him asking about Mrs. Payne's death sunk in. "Um, you asked me if I killed your grandma? Was it a joke or…does…does that mean you don't think Ms. Eldonforth did it?"

He looked me in the eye. "There's no fucking way she did it." He spoke with more confidence than I'd ever heard him use. "In her own weird way, that woman loves each and every one of us." He nodded at me to show I was included in the list.

"You think?"

"I know. She was frustrating. She'd hide my pills. Flush my vodka. She was our surrogate grandmother long before the fire." He pointed at the floor for emphasis. "Crystal was her family too. I'm still her family." He pointed again. "What's happening now is a fucking disgrace."

"Got it," I said.

He stared at me. "Do you know something more?"

I shrugged. "Do you remember a kid named Ryan?"

"Ryan?"

"Yeah, a blond boy, maybe?"

He remained silent for a moment. "Maybe? When we were little—before the fire—Grandma would invite people over to network and schmooze. After the fire, it was family only."

"Oh." Neither of us moved. The noose pinged. "Steve?"

"Yeah?"

"Do you think the fire was an accident?"

"No." His face looked steely.

"What makes you think that?" I stepped closer. I rubbed at my arms where goose bumps rose.

"The s'mores."

"What?" I shook my head.

"Talc was the only one of us kids at the cabin. Like, the accepted story is that he woke up and asked the adults to make him s'mores because he couldn't sleep." He shook his head.

"Oh. So?"

"He didn't like s'mores. He'd just eat the chocolate and sneak me his marshmallows."

I gulped and cleared my throat. "What does that prove?"

"There were two marshmallows skewered on sticks just waiting by the firepit. Supposedly, they built the fire back up to have Talc roast marshmallows, and the fire jumped to a tree and then to the roof."

"Huh."

"Yeah."

"Did you ever tell your grandma, Ms. Eldonforth, or anyone else about this?"

"I didn't think they'd believe me," he said. "This is a twin thing. I just know the s'mores by the firepit weren't his."

"Got it."

"I haven't eaten a marshmallow since," he added as though I'd find it funny.

Tears stung my eyes at hearing him make such a familiar punishing rule for himself. "Steve, stop punishing yourself," I said as a dam that had held my compassion at bay broke. "Eat a fucking marshmallow if you want."

"Easier said than done," he admitted before staring at me.

I fidgeted but didn't shrug.

"You too," he finally added, seeing what swirled below my surface. "However you're punishing yourself for still being alive while Dalia isn't. Stop it."

I took a shaky breath. "Easier said than done."

"Yeah. But we're going to figure it out."

I tried to smile but couldn't manage it. *Tink. Tink. Tink.* The air-conditioner had kicked on.

The swinging noose drew Steve's attention again. "God, that's annoying." He pointed to it.

"You don't even notice it after a while," I lied.

"Do you mind if I?" He waved toward the noose.

I shook my head no, and he shuffled to the window, releasing the curtain from the rope. The noose fell to the window's side, swung side to side, but now—removed from being under the AC vent—slowed and stopped. *Silence.*

"Thanks," I said.

"No problem." He tucked his hands into his pockets, looking awkward.

"Don't be a stranger. Call any time you need to talk." I'd answer, I realized. I didn't think I would have said that an hour ago.

He nodded, gave me a thumbs-up and turned to go, opening my door and stepping into the hall.

"Steve?"

"Seriously?" He turned back to me. "I can't get better if I never leave this room."

I gripped the water gun by the trigger and aimed at his head. "Take better care of yourself. Or I'll shoot."

He held his hands up in surrender before smiling, turning, and walking away. Maybe it wasn't the sweetest good-bye, but it worked for us.

CHAPTER TWENTY-TWO

An hour later, after mentioning to Alex and Gwen that I needed to go to Sandusky with my parents for a weekend at home, they turned the trip into an elaborate plan: all three of us would go. Kind of. Alex would just go for his weekly groceries, but Gwen hoped to stay in town.

"We can have that dance you owe me," she said bumping her hip against mine. "If you're nice to me."

"Maybe," I said. "Assuming Charlotte even gives both of us permission to go, my parents may want me to stay home with them after everything." I also found myself wondering if Rose would be in town for the weekend, home from college.

"You owe me." Gwen leaned close, bringing me back to the moment. "And I collect."

"She really does," Alex confirmed.

"Yeah, but...I'm not out," I said, letting my frustration tinge my voice. "And I'd really like to wait to tell them a little longer. Since we're all having a difficult time." What I said was mostly true. *Mostly.*

Gwen shook her head at me and sighed. "We've all been there." Then, she smiled. "Now you owe me two dances."

I nodded, but I also gritted my teeth at her pushiness. Maybe Charlotte would have a reason that Gwen and Alex couldn't go with me. I found myself wanting a break from both of them.

Copper had accompanied Steve as he checked in at the rehab center and had said he'd most likely stay in Cleveland for a few days to do business-y things. He might sleep better away from the murder house too, I thought. Charlotte and Rock would be the only ones on the island. They'd ask Gwen to remain close, right? Just in case.

This was another moment when Skirty would have saved me. When we were little, it would have just taken the briefest flash of a thumbs-down for us to make excuses for each other. As we aged, it had only taken a glance to get the same result. Now, I had to fend for myself.

"I'll still need Weston to take me and the groceries back to the island tonight. No vacation for me," Alex said. "And it's probably best not to leave Rock and Charlotte completely alone. Especially not when Rock has put in a request for a meal with octopus in it." He smiled at the grocery list he'd written. "Things are about to get much more interesting food-wise without Ms. Eldonforth on the island."

Gwen and I trooped up to Rock's room, where we found him and Charlotte lying side by side on the floor, drawing. They'd taped together twelve sheets of paper and had started to outline a school of fish in a large ocean scene. Based on the smile on Rock's face and the way he hummed, he relished his mom's undivided attention.

"We'll have a shark lurking in the shallows," Charlotte suggested. She wore an orange, fish-shaped hat, and she looked up at Gwen and me from between the fish's fins.

"Morning," I said. "Coffee?"

She nodded, the fish fins flopping.

"I'll bring up a juice for Rock too," Gwen said.

"Um," I exchanged a glance with Gwen. "I'm sorry for the short notice, but since you're on the island until Sunday night, would you mind if I went home with my parents for the weekend?" I asked. "I can be back before you leave for OSU."

"And I'd also like to visit my family," Gwen lied. "It's been a stressful few weeks. But now that everything is resolved with Mrs.

Payne and Ms. Eldonforth, I'd really love to see family. You know, give my dad a hug."

I glanced at Gwen. She'd known just what to say, her tone perfect. The way her head tilted and her eyebrows curved, she even looked sincere. I didn't see any tells or hints that her real motive for leaving involved relaxation and partying. This was a very different Gwen from the night we'd played chore poker. I now stood beside a professional actress. I couldn't detect any tells. For some reason, the idea needled me.

She's not authentic the way Rose always is with me.

I shifted away from her side.

"Of course, yeah." Charlotte said, drawing my attention back to her. "I don't have much homework yet. So we can make it work. When the ferry returns me to Sandusky for my drive to campus Sunday night, it could pick you up. It'll be perfect. Alex will only be on Rock-sitting duty for about an hour. Can you check that he's okay with babysitting when you get the coffee?"

"Yeah," I said, my hopes sinking.

"I doubt he'll mind," Gwen added.

"Oh, tell him to add sour cream and onion chips to the grocery list," Charlotte said.

"And fish," Rock shouted, shaking his crayon in the air.

"And gummy bears." Charlotte matched his tone. She seemingly reveled in the idea that she was the sole Payne to consult about groceries for the moment.

"And *two* more octopuses," Rock added.

"No, four more octopuses."

"Ten bazillion and one octopuses," Rock shouted.

"Or is it octopies? Octopods?" Charlotte asked.

"Octopuses," Rock shouted again. "Octopus pie."

"Excellent. Let's not steal all of them from the ocean. Let's stick with three octopuses, Rock," Gwen suggested.

"Yay, three octopuses for dinner. That's twenty-four tentacles. Twelve for each of us," Charlotte said with no hint of sarcasm before clinking her crayon against Rock's as though they were glasses of champagne. "But, yeah," she said to us. "I think Copper's going to want a few days to reset and reevaluate the way we've been running the island."

"Understood," Gwen said, and we left Rock's room.

"Text me about going dancing tonight," Gwen whispered in the hallway.

I nodded, keeping my face neutral but feeling as though she and Charlotte had officially sunk all my battleships.

Gwen charged ahead of me down the stairs to get coffee and juice and to tell Alex about the additions to the grocery list. I moved to stand outside the guest room where my parents still hadn't emerged to start their morning.

I was going home for the weekend. With my parents. And Gwen, who could unintentionally reveal one of my secrets or overhear me asking Mom about the mysterious Ryan. I wouldn't call this a rest. I knew Steve was right about telling the truth. Logically, that was the answer. But also, maybe I could delay? When I finally got Mom alone, I'd ask her about Ms. Eldonforth and this Ryan kid. That needed to be the priority.

After I told Mom all my secrets, she might never speak to me again.

I finally knocked on the guest room door. When I told my parents that I'd be going with them to Sandusky—*just for one night*, I repeated a few times—I saw them smile for the first time in months. I wondered how long it would take them to smile again after we had our overdue conversation.

I stood on the small deck of the ferry, trying to keep my distance from Gwen while my parents remained inside the cabin and out of the wind. We'd left our stuff inside with my parents and Alex. Not that I was bringing much home for one night: only one small bag with the phone—still off—and the copy of *One Fish, Two Fish* with Gerald's letter tucked inside.

The wind dragged tears from my eyes, made my hair whip at my face, and muted my worries over Mom judging me or not helping. Gwen whooped into the wind, and we exchanged smiles, but she left me alone, thankfully. As we sped by Cedar Point, I could see the roller coaster cars tumbling, twisting, and flipping. I imagined the screams of the riders and the sense of breathlessness. Growing up so close to the coasters had meant mooching from friends who had season passes. I had each turn, twist, and dip on the Millennium Force, Raptor, and Steel Vengeance memorized.

Skirty had always preferred the kiddy rides. Cedar Point had been one of the few places where we'd separated and didn't see each other all day. Dad explored with me and Mom with her. Maybe Skirty's dislike for roller coasters had been one of the reasons I'd shrugged that day on the beach.

I closed my eyes and tried to enjoy the sensations of the boat crashing against the small waves. I enjoyed the *thunk, thunk* rhythm of it. Skirty would have hated this. She would have remained inside with our parents.

Which meant, maybe I should go inside.

Maybe.

And maybe that day on the beach, I'd just made a stupid shoulder movement in a moment, and I shouldn't have punished myself for that.

Or maybe I hadn't shrugged out of evasiveness. Maybe I'd felt confused. Maybe I was a teenager at the beach with my sister. Maybe Rock shouldn't have thought a hug could hurt a family member. Maybe Steve should have eaten marshmallows whenever he wanted.

Maybe I should live my life.

Maybe. Maybe. Maybe.

CHAPTER TWENTY-THREE

Home. I swear, our small, two-story house smelled different without Skirty.

We didn't live in the nicest part of Sandusky. Not that tourists from bigger cities thought there was much *to* Sandusky. But our parents had resided here since before we were born.

I couldn't bring myself to go upstairs to see the changes Mom had made to our bedroom. Instead, I sat in our slim backyard: a patchy lawn exactly as wide as our house, plus one foot on each side. A tall, peeling, white fence caged me, clearly marking our territory from the neighbors'.

Mom had managed to string up a laundry line to dry bedsheets and—much to our horror—Dad's underwear, since our dryer had never worked well. She had just hung one of our old sheets, decorated with small purple flowers, a few minutes ago. "So you'll have fresh sheets for tonight," she'd said.

The best part of our backyard was its sole cherry dogwood tree that had taken root in the middle. We'd helped Dad pick it out as an anniversary gift to Mom when we were eight or nine. Dad had beamed when I'd thought to ask the Molyet's employee how much sun and water the tree would need.

The cherry dogwood had taken root and bloomed in May, an annual advertisement that the end of the school year approached. I sat in an Adirondack chair beneath the branches now, trying to list all the questions I needed to ask Mom about Gerald and the fire. I was glad I'd waited until we were home to talk. I wasn't sure I would have gotten the real answers if the Paynes had been nearby.

Wind chimes collided, and the sound echoed. Since I'd been gone, Dad had hung a bird feeder on one of the dogwood's branches near the small silver wind chime that had been there for years. He'd also hung a hummingbird feeder that contained sweet water.

"To honor Dalia," he'd said the day after the funeral. "This was our Shorty's favorite spot."

He knew us well. I smiled grimly. *It's only a matter of time until they figure it out.*

The back door from the kitchen squeaked, and Mom joined me outside. She had been silent on the ride from the dock, but now, her lips pursed in a Ms. Eldonforth-like manner. "For the love of God, please behave like a normal teenager and keep this by your side," she said, extending the cell phone. "It had less than ten percent left on the battery."

"Did you take that from the bag?"

"Yes, of course, I did."

"Mo—"

She held up a finger for silence. "Something has got to change. This isn't like you." The only thing missing from this rant was for her to ask, "What is wrong with you?" I could tell the question was at the tip of her tongue. But she didn't ask it. She had an excellent idea of at least some of what was wrong. "We can't go on like this."

After a moment, she added, "There is a message for you," in a softer tone. "I think you should answer it. And then, tonight, we are going to talk. *Really talk.*"

I nodded, gritting my teeth. She had no idea.

She'd used *we* to mean her and me. I'd rarely thought of Mom and me as a we. Usually, it was *your sister and me* or *Mom and my sister* that had formed a we. Never Mom and me.

"Do you have your SD card?"

"Huh?"

"For photos you want me to print. I'd figured you'd have a bunch of new ones."

"Ah, no. I didn't...with everything..." I resisted the urge to shrug. "I didn't want to be rude and wander around the island with a camera while everyone mourned."

Her brow wrinkled, but she said, "That's thoughtful. We should look among your old photos for ones of Aunt Crystal that we can send to your cousins."

I nodded again, lips pursed. We'd finally become a we. I didn't know if we'd still be after we talked. "Good idea." I held up the phone. "I'll be better with this. Promise."

"Please be," she said before making a *teenagers are so exhausting, why must I suffer so?* gesture at the sky and going back into the house.

I opened the home screen on the phone. Mom had charged it for me. Rose had sent the new message: *Heard you were in town. Just got back from U of M for the weekend.*

Gulp. Who'd told her I was home? I'd been here for an hour and a half, and I hadn't left the house.

Mom. I answered my own stupid question, shaking my head. Why had she called Rose and not Derek? The question worried me.

I'd just set the phone on the arm of the chair when several more texts came through:

Will you please go to Dalia's grave with me? I can't do it alone.

I need to leave a poem for her.

I slumped in my seat. I took a deep breath. *Okay*, I sent. *In an hour?*

❖

The small cemetery rested a few blocks from our home, near the train tracks. I could see employee parking, dumpsters, and the back of a strip mall through the trees and beyond a chain-link fence. The trees prevented some of the mall noise from pervading the cemetery, but the sounds of traffic still reached me. A slight breeze and the shadows of waving tree branches prevented the sun from feeling antagonistic on my shoulders.

I would hate to be buried here. But my sister? I wasn't sure. She never wanted to leave Ohio the way I did. She was the only Smith or Payne buried here. Dad had arranged to have his parents cremated and had spread their ashes before I'd been born. The Paynes had plots and statues in a picturesque cemetery near Cleveland. Mom always talked about visiting it at some point, since her mom was also there, but we'd never actually gone. I guess we'd visit soon for Mrs. Payne. When the police finally released the body.

I wondered if Mom had hoped that Crystal would have invited my sister's body to rest in the Paynes' family plot. Maybe it would have been better if she had been buried there. The thought that she was alone here and might remain that way for decades broke my heart.

A hint of movement outside the cemetery gates had me adjusting my hair and checking that my tank and shorts looked okay. I could hear my heartbeat in my ears as Rose strode toward me from the entry of the cemetery's drive. She must have parked on the street. I forced my body to remain still—no bouncing knee, no shoulders hunching—as I leaned against my mom's car where I waited for her.

She carried two large, clear plastic cups of lemonade from Crimson Cup. She wore a maroon tank top that I'd seen her in dozens of times throughout our senior year. She also wore black jeans that would make her too warm in this weather. She joked that she had three hairy moles that would get ideas and form their own face if she wore shorts, and they saw enough daylight.

I swallowed the urge to tell her how beautiful she was, her hairy moles, thoughtfulness, passions, and insecurities included. "Wow." I couldn't help myself. "You look—"

"College agrees with me." Rose paused to pose, holding the drinks above her and framing her face while singing as though an angel was present. "I feel a bit safer to be myself there," she said. "So many poetry slams to attend and so many weak-ass poker players to beat."

"I'm so happy for you." It felt foreign to smile so wide and mean it.

"There are even multiple organizations for students of color who are also queer." I could see her dimple on her left cheek as she smiled big and genuine.

"Cool," I said, trying to fake excitement. She'd never had choices like that here in Sandusky. Would she still have been *all in* with more options and more people?

"Oh, shit." Her smile fell, and she swept her braids behind her shoulder. Her tell. She was nervous. "Sorry. I didn't mean to—"

"I think it's not only a college thing but also a bigger town opportunity." I tried to bring back her smile. "I'm so glad you've found a home and people who welcome you."

She came closer, extending one of the drinks. The sound of traffic from the nearest highway whirred too loud.

"I'm not thirsty," I said. "But thanks."

"Are you sure? It's hot out."

"No, no thanks." I hated the thought of acidic lemonade right now, with my stomach already so nervous. But even more, I feared Rose stepping close to me, having to inhale her perfume. I wouldn't be able to maintain my poker face through that.

"Okay, I'll ask you again when we leave, but it won't taste as good since the ice will melt."

"My loss," I said, standing up straight.

She set both lemonades on the curb in the shadow of Mom's car.

"It's over here." I waved in the direction of the grave. Rose had been at the funeral, but her mom had declared her too upset to stay for the actual burial. I'd been thankful she'd left. It had hurt too much to see her pain while THE BOYFRIEND had repeatedly hugged me or patted my back.

Our feet *swish, swish, swished* against the grass as we approached the small plaque to mark my sister's spot. Someone had typed the name, *Dalia Smith*, on a small rectangular paper and wrapped it in clear plastic to mark the grave. It'd be months and months before the gravestone would arrive.

We remained silent as we stood at the edge of the grave where shoots of grass had begun to grow. I should've planted flowers. Why hadn't I thought to do that weeks ago? Maybe some purple hyacinths. They'd do well in this sunlight and would bloom in the spring. Her favorite color, purple. I could plant them in a few weeks.

Rose strangled a sob as she pulled a folded paper from her pocket.

"I'll...I'll give you some space," I said before swishing through the grass and back to Mom's car.

The lemonades still sat on the curb, condensation pooling around the base of each cup. I resumed leaning against the car and watched Rose mourn in the distance. I could see her unfolding the paper, reading from it, crying over it, setting it in front of the grave, burying it under a layer of dirt.

I fought back tears and stared at the sky for a while and wished it would start pouring.

Rose placed a small stone on the corner of the name plaque. I knew this was Jewish tradition from when a few of us had attended her father's funeral. She swept her braids behind her shoulder again and shuffled to me.

I wanted to hug her, hold her close, and whisper the truth to her. Then I'd kiss her temple. I'd...

The muscles in my arms tensed to do just as I imagined, like it was natural. So instead, I crossed my arms to help keep my distance as I asked, "How are you?" I managed. "I mean, aside from...." I waved in the direction of the grave. *I'm such an idiot.*

Rose leaned against the car by my side, her hip and shoulder millimeters away from contact with mine.

I inched away.

"Did Dalia ever tell you about the Plan?" she asked.

I nodded slowly. All in: leaving Ohio. College together. Swim scholarship. Spoken word poem performances in cafés. Attending queer student alliance events. Texting the family daily. Nightly poker games. Eventually, studying abroad together. Happily ever after.

"Yeah, well, I'm doing my part. University of Michigan, preparing to become an English teacher. It just really sucks not having her with me."

"I know what you mean," I said.

A few bird songs complemented the distant whoosh of cars. The breeze picked up just enough to carry the scent of eucalyptus to me. Rose's perfume. I'd missed this smell so much. Combined with a product that she put on her scalp, the scent seemed richer than it had on Gwen.

Rose. Rose. Rose.

I stood straighter, clearing my throat. "Well, I should go," I said, turning to open the car door.

"Here, wait, the lemonades. Don't drive off without one." She came close, reaching around me to rescue the drinks, and we collided a little as I opened the driver's car door. She put her hand out to stop from falling and gripped my arm.

I felt the warmth and nervous tingles she'd always caused. What if she felt them too? Could sense the truth? See through my poker face? I should have pulled away, but my heart stumbled and raced. I studied the curves of her eyes, the tilt of her dark eyebrows. She still looked sad.

She didn't recognize me. Didn't realize. Maybe didn't feel the tingles that she had once written poems about. My heart shattered at the realization.

"Here you go." Rose handed me one of the lemonades, the sides of the plastic cup slick. The wind shifted just so, and she shifted close enough that her eucalyptus scent surrounded me fully.

Suddenly, I returned to myself. My *real* self. Me from three months ago surfaced. Me without the guilt, the rules, the lies, the knots, or the punishments.

Just for a moment and without thinking, I started to say, "All in," but I remembered, submerged, and stopped my mouth from forming the *in*. I tried to cover the slip by coughing.

Maybe part of me had wanted her to know. Had slipped up on purpose.

I heard my pulse in my ears, the way I had when I searched the Erie for Skirty. But this time, instead of seeing green tinted rocks and seaweed, I watched as Rose's brown eyes widened, and her mouth went slack. She'd heard me. She'd heard the phrase I'd almost said, and her hand loosened on the cup of lemonade.

It fell.

Neither of us moved and the drink's top flew off when the cup impacted with the ground, lemonade and ice splattering on our shins and feet. Rose didn't seem to notice the liquid, but I backed away.

"What?" she demanded.

"Swallowed wrong," I said, my words sounding reedy. I tried to cover. "I'm sorry. I know the poker phrase was important to you. I'm sorry. I wasn't thinking." That part was true.

She stared, her eyebrows furrowed, her lips downturned. This was what I'd feared. This was why I'd ran. She *always* brought out the real me, always could tell when I bluffed. Would she tell my parents the truth? Would she think I was insane? Would she hate me forever for what I had done?

"I'm sorry," I repeated. "I have to go." And I fled into Mom's car, locking the door.

I drove away, leaving her standing there, dripping acidic lemonade, watching me.

CHAPTER TWENTY-FOUR

Mom and I stood in the kitchen, stomachs growling. I'd washed my feet and changed the subject when she'd asked about Rose.

"I wish we had a personal chef," Mom mumbled, opening and closing a few cabinets to take stock of the shelves. Dad had gone to work. The middle school teachers would hold in-service days next week, and he had wanted to get the rooms organized for them. Our house rested, lacking the usual noise of the school year, no monologues to memorize. No swim meets to recap. The silence felt like a heavy blanket over the house, suffocating me.

Rose hadn't texted. Not that I would have answered her. But I also half expected her to call my mom about my lies. Rose was too honest. She wouldn't want to hold on to the secret for long. I felt like I would hold my breath, legs jittery and ready to push off a starting block to help me flee, until she showed her hand.

I slowly set the table, puzzling out a way to ask Mom about Uncle Gerald, the letter, or Ms. Eldonforth without her immediate response being, "Why do you want to know that?" and, "How'd you get this letter?"

I heard the ice clink in Mom's water glass as she drank. She swirled it. "Fuck, I miss Dalia," she said.

I looked up from the paper napkin I'd been folding. *What did she just say?* It was the first time I'd heard her use that name in months.

"It's too quiet without her. Without the two of you always conspiring. Asking if Rose can come over. Doing her god-awful calisthenics all over the house."

"We didn't conspire."

"You conspired *constantly*."

"Okay, yeah," I admitted, not sure what else I could say.

"I miss fighting with her about not waking us when she left for her stupid five a.m. swim practices," Mom continued. "Bitching at her about hanging her stupid swimsuits all over the house to dry. About not cleaning up after her game nights. I'd give anything to yell at her again."

Laugh or cry? I couldn't decide. The laugh bubbling inside me and the sting of tears threatening to fall might have meant I'd do both. So this was what it felt like to have Mom confide in me.

"Well, if you want, I can leave a few swimsuits on random surfaces," I offered.

Mom's lips quirked up. "Don't you dare," she said, shaking her head. "Why did she need so many swimsuits anyway? Some of them had holes, but she yelled at me when I tried to throw them away. And why couldn't she just hang up the wet ones on the line like I asked?"

I answered what I could. "You wear the suits in layers. When you practice, you wear loose, old ones on top of tighter newer ones. The old ones create drag, and you have to push harder as you swim."

"Really?"

I nodded. "That's what she told me," I lied. "It may be more mental than anything else. Like how swimmers don't shave their legs until a big swim meet. Then, on a race day, when you're wearing only your team's suit, your legs feel slippery, and you dive in, and you feel so much lighter, faster. Smoother." I imagined the feel. Nothing holding me back. No resistance as I moved through the water.

I was all drag and knots now. I folded a second napkin. I'd never need to fold four when our family ate together again.

"I guess I should have asked her," Mom said. "Asked her more questions when I could."

"She may not have answered," I said. The truth.

Mom looked into her cup, swirling her melting ice again.

"I'm sorry," I said.

She finally looked at me. "What are you apologizing for?"

"I don't know," I lied and shrugged, then internally cringed, wondering if she'd noticed the gesture. "The situation, I guess." *Everything I'm going to tell you as soon as I stop being a coward.*

Mom stared at her melting ice and not at me. "Don't apologize. That's one thing you should take away from Aunt Crystal and your sister. Don't apologize if you're not in the wrong."

I worked to keep my face blank.

"Your sister was a lot like Crystal in that way. *Strong.* Going to do what she was going to do. And not going to apologize for it." Mom smiled wistfully. "I think that's why Crystal didn't take to Dalia."

A few tears lumbered down my cheeks, just like the condensation on the side of Mom's glass. "She wouldn't be tethered," I whispered.

"Damn straight." Mom shook her cup as if to hear the few remaining chunks clank. "To my girl who wouldn't be tied down."

I sniffled and held up an imaginary cup to toast. Mom took a long pull of her melting ice water, and I looked at my hands. Just dive in, I thought. "Hey, Mom?" I finally asked.

"Hmm?"

"What do you think of Ms. Eldonforth? You must know her a little. Do you think she could murder someone?"

"Yes. Definitely capable." Mom laughed. "But not Aunt Crystal. I think she'd kill a delivery person who gave her the wrong package or maybe a decorator or event caterer who didn't meet her expectations." She sighed, leaving the kitchen counter and sitting at our small circular table.

I slinked into the seat across from her, Skirty's seat.

"She was a tough lady," Mom continued. "But she loved those kids, the whole family."

"That's what Steve and I think too." It made me want to claw out of my skin, the thought of Ms. Eldonforth admitting guilt when she wasn't. She must have somehow felt trapped like me to do something like that. To—

"Remember when you were three or four, and we stayed with the Paynes? No, probably not. She was the reason Uncle Gerald opened the cabin for the kids."

I worked to keep my expression blank. Mom had just brought up Gerald herself, and I was officially the best detective in the world. *Just let her talk.*

"Ms. Eldonforth liked to work behind the scenes. She'd encourage Cinnabar and me to read to all of you. She convinced Aunt Crystal to let all seven of you kids stay for an entire summer."

This matched the vague memories I had: the red hammock, a crackling firepit with s'mores, and a blanket fort. I wondered how much of it was real and how much I'd imagined. *The acrid odor of burned wires, burning wood, and shouts for Talc.*

Wait. How many children?

"*Seven* of us?" I asked. Four Payne children while Talc was alive and two of us. "There were six. Copper, Talc, Steve, Charlotte, and us."

Mom stood and rummaged in the fridge, opening the crisper drawer, pawing among clear bags of veggies. "Mmm, no. The summer of the fire, there was a seventh child. He'd visited before. Some relation of Ms. Eldonforth's, I think. The boy was around Talc and Steve's age. I never saw him after the accident."

Goose bumps. "Was he blond?"

"Oof," Mom said, shaking her head. "You're testing my memory. Maybe? I don't really remember *him*. I just remember he didn't really play with the rest of you."

The boy in the pictures. Ryan.

"Your father and I liked to joke that he was Ms. Eldonforth's secret love child."

"What...what would make you think that?"

"Oh, I don't know. She did quit for a while."

"Really?"

"Yeah, before Steve and Talc were born," Mom said. "I wouldn't be surprised if not even Copper remembered it. But that boy was the right age to have been born while she was gone."

"Uh-huh."

"And Gerald was the reason Ms. Eldonforth came back."

"Really? Why?"

"Aunt Crystal had always referred to her as their best employee, and she'd never understood why she'd left. It was part of his anniversary gift to her to bring Ms. Eldonforth back," Mom said. "Aunt Crystal would tell the story at parties. Before the accident."

The, *I choose you*, Post-it. What if Ms. Eldonforth wrote it to choose her biological son? But she'd given it to Alex. Alex, who was also around the same age as Steve. *Could he be using a fake name? But why? I mean, none of us even remember him if he is Ryan.*

Unless Ryan had done something he needed to hide.

Fire and s'mores.

"Lyla, you okay? You look pale."

"Mom, was the fire on the island investigated? Like, truly investigated by police?"

"I mean, I guess, routine procedures. Nothing like the investigating going on now with Aunt Crystal, if that's what you mean."

I nodded. "Weird question, do you know what Ms. Eldonforth's first name is?" I asked, suspecting I already knew the answer.

"Suzie or Susan, I think. How do you feel about salad?"

Goose bumps. Maybe Ms. Eldonforth and Gerald had an affair. *Maybe* Mrs. Payne did know everything and had demanded her husband never contact his son. *Maybe* Gerald couldn't live without the money. *Maybe* Ms. Eldonforth couldn't live without Gerald. *Maybe* she'd abandoned their son to remain on the island.

Except for one summer. One summer to try to be a complex family. One summer that had ended in tragedy. And what had Alex told me? He'd wanted Ms. Eldonforth to make him a blanket with fire and s'mores on it. To commemorate that summer?

I gulped. I was making a lot of assumptions. I wasn't a real detective. Actual detectives hadn't arrived at any of the same conclusions as me.

No, they hadn't. Because Ms. Eldonforth confessed, ending their investigation. *I choose you.* Was she making up for past mistakes? Did she confess because she knew her son had killed Mrs. Payne?

Holy shit.

"Lyla. Lyla?"

"Huh?"

"Salad?" Mom repeated, twisting to look at me from her place in front of the fridge.

"Mom, I have a letter I'd like to show you. I'm having trouble reading it because its faded and in cursive."

Mom *tsked.* "See, this is what is wrong with education today. No longer requiring you to learn cursive. You need to be able to read and write—"

"I can read just fine. It's the handwriting."

"Yeah, I can look at whatever you want. But can it wait? My reading glasses are upstairs, I think."

I nodded.

"Besides, I'm ready to commit to making salad." She extracted a bag of greens and moved to the counter. "Please choose your dressing."

"Mom, do you think I could visit Ms. Eldonforth in police custody?" I took her place in front of the refrigerator to search for the ranch, Skirty's favorite. "Would I be allowed to do that?"

"You don't have to go to the police station. She's out of jail," Mom said, her back now to me as she tore open the bag of spinach.

"What?"

"Yeah, I saw her walking by Cleveland Road. Out on bail or whatever. I pulled over and asked if she needed a ride, but she refused. Too proud, I guess. Poor thing. She can't go home to the island. Copper was asking if I'd help arrange to send her stuff after he has movers pack everything. He didn't want to contact her himself."

"Did she say where she's staying?" I asked, gripping the ranch and Italian dressings too tight.

"Yeah, um, that motel we used to drive by to take Shorty to the old Y pool." She used a childhood nickname I hadn't heard in years. Mom was leaning into healing and using names again. She continued to ponder, "Shoot, what is that place called?"

I didn't need Mom to remember the motel's name. I knew which one she was talking about. I could run that distance in ten minutes. Fifteen tops, since I was out of shape.

I went for a walk after we finished our salads. It was a bit out of character, and my announcement made Mom's forehead wrinkle in confusion, but she didn't say anything as I put on Skirty's only pair of tennis shoes and left. The shoes fit strangely, since I had never had need to borrow them before. Where Skirty had used to lean in different ways then me, she had worked in the padding at the bottom of the tennies in unexpected ways.

The muggy air and crunch of gravel made it feel as though I jogged through soup, and a cacophony of crickets warned me that night approached.

As I wiped stinging sweat from my eyes, I took in the sight of the Cedar Buckeye Motel. It would not appeal to the tourists coming into town to visit Cedar Point. No, they would reverse out of the pot-holed parking lot at the sight of this green, paint-chipped, run-down motel. Each door and window of the long line of rooms looked out on the dimly lit lot. Shards of glass from broken bottles glittered on the pavement. A few busted medical needles decorated the sidewalk. This was the kind of place where some kids at school stayed after landlords evicted their families from their apartments.

I went down the line, knocking on doors, trying to peek into any windows that didn't have the thick beige curtains fully closed. I got lucky and unlucky with a single glance into the fifth room along the row. The occupant had the curtain open. I had a partial view of a prone body lying on the gray-carpeted floor near the door. The bed blocked my view of the head from this angle, but I could tell the pants matched Ms. Eldonforth's usual uniform of black slacks. The feet were bare and pale.

I knocked on the glass.

No movement.

I tried the door, but it was the kind that locked automatically. I ran to the motel office, lied and said that Ms. Eldonforth was my aunt, and asked the motel clerk to call an ambulance. I hoped I was wrong about what I'd seen, that I was about to interrupt the drug trip of some high stranger. It wasn't difficult to look scared as I begged the motel clerk to unlock the door for me, but once he had, I remained outside, too afraid to step into the room.

A sickening scent tinged the air.

"Aw, shit." The clerk waved his hand in front of his nose.

With the door open, I could see more of the body. Her ashen face was turned toward me, and I could see her unblinking eyes. The wrinkle lines protruded along her blue, thin lips. Dried froth stuck to her chin and the corners of her mouth. *A froth...just like what had happened during Mrs. Payne's seizure.*

I couldn't breathe.

Ms. Eldonforth's face had finally relaxed.

She was dead.

CHAPTER TWENTY-FIVE

As we waited for the ambulance and the police to arrive, I stood in the motel room's doorway, trying to take in the dingy scene. I couldn't even see that Ms. Eldonforth had any personal possessions here aside from her purse since Copper hadn't allowed her to return to the island.

The bed was made, its corners perfectly tucked and square. The TV was off. The remote sat on the nightstand beside a lamp. The closet had no door, revealing empty hangers and a dingy ironing board. The hangers encircled the bar across the top of the closet so nobody could steal them. Ms. Eldonforth's practical, black, slip-on shoes rested on the floor of the closet, perfectly aligned. A rolled pair of black socks had been stuffed into the left shoe.

I couldn't see much of the bathroom. The sink was in the main room beside the door to the toilet and shower. Only a tissue box rested on the tabletop. The sink's pipes snaked out below. No cabinets to store things, no drawers to snoop through.

A narrow table stood under the room's only window and to the right of the door. The curtain had blocked my view from outside, but now, I could see a medium-sized plastic cup with the Live Aloha Nutrition logo on it. Blue, green, and pink bits of fruit and vegetables lined the inside.

I'd never seen Ms. Eldonforth drink a smoothie while on the island. Alex had occasionally made them for me, Charlotte, and

Gwen, though. He'd always try new recipes. I leaned closer, trying to smell the liquid. Could Alex have mixed poison into a smoothie and then used the Aloha Nutrition cup to prevent suspicion?

I focused on the green bits of leaves. I thought back to the puddle I'd put my knee in under the dining room table right before Ms. Eldonforth had been arrested on the island. There'd been green bits on my hand. I'd thought they'd come from the carpet.

Maybe Alex had been trying to poison Copper or Charlotte, and Ms. Eldonforth's weird outburst had prevented that. She'd ensured all the drinks had spilled. But why would Alex poison his mom now? Assuming I was correct about their relationship. If my ridiculous theory was right, then Ms. Eldonforth had finally chosen him, protected him. Maybe even taken the fall for him. He should be happy, right?

Alex hadn't brought a smoothie on the ferry today. But there had been a cooler on board for when he brought groceries home. Would Weston notice if Alex had sneaked a smoothie mix aboard?

I leaned closer, trying to get a whiff.

"Stay out of there," the motel clerk yelled from the parking lot.

I startled and stepped back outside. I checked for glass shards before sitting on the curb just outside the motel room door. I was being an idiot. Green bits in a smoothie weren't clues. What kind of killer would poison someone and leave the cup they'd used to do it? A cocky one? Someone trying to frame someone else?

Skirty had run through those kinds of scenarios when we'd discussed the plot of the Agatha Christie mystery that our school had done as the fall play last year.

I shook my head. Besides, I drank from each and every different lemonade and smoothie Alex had given me while on the island. I felt fine. There was one thing I was certain of, though: I'd seen way too many dead bodies this summer. I feared the police would think so too.

❖

After a police officer, who kept looking at me from the corner of his eye, drove me home, I sat in our small living room.

I couldn't believe Ms. Eldonforth was dead. I distracted myself by looking for changes among the photos on our walls. The largest and oldest photo was a selfie that Skirty had taken when we were around nine or ten, and she'd been so proud, Mom and Dad had thought it was worth enlarging and framing. I think that sparked her interest in photography. She'd taken it during a family game night. We sat on the living room floor playing Go Fish. Mom played with her water glass, her most obvious tell. Dad stared at his cards. Only I noticed that Skirty had been taking the photo. Our smiles matched, and we both flashed the thumbs-up sign.

My parents had added more pictures since I'd left. Ones of us with Derek and Rose. The photos with Rose surprised me. Mom hadn't always welcomed her. I focused on a photo of the four of us playing poker from early in our freshman year. That had been a few weeks after Rose had started teaching me how to bluff. Her dad used to fly to Las Vegas to compete in tournaments before he died.

Dad shuffled into the room carrying a steaming mug. He held it out to me. He'd come home from the middle school just in time to see me brought home in the police cruiser.

"Thanks," I said, taking the warm mug and wrapping the string of the tea bag around one finger. The skin went white with the lack of blood I loosened my grip and looked at the label: pink rose lemonade. *Of course.* "You didn't have to make me this."

He waved off the idea. "Bought it special just for you." He turned to head upstairs for the night, the stairs creaking with each step. That was as close as he got to making a speech. He'd always been a person of small, quiet gestures. He made us drinks instead of using the words, I love you. He didn't say more than, "Hot chocolate for Dalia, the Wave Warrior; lemonade for Lyla, the Sweet Star; and ice for my Lady Love."

Rose, somehow, had picked up the habit as well, bringing drinks from Crimson Cup to school. Derek was less clued in to the family tradition. And Gwen? Her job involved bringing drinks. I wondered if it would ever occur to her to do it when we were off duty. Maybe I should have brought drinks to her. I grimaced. Not that I really wanted to anymore.

Someone tapped on the front door. I set the tea down and made the mistake of answering the door myself.

Detective Wilhelm. Didn't Sandusky have any other detectives?

I escorted him into the living room and retook my seat. I waved for him to sit, but he chose to loom over me.

"Hello, Lyla."

"Hi," I said.

"You've had an eventful evening."

"Yep."

"You doing okay?"

I took a deep inhale, paused, and breathed out with a, "No."

He nodded but didn't try to comfort me. "What were you doing at the motel? Why'd you go to see Ms. Eldonforth?"

"I told the officer there."

"Tell me."

I shrugged. "I was worried."

"Worried about what?"

"About how she was doing," I said. "It just…it just didn't seem like her." I told the truth but also avoided revealing my ridiculous speculations. "To do any of this. So I wanted to check with her."

"What makes you think this was out of character for her?"

I shrugged again.

"Oh, come on," he said, sitting on the worn armchair across from me. "You must have a theory."

I shrugged once more.

He raised an eyebrow and waited me out.

"I don't think she was a killer. I think she was protecting people," I finally admitted.

The lines on his face deepened as his eyebrow rose even higher.

"Look, that woman was scary," I said. "And efficient." I thought of the intentional capitalization of her notes and her perfectly aligned pair of shoes in the motel closet.

Detective Wilhelm pursed his lips like he was trying not to smile. "So you're saying that if Susan Eldonforth wanted people dead, they'd all be dead?"

"Yeah, I guess," I said before taking a sip of tea.

"That's an interesting theory."

"Is it?"

"Yes, because I've been in touch with the drug chemistry section of the crime lab."

"Was the smoothie poisoned?"

He hesitated.

Maybe I shouldn't have asked him about the smoothie.

"I don't have those results yet," he finally said. "But there was evidence that there was a poisonous compound in Copper's glass from last night. Ms. Eldonforth's confession and breakdown probably prevented him from consuming it."

"Wow." Uncertain what to say next, I sipped my tea.

Detective Wilhelm cleared his throat. "What do you know about plants?" he asked.

"Plants?" A lightning strike of nervousness charged through my gut.

"Yes, plants. Trees, bushes…flowers."

"Um, not much." I shrugged and nervously fiddled with the string of my tea, accidentally tearing off the label. "Do you mean like about plant cells and photosynthesis? I learned that in tenth grade biology."

"No, not photosynthesis," he said, his voice lowering as he leaned toward me. "Copper had mentioned that your sister used to love botany, and I wondered if she ever discussed plants with you."

"I…ah…she….are you—" I shrugged once more, and my foot bounced in a fast pattern.

Detective Wilhelm noticed the tell.

I stopped bouncing my leg and tried to reform my poker face.

"Relax." He leaned back in his seat. "What I'm wondering is if she ever noticed any poisonous plants growing on the island. This would have been one that isn't quite right for this climate. It may have stood out to her."

I almost shrugged again and worked to keep my legs still.

"When we searched the island, we didn't see anything suspicious. I just wondered if someone more knowledgeable had noticed something unusual in the past."

"No." I shook my head. "My, ah, sister hadn't been out to the island for several years, though."

I slurped my tea again and looked at the ceiling, my gaze briefly landing on the overhead lamp. "Oh."

Detective Wilhelm raised his eyebrows in question.

"The grow lights," I explained. "In the basement. I didn't see any plants under them. Alex told me Ms. Eldonforth had wanted to try to grow vegetables in the basement."

He nodded. The information didn't seem to be news to him.

"Alex apparently helped Ms. Eldonforth." Had he grown something dangerous?

"Lyla?"

"Huh?"

"Have you ever heard of oleander?"

Nerium Oleander. Used for landscaping. Hardy. Purple flowers. I didn't say any of that out loud, of course. I shook my head as I thought about the oleander bush and how it wouldn't grow this far north. I'd never seen one on the island. But I supposed someone—Alex—could have been growing it in the basement and hidden it or discarded it by the lake. Ms. Eldonforth probably would have happily set up a grow light if her secret son had asked. It even made sense for him to want to grow fruits and vegetables year-round to cook. *Should I tell Detective Wilhelm what I suspected about Alex?*

The detective still watched me, his expression impassive.

I sipped from my almost empty cup. I needed to either take smaller sips or find a new way to buy time. We continued to stare at each other as if checking the other's reactions. *Wait.* A sense of dread crawled over my skin. "Should I have had a lawyer here for this?"

"I wouldn't go that far," Detective Wilhelm said. "I am a bit concerned about you and your location. You are now the only person that has been present at all suspected poisoning attempts."

My mouth fell open. "My location...me?" I pointed to my chest. He thought *I* killed Mrs. Payne, Ms. Eldonforth, and maybe even tried to hurt Copper?

He nodded, and I stared.

Should I get the letter from One Fish, Two Fish *and show it to him?* But I still wasn't certain of what all parts of it said, exactly. And then, he'd want to know why I had it. Plus, if I accused Alex, Detective Wilhelm might suspect me of being both guilty and desperate.

Fuck.

"I think I need a lawyer here if you want to continue this conversation," I finally said in my best imitation of a character from a crime show. Not that there was any way my parents or I could afford a lawyer.

He nodded and stood. "Please don't leave the state."

"I won't. But I do have to go back to the island."

"Before you do, please come by the police station to get fingerprinted," he reminded me.

I nodded.

"Tomorrow," he added. "Please do it tomorrow morning if possible."

I gulped.

We stared at each other for another moment. *Appraising.*

"Good-bye, Ms. Smith."

It was only after he'd gone that I breathed again.

I was a suspect. He acted like I was the *main* suspect. I shook out my legs, rolled my shoulders. I felt the familiar jittery sensation of nerves, and I shook my arms and hands and bent my knees to loosen my muscles.

Motivation, I thought. *I am motivated to finish this.*

Was Alex framing me? I had no idea how he could have had the time to kill Ms. Eldonforth today. And he didn't look much like the boy in the photos I saw, but it wasn't unusual for a little kid's blond hair to change color to red as he aged, right? Either way, he was the person I needed to talk to.

He was still on the island. A coldness seeped through me. *Still mixing drinks for others.* If he'd tried to hurt Copper, then he could also go after Charlotte. Or Rock.

Right now.

CHAPTER TWENTY-SIX

I picked up the cell phone to find seven texts from Gwen. I didn't bother to read them, just replied with an apology about not going dancing with her tonight. Next, I found Charlotte in the phone's contacts listed as a favorite. Sending, *I think you're in danger*, in a text seemed like a B horror movie cliché. So I called.

No answer.

I hung up without leaving a message.

I called again. Still no answer. I paced for a minute. Called again. No answer.

I looked out the window; the shadows ruled the night.

I didn't have Alex's cell number or the landline on the island. Gwen would have his number, but I didn't want to drag her into this. What could I even say to Alex over the phone?

Contacting the police wasn't an option. What else could I do? I shook and paced. I only knew one other person who had easy access to a boat. I sighed and dialed Derek, almost hanging up before it rang, feeling certain I'd regret this.

He picked up after only two rings and immediately agreed to drive me to the dock and take me in his dad's boat back to the island. No questions asked.

Well, there was one question, couched in a series of rambling ones: "Should I pack a bag for overnight?" he asked. "To stay with you on the island? I mean, not *stay* with you, right? Unless you'd want me to? I mean—oh, man." He trailed off.

"Um, okay," I said, fearing that I told him I didn't want him to stay with me, he might not take me at all. *He will hate me when this is over.*

"Great."

I cringed.

"I'll be over in just a few minutes," he said before disconnecting.

I jotted a note to my parents, telling them where I was going, saying I was sorry for being so weird and sorry for what had happened at the beach, saying I suspected Charlotte and Rock might be in danger and that I didn't think the police would listen to me. I wrote that if I didn't come back, they should tell the police to investigate Alex, the cook on the island. I said to check in the book *One Fish, Two Fish.* I wrote that I loved them.

And then I hesitated.

I decided not to sign my name, not wanting to share my worst secret this way. I hid the note in the refrigerator with the bags of vegetables. Hopefully, I'd be home later tonight to reclaim it before either parent could discover it tomorrow.

I went upstairs, and I avoided a direct lie and only said Derek and I were going out for a bit. "We'll probably be gone late," I said.

They didn't exchange glances before they nodded yes. It seemed I'd finally chosen a daughterly behavior they deemed acceptable and normal.

I tried calling Charlotte again and again while the dark settled in for the night, and I waited by the window looking for the headlights of Derek's truck to come into view.

Still no answer.

When light finally slid across our living room as Derek turned into our thin drive, the motor of his old pickup whining, Mom called from upstairs, "Have fun."

"Thanks," I shouted. "I have the phone."

"It'd better be charged."

I left the house, tucking the cell phone into the back pocket of my jean shorts.

Derek remained quiet as he drove to the dock and as he prepped the speedboat. Both his truck and boat were ancient and finicky, inherited from previous generations of Steyers. His family had lived in the area for as long as the oldest houses and buildings in town had stood. Teachers always compared his behavior in class to one of his parents or uncles. When Skirty, Rose, and I would go around town with him, many older people always seemed to know him by name and wave. Some of those same people would give Rose dark looks a moment later. I didn't know if Derek realized he was a pre-approved member of the small-town, white privileged, and old boys' network. He never seemed to use his status to his advantage in any intentional way that I could see. He just returned smiles and waves and then would return his arm to encircle his girlfriend. *Like a claim.*

But it wasn't just that simple. He liked to touch.

Even now, while prepping his boat, he looked for opportunities to close the distance between us, to touch my thigh or arm, to lean in close as he untethered the boat. Skirty showed she'd cared through conspiratorial glances and thumbs-ups, Dad used drinks, Rose spoke. THE BOYFRIEND preferred touch.

I had to resist the urge to back away with each caress. My knee bounced faster whenever he got too close. I was filled with so much nervous energy, I imagined diving into the lake and swimming to the island myself. Just to feel like I was making progress, to know that Rock would be safe.

Finally, Derek's speedboat cut through the current. The bright cell phone screen burned my eyes in the dark. I still couldn't connect with Charlotte. A few stars spied upon us as we sped beyond the light pollution of Cedar Point. The wind whipped around us, and the roar of the engine thankfully prevented discussion.

As Derek reached to take my hand, I pretended not to see and moved to the back seat of the speedboat, trying to look fascinated by the dark, Erie water churning below. It wasn't long until the island came into sight. I returned to the bow of the boat, craning my neck to see around the trees to peer at the mansion. Relief flooded my chest to see the warm glow of lights emanating from the windows in both Rock's and Charlotte's rooms on the second floor. But the feeling immediately ebbed. *Rock should have been in bed a couple of hours ago.*

Strings of lights and lamps illuminated the dock and the path leading up to the mansion. A small golden aura encircled each light, welcoming us. I told myself to breathe easy just before Derek cut the engine about one hundred yards from the dock, and my heart stuttered with it. The speedboat slowed and then bobbed up and down in the waves.

"Um, Derek. What's wrong?" I asked, swiping at my hair since it'd gotten messy in the wind. "We're almost there."

"What's going on with you, Lyla?" he asked. "You're gonna tell me, or I'm not going to take you the rest of the way." His shadowed outline crossed his arms.

"Is this a joke?"

He didn't answer.

"Derek." I shook my head.

"Lyla."

I stared toward the dock. It would have been an easy distance to swim. If that was an option. "Come on, Derek. I'm not in the mood for this." The boat started to drift in the gentle waves, no longer pointing to the dock.

"You haven't been in the mood for anything. It's like you hate me ever since…" He didn't say *since she died.* He knew better. "And I don't know why. I get that you're in pain. I know that things aren't okay. And I'm fine waiting for you to heal. I want to help you. But I don't get why you're mad at me. Why you gotta take it out on me?"

I put my head in my hands and rubbed at my eyes. "I don't mean to. I just feel stuck. Trapped." Unknowingly, he served as one of the prison guards.

"Lyla."

"I'm sorry. I didn't mean to hurt you over the last couple of months. I didn't. I just—I just." I shrugged. I didn't know if he saw my tell in the darkness.

"Lots of people lose siblings." He seemed to be working to keep his tone gentle, his words coming slowly.

"*Don't.*"

"I know she was your best friend," he continued. "Your twin."

"Nothing compares—"

"Half of you. But you will get through this."

Will I? "Maybe. But not with you." There, I'd said it. "I'm sorry. I know I've been weird. I know that I've tried to break up with you only to keep calling. Grief is fucking weird, and it's making me insane. But I mean it this time." I took a breath and kept going. "You're free. You should date someone else, someone who's not as screwed-up as me. I want you to be happy. I do. And you'll never be happy with me. And I'll never get through this or be happy with you."

I felt lighter, like it was a little easier to breathe, or like I'd finally cut one of the ropes anchoring me. The boat bobbed up and down in the waves for a few moments, and I listened to the water's rhythm as it struck the hull.

Finally, Derek spoke barely above a whisper. "You don't have to suffer because she died. She wouldn't want that."

I was learning that. Or trying to. My eyes once again stung. I logically knew Skirty would want me to be happy. Just as I would her, if our positions had been reversed. She'd want happiness for Derek too. And my parents. Rose. Charlotte. And Rock. And everyone else.

How could I be happy when half of me had drowned? Had been scared and alone and cold? Pulled down by a riptide? Shredded by rocks and coral? Had her lungs invaded by water? All because, "I *dared* her to go, to swim."

I'd said the words out loud. I didn't realize it until after they were in the air like buzzing mosquitos or brief flashes of lightning bugs.

"It was my fault."

Derek's shadow shook his head. "She was a strong swimmer, but riptides can hurt anyone. It was brave of you to try to swim and help. Do you really think, if you could talk to her now, she'd blame you?"

I blinked, and the tears fell. I pictured Skirty in my mind. Not with the blue lips and dripping, tangled hair; but I pictured her whole and alive in the sunshine on the beach.

Her expression and eyes said it all. She *would* be mad at me but not for daring her. She'd rage at how I was torturing myself. For only being an *I* instead of reaching out and being with *our* parents, with *our* friends. For not being honest and allowing each of us to mourn properly *together*.

More tears fell, and I sniffled. "Derek?"

"Yeah."

"I think you're the smartest person I've ever met."

He laughed. "I know," he said, and then, he sighed. "We're going to be okay someday."

"I hope you're right. I'm sorry I've been so mean to you since…she died. But this is how it must be from now on. Just friends. That's it."

"I mean," he clarified. "You and I will be okay. As separate individuals who occasionally get coffee when we're on breaks from our separate colleges."

I smiled through my tears. "Thanks, Derek."

In the light of the helm's controls, he fiddled with the wheel then looked at the few visible stars. I didn't think he was stargazing though. He was giving himself time to prevent his own tears from falling.

"Derek," I said. "I—"

"It's fine." He lied. "I get it." And he powered on the boat again to take me the rest of the way to the island, working quietly near my side, the way he used to do in our Chemistry labs.

He took my hand and guided me off the boat, asked if I was okay, and then pushed the boat away from the dock, saying, "I guess I won't be spending the night after all. You want me to wait for you?"

"No," I said. "I couldn't bear to inconvenience him anymore. I'd find another way home tomorrow morning.

"Good-bye, Lyla. Have a good night." The boat puttered a few yards before his shadow looked at me one last time and increased the throttle to speed back toward Sandusky.

A good guy to the end.

CHAPTER TWENTY-SEVEN

Stones crunched under my feet, and a few toads called in the dark beyond where the golden lights reached. The bulbs entranced moths and other circling insects.

My cheeks felt sticky from crying on the boat, and I swiped at them. Glancing up at the windows of the snoozing, dragon-like mansion, I noticed Charlotte and Rock's bedroom lights were off now. That meant they'd both must have gone to bed, right? They were probably fine. Only the kitchen light blazed, the eye of the dragon searching for intruders.

Tiptoeing and easing the servants' hall door open, I decided to snoop in Ms. Eldonforth's room first instead of going directly to the kitchen. Too afraid to turn on the overhead light, I stood in the center of the room, looking around, breathing in the faint scent of flowery perfume.

I switched on a lamp. The room was—as I expected—very tidy. No clutter. Muted colors. No photos. If I'd guessed, I wouldn't have thought that the person occupying this room had lived here for decades. It was a bit sad, really. Was this all there was of her after her decades of devotion and care? I'd make sure her truth came out.

Her bed looked slightly mussed, like someone had slept on top of the comforter and not under it. I couldn't imagine Ms. Eldonforth leaving it imperfect. Alex maybe?

I switched the lamp off and gently closed the door. I heard distant clanks and whispers from the kitchen. I sneaked into the entryway, finding the kitchen door ajar. I peeked around the corner and blinked at the brightness of the well-lit room. Rock perched on one of the chairs beside the high counter. His feet kicked back and forth in the air as he sang to himself.

Alex stood at the gas stove. The open flame simmered as he stirred a small pot. Two red mugs sat on the marble counter of the island. I noticed a small pile of green leaves on a cutting board near the stove beside a large butcher knife.

I gasped and rushed into the room, demanding, "Where's Charlotte?"

"Lyla," Rock shouted, throwing his hands up at me for a hug.

Alex twisted, a spoon in his hand. He didn't answer my question.

"What are you doing?" I asked, glancing around before refocusing on the leaves. And the knife.

"Making hot chocolate. I said I'd do it, so Charlotte went to bed," Alex said. "This one discovered pop tonight. And refuses to sleep." He pointed the spoon at Rock. "Apparently, Mrs. Payne was right to forbid us from having sugary stuff on the island." He looked confused. "How did *you* get here? Is Gwen back too?" He resumed stirring.

"Rock, go upstairs, please," I said, lifting him out of the chair and setting him on the tiled floor.

"But I want hot chocolate." He looked back and forth between me and Alex. "Please? It's fancy. With seaweed."

"Mint," Alex corrected.

I stepped beside the cutting board, looking at the chopped plant. A longer piece with a stem stuck to the blade of the knife.

Mint.

I sniffed for confirmation, inhaling a scent I associated with desserts, winter hot chocolates, and nervous early kisses with Rose. I picked up a small sliver and crushed it between my teeth.

Definitely mint.

I sighed and felt my shoulders relax for the first time in hours. I'd been an idiot. I was wrong about everything. I needed to get back to Sandusky. My parents would have me committed if they found that note in the fridge. I hoped Weston would be willing to take me. "Yum, hot chocolate." I forced myself to smile and clap. "I'll have some too."

Alex gave me a weird look but didn't comment and kept stirring the pot. He reached into a cabinet to pull out a third red mug to set beside the first two.

"I came back after I found Ms. Eldonforth," I said. I lifted Rock back into the tall chair.

"Will you chop up some chocolate for me?" Alex pulled a few bars out of one of the cabinets above the stove, still maintaining his grip on the spoon and swirling the milk constantly. "How's she doing? She must be pretty freaked out. I imagine she's never been arrested before." He chuckled, seemingly at the image of a felonious Ms. Eldonforth.

I couldn't laugh. Did he not know? I'd assumed the police would have called here. But maybe they'd only told Copper.

Alex's amusement seemed real: his lips turned up, and his shoulders relaxed. He didn't know. He hadn't killed her, and he didn't seem worried about her the way I would have worried about my mom. Had I been wrong about everything? "I bet she even tried to tidy her jail cell," he said. "Did she demand they bring her bleach and a mop?"

"Um." I shrugged and glanced at Rock. "She seemed...*okay*. Ish."

The lies we tell the children chanted in my head as I shifted to Alex's side near the stove and began unwrapping the dark chocolate bars. The paper came off easily, and small splinters of chocolate flaked from the bar and threatened to melt against my fingertips.

Alex seemed to hear the strangeness in my tone and focused on me. I glanced at Rock to see that he was quietly humming before I mouthed the word, "Dead," in explanation.

He dropped his spoon. He mouthed, "D-E-A-D?" his face paling.

I nodded. "You okay?" I asked aloud. "I know you two were close."

He turned his back, lowering the temperature on the stove for a moment before changing his mind and twisting it too high. Blue flames sprang up and punched along the sides of the pot in orange and red.

"Alex?" I asked.

"How?" He spat. "Why'd you—"

I gaped at him. "Uh. I didn't."

"What's going on?" Rock asked.

"Everything's fine," Alex said, turning his back on both of us.

I held my breath, letting go of the chocolate. I wiped my hands on my shorts. I jumped when Alex slammed a fist against the cutting board, causing it, the knife, mint, and chocolate to flip up and tumble to the floor. The knife clattered out of sight.

My pulse once again a fast beat in my ears, I asked, "Alex?" as I bent near the mess, calculating the best way to get Rock out of the room. His chair was on the other side of the island from where I crouched. Alex could reach him faster. I either needed to get around him, or I had to take the long way around the counter.

I looked among the chocolate and mint strewn across the kitchen tiles. Where had the knife slid? "I'm sorry," I said. "I should have told you in a better way." I picked up the cutting board instead.

He chuckled, and something about the sound made me freeze. Holding the cutting board like a shield, I rose to my feet. "How'd she die?" he asked. "I'm guessing it wasn't peacefully in her fucking bed."

"Oh, bad word," Rock called.

"Maybe we should talk about this later, when you're calmer," I said as I stepped away from him, only to accidentally back into the island.

Shit.

"Don't fucking talk to me about calm, Lyla," Alex shouted and slammed the spoon he'd been using on the counter. The bubbles of the boiling milk popped, and a sickeningly sweet caramelized scent filled the room.

"I...I'm not," I floundered, the marble top of the island digging into my waist. "I'm not talking anymore."

"Did you kill her?" he demanded, picking the hot spoon back up and pointing it at me like a sword. A droplet of hot milk struck my neck, making me flinch.

"What? No. Of course not. Alex, you're scaring Rock." And me.

He glanced between us, lowering his arm. "Sorry," he said, turning to face the pot. His hand shook as he twisted the dial off. "Sorry," he repeated. "Sometimes, when I'm upset, I—"

Rock wailed in delayed fright. I baby-stepped sideways to go the long way around the island to reach him. Alex's hand shook as he raised it to hover over the pot's handle.

"Alex?" I asked, rounding the corner of the island. My legs tensed, ready to dive and pull Rock to me.

Alex mumbled something I couldn't hear. He shook his head, then twisted to glare at me, his expression dark, his lips pulled back into a snarl. He clutched one of the red mugs. "*She* told you to do it, didn't she? She manipulated you too."

"What? No. Ms. Eldonforth was already dead when I found her."

His rage blazed. "You have to pay."

I dove toward Rock, pulling him from the chair and shoving him toward the doorway to the servants' hall. "Get out. Go hide," I shouted.

Alex engulfed me, and I tried to scream. The mug *thudded* into my head, shattering. It was a moment before I felt the sting, and the waves of pain dispersed through my scalp. Alex raised his fist, now only holding the sharp-edged remains of the mug's handle.

Rock screamed as I fell. My hip, then my shoulder, and finally, my head collided with the tile floor.

"Shut up," Alex shouted.

Rock hesitated at the mouth of the dark hall. I could practically see him worrying that Smoky Shadow would be there waiting for him.

Alex reached out to ensnare Rock, and waves of nausea carried me away.

CHAPTER TWENTY-EIGHT

When I broke the surface into consciousness, my head pulsed with the sound of crying.

Rock.

I wanted to say, *It's okay. Everything will be fine*, but only a slur of quiet vowels and drool escaped my mouth.

I had the vague sense that I rested on my side. I couldn't quite command my limbs to move. My right arm flopped on the floor, caused by a rocking motion. A jarring movement up and down made my head storm. Where were we?

A constant buzzing accosted my ears. For a few minutes, I thought it was all because my head had collapsed in on itself. But eventually, *eventually*, only after I heard Alex's voice from a couple of yards away, I recognized the sounds and rocking motions as those of the Paynes' speedboat, the one normally stored in the shed. I couldn't understand any of Alex's words over the noise and rush of wind above me.

I kept my eyes closed, hoping everything would start to make sense soon but fearing it never would. Something small and warm leaned closer against my front. Rock. Still crying.

The buzzing engine cut, and the up and down skipping motion became gentler but remained nauseating. "Maybe Lyla deserves worse. Should I go back?" I could hear Alex clearly over Rock's sobs now. He must have been seated at the helm.

I fought the urge to open my eyes to tell Rock I was awake. I doubted he'd keep his reaction quiet.

"I'm telling you, I don't know how to get the stone to stay tied in the rope. I need, like, a net or bag…oh, like you're the expert on weighing a body down. I can still go back and roast her."

I put the words together in my sluggish brain and held my breath. Alex was talking about me. He'd thought I'd died and was trying to dispose of my body.

"Stop crying, Rock. Or I'll hit you again. Is that what you want?" Alex's voice came closer.

Rock angled closer to me, his shoulder digging into my gut before his little hands clung to my thighs, trying to wrap his arms around one of my legs. His sobs quieted a little. "N…no," he whispered.

"Well, I'm sorry, but you still haven't exactly explained what happened with my mom," Alex said to someone over the phone. "She was cooperating. We just need to find the proof. Why the fuck did you and Lyla kill her?"

Still keeping my eyes closed, I tried to make sense of my exact position. I suspected I lay against the floor of the speedboat, jammed between the back seats. Alex was probably now standing in the middle, talking on his cell. Who was he talking to?

"I'm not swearing at you. You stop fucking swearing at me," he yelled.

Skirty's phone. Where was it? I'd left it in my back pocket. My shorts were tight, so I could feel that the phone wasn't there anymore.

Rock shook against me as Alex remained silent for a moment. "I don't want to do this," he finally said, his voice strained. "I didn't want any of this. You said nobody but Crystal would die. The kid is like my great-nephew or something, and he's so little. Can't we just—"

A pause as Alex's partner spoke.

"I know we said, but…you swore everything would be okay, my mom would—that they'd welcome me once they learned." He fell silent. I listened to Rock's unsteady breaths and to the sound of the small waves shattering against the boat's hull.

"Fine," Alex snapped. "I'll call you when it's done." A moment later, I heard the familiar chime of a cell phone powering down, and then, a splash. He'd made that call on the phone I'd brought and had just thrown it into the water. He'd been using…he'd tossed Skirty's phone in the lake. All the photos and texts, gone. Energy and rage like I had never experienced before surfaced in waves. I could have murdered him back.

Still, I remained motionless. I'd have one chance. I had to surprise him.

The boat undulated. The sound of water breaking against the hull kept a slower beat than that of my heart. Finally, Alex cursed under his breath, and his footsteps approached, making the boat bob to a rhythm incongruous with the small Erie waves. I heard him drag and shift something heavy. It thudded against the hull, and he grunted at the effort. More thuds and scrapes coming closer. A few moments of quiet. More swearing under his breath, then, "It looks like a fucking Christmas bow."

A few more footsteps. Clammy hands pawed at my ankle, lifting my right leg. I bit the inside of my cheek to stop myself from crying. Alex encircled my ankle in rope. As he knotted it, the fibers bit into my skin.

No!

I struck out, muscles protesting as my foot collided sloppily with Alex's chest and then up against his chin. He swore. Rock screamed as I reached over him. Alex lunged, grabbing at my hands and arms while I scratched any skin that I could reach. Each of us cursed at the other while Rock cried, trapped under both of us.

"Crawl away, Rock," I yelled, not wanting to strike him.

Rock did as I ordered as I sat up and tore at Alex. I resumed kicking, managing a lucky strike to his groin, and he rolled away from me. I forced my aching body to my feet and reeled toward the stern of the boat to draw Alex away from Rock.

The rope bit harder into my ankle, and I fell on my face between the leather passenger seats before I got more than a few steps. Alex jerked the rope, tugging it again and again. My knees and thighs dragged painfully against the boat's floor.

I heard the loud splash of the small boulder hitting the water. The rope bit deeper into my ankle, sliding me toward the railing and threatening to pull me overboard. I clawed at the back of one of the passenger seats to stay aboard, scratching the upholstery and tearing my fingernails.

Alex climbed to his feet and laughed at the sight of me: my right leg extended over the side while I struggled to maintain my grip on the seat. "It's almost better that you're still alive," he said. "You deserve to suffer."

"I didn't do anything."

"Liar!"

Rock screamed for help, his shouts echoing into the bleak darkness. He'd lodged himself in the foot space of the captain's chair.

"What are you going to do to Rock?" I asked.

"He'll join you soon enough. Can't have witnesses. I'll make them think you kidnapped him and ran. Charlotte will be devastated. She'll hate you." He inched near to pull at my wrists, trying to dislodge me.

"No, just take him home," I begged. "You don't have to do this. I didn't kill Susan, Ryan." I tried using his real name. "I can help you. Help you find out who did. I think they're framing us. They left a smoothie in her room. I'm betting there was oleander in it. I'm betting the smoothie was bought with either my or your debit card."

He stared, his face inches from mine and his breath hot and sour against my cheek. "You're fucking bluffing," he finally said and slammed a fist against my fingers.

I lost my grip on the seat with my right hand. "No," I yelled, trying to slap him with my throbbing hand while maintaining my grip on the seat with my left.

Alex had the advantage, and my remaining fingernails tore and ripped as he struck them. My side scraped along the speedboat's railing, and the rope pulled me over and into the water. I managed to inhale just before I sank.

Cold.

Tiny, sharp pinpricks poked at my head, my fingertips, and my knees as the lake water caressed my open wounds and scrapes. I let my arms and feet go limp. My body knew what to do. I held in oxygen, blowing out a little from my nose to prevent the water from invading.

I could only see blackness, and my ears popped with the sinking pressure. The boulder pulled me down steadily, the rope biting at my ankle as I prayed we weren't over a deeper part of Lake Erie. I kicked my right foot and tried to bend my knee. I felt the rope and rock respond. A lightning strike of joy traveled through me. *Keep going.*

Not wanting to raise bubbles at the surface, I curled in the water, bringing my face close to my knees, reaching out for my right ankle in the cool darkness to pull at the rope and feel the knot.

The pressure in my ears increased.

I pulled off my right shoe, and it collided with my face as it floated up. The knot remained too tight around my ankle to pull it off. I blindly scratched at the rope, and what remained of my fingernails tore more, triggering more prickles of pain. I pulled at the knots, feeling them give a little.

Alex had used simple bows, thinking I would already be dead.

My lungs burned.

I heard a muted splash. Then the sound of the boat's engine starting above me.

Rock! Alex had thrown him into the lake.

My fingers worked faster at the rope, until…

Freedom. The rope uncurled and fell away. The cool water both massaged and stung my newly exposed skin. I kicked and pulled toward the surface, my eyes wide as I sought Rock. I exhaled what little air I had left, the bubbles tickling and rising against my cheek and forehead led me up.

I broke the surface, gasping and greeting the inky dark of the night sky. Alex's haste to leave us meant the boat had already sped far away. The buzz of the engine receded more and more.

I couldn't hear Rock or see his shadowy form struggling to tread water. "Rock?" I called softly, fearing my voice would carry over the water.

No answer.

I dove, my arms outstretched, feeling for him.

Nothing.

I dove again and again.

What if Alex had weighed down Rock's body as well? The thought made me desperate and hysterical. My eyes burned. I'd never find him. How could this be happening again?

I dove and surfaced, dove and surfaced. "Rock? Rock?"

I might have called Skirty's name too. I was losing another to the lake. I dove again. I'd drown too.

CHAPTER TWENTY-NINE

Rock screamed underwater. The air bubbles from his last breath brushed against my left shin. I knew where to dive next. I clawed into the dark and clasped his small body. What remained of my fingernails caught against his shirt.

I pulled him to the surface. He coughed and sputtered, his limbs useless. After a moment, he clung to me as breathing brought life back into him. "You did well. You did so great," I whispered between ragged breaths.

I wrapped my arms around him, holding him above me, his back to my front in a dead man's pose to let us catch our breath as the small Erie waves broke and rippled for us. His breath finally caught, and he resumed crying.

"Shh," I hissed. "We have to be silent, or he might come back."

That quieted him, but he continued to sniffle and gasp, hyperventilating.

"We're okay. We're okay," I assured him. "I've got you now, and I'm not letting you go. You can breathe...look at the stars." I squeezed him around the middle before extending one arm to help keep us above the water. "Just float. Catch your breath. I've got you," I repeated.

I looked around. Dark in all directions. Alex must have taken us far out into the lake. No land or light pollution in sight.

"I'm gonna sink." Rock flapped his arms. "I don't have the floaties, I'm gonna sink," he whispered, unbalancing us and making me tread water while still holding him to my front.

"I won't let you sink." A short wave took me by surprise, catching me with my mouth open. I sputtered. "Just breathe and hang on to me." I said, changing my grip to hold on to his arm and pull him around to my back. "Let's be frogs. You're a tadpole, and you'll ride on my back."

"Frogs?" he asked, his curiosity piqued.

"Yes, put your arms around my neck, tadpole," I ordered. He quickly followed my directions, his knees digging into my sides. "Not so tight," I said. "I have to breathe too." My face bobbed below the surface again. I spat out water. "Okay, we've got to swim to the mainland."

His grip loosened a little.

"Good, I've got you," I said. Using my toes, I kicked off my sister's remaining tennis shoe.

"But you can't swim," he whispered against my ear.

"Rock." I inhaled. "Did I ever tell you about my identical twin sister?" I moved my arms to pace with the waves, considering in the dark which direction the boat had taken and which direction I should swim.

"Dalia?"

"Yep. What did I used to tell you about her?"

"Um, she was quiet. She loved science. She was your best friend."

I smiled before twisting us around, feeling for an underwater current, searching again for any hint of light pollution. "Did I tell you anything else?"

"She loved swimming."

"Yes." I pointed my toes, straightened my knees, and began to execute small kicks while I did the breaststroke, cupping my hands like paddles in front of me, extending them to the sides, bringing them together again at the center of my chest, and out in front again. And again. Around, together, extend, around, together.

I began to move us with the water. "Did I say anything else about her swimming?"

"Um, that she…she won stuff."

"Yes, in swimming." I inhaled and spat out water in quick succession. "Competitions are called meets."

"Meets?"

"Mmm-hmm." I couldn't see our progress. Not in this darkness. But I kept my eyes focused ahead as best I could.

"That's a silly word."

"Yep. And during one meet, there are races, lots of races."

"Like running in water? Like I did with my arm floaties?"

"Kind of. They swim different types of strokes." Steve's swimming lessons clearly could have been more detailed. "Backstroke, butterfly, freestyle, and breaststroke."

Breaststroke. Not my favorite or best stroke. But the one that kept my shoulders steady and would make it easiest for Rock to hold on. His body coasted above me, half out of the water as we moved.

"And there are rules," I added. "Like no touching the bottom of the pool. Which means we're not allowed to touch the lake bottom until we reach a beach."

"Okay."

"This'll be like a real race." Water got in my mouth and nose. I felt no fear. I knew how and when to exhale to expel it. I knew how to keep breathing through this.

"Okay."

"Instead of racing other swimmers, we can pretend to race fish."

"Really?"

"Mmm-hmm." I had the rhythm now, knowing just when to bend my middle to keep our heads above the waves as much as possible. "What fish do you want to race?"

"Um, a shark. No. A dolphin…or a pipefish. Mommy showed me a video of them. And she drew one for me."

"Tell me about the pipefish," I said.

"They look like snakes. They're good at hiding right in front of you, and…" He tried to remember more. "They have…they're like knights."

"What do you mean?" I spat out some water.

"They wear silver stuff."

"Oh. You mean armor?"

"Yeah, they have armor." He started to chant to the beat of my strokes. "Armor. Anvil. Armor. Anvil. Armor." I could feel his breath as little puffs of warmth against my right ear. "Maybe my brother will save us. He's underwater."

"Maybe."

"He says he'll swim below us and keep any big fish from eating us."

"That's good," I said and spat out water. "Tell me more about the pipefish." My fingers had gone numb. Maybe it was my loss of blood from my head affecting me since the water didn't seem too cold for Rock.

"They're not the best swimmers," he said, and it took me a moment to focus enough to realize he was referring to the pipefish.

"Uh-oh," I said. "We can't race pipefish, then, because we're *strong* swimmers."

"Uh-oh," Rock echoed.

"What's a fast fish?" I asked. "Let's pretend to race fast fish."

"Um, uh, the wahoo." His voice grew steady. "Wahoo. They have the best name." He used the same tone he would have used when we discussed fish as he prepared for bed.

I declared my distraction technique successful.

"But they're really fast," he finished.

"So are we. Do you know what my sister's favorite event, er, race is?"

"No."

"The 500 free." My arms and legs were in constant motion. It was familiar, comfortable. I could probably sustain this for hours if necessary, assuming I could withstand the chill…and my head wound. "Now, five hundred yards doesn't mean much to you."

I spat out some water. "But that's the farthest distance that a swimmer can race while at a high school meet. That means going back and forth in a big pool ten times. Twenty whole lengths of the pool."

"Wow! I only did two with the floaties."

"Well, in a few days, I'll teach you how to go farther."

"Really?"

"Mmm-hmm." My muscles had warmed up. "I'll be a *really* good teacher. I promise."

"You will?"

"Yep. You see, I have a secret, Rock. But I'm not going to keep it a secret anymore. And you're the first person who gets to hear it."

"Really?"

"Yeah," I said. "D...Dalia was the fastest female swimmer to compete in the 500 freestyle competition for three years in a row." Around, push the water in, and extend the arms back out. "She was ranked number one...out of all the girls in Ohio who competed between the ages of fourteen and eighteen. She beat them all...she beat them all three years in a row. She had a scholarship to swim... at the University of Michigan."

"Oh." He didn't sound impressed. He probably had no idea what a scholarship was.

I had to say this. "But that's not the secret," I continued.

"Then what is it?"

Four waves collided with us before I finally found the words:

"Rock. I'm Dalia." I finally admitted aloud, my voice cracked on my own name. "I'm Dalia," I repeated. "It was Lyla who died. Not me. Nobody knows that but you and me. And I'm going to get you to the beach, okay? You just have to hold on."

After a moment, he asked, "Is this why you were bad at hide-and-seek this visit?"

I laughed. I couldn't help it, even though it made my head pound. "Yes. But I'll make up for it now." I kept swimming, Rock clinging to my shoulders.

"I'm like a, what you call it? A re…remora on a shark." If his little fingers hurt or if he was getting cold, he didn't complain.

"Yeah, just like that." My breath was steady, my pattern established. Every few breaths, I'd remind myself to keep going, and soon, it felt like I was swimming in a regular practice where I could just keep moving and propelling. My body remembered what to do, pulling us forward and closer to shore…I hoped. This was me breathing, and we struggled on, hoping we'd find light and land soon.

❖

A few stars still spied on us as we swam through the dark waves, and I wished I knew how to use them to navigate. An itching panic in my chest grew worse as my fearful thoughts that we'd never find the shore chanted louder and louder. Could I be swimming in circles? How far out had Alex brought us? For all I knew, I'd been unconscious for hours while he'd driven the speedboat. Were the waves pushing us off course?

Every part of me ached and struggled; my back and shoulders throbbed from holding Rock up. My muscles protested with each stroke of my arms and kick of my legs. My energy levels were plummeting. I desperately wanted to stop and float, but I suspected that would worry Rock. Or worse, after I rested, I might never find the energy to resume swimming.

Fuck. So much for my master plan to save the day. I bit back a sob.

But I kept moving.

I kept my feet kicking a slow, familiar rhythm.

I kept my arms circling.

And we kept breathing.

It was only when the doubts shouted loud in my mind and my hope had been reduced to a mere whisper that I heard Rock say, "Hi, birdie."

"Huh?" Then, I noticed the shadowed buoy rocking in the waves to my right. I hadn't even realized that I was almost on top of it. I could just make out the dark letters that spelled, *swim area* along its side. On the base of the buoy slept a seagull, just inches above the small waves. I would have cried if I hadn't been too tired and dehydrated.

I saw it now. Ahead of us. A beach. When I rode a wave up, I could see the lights from houses in the distance. I almost laughed. I couldn't believe it.

I tried putting my feet down. Seaweed caressed my toes. I stumbled and swam on. After a few more times of trying to stand, my feet finally collided with the rocky bottom. I pulled Rock from my back to carry him in my arms, almost tripping twice on my unsteady legs. He remained still against me. The waves pushed at my shoulders, then at my back, then at the back of my thighs.

Yes, yes, yes. Almost there.

Every muscle screamed, and I lost my footing. I fell forward, and we both plunged back into the water for a moment. I coughed and crawled on my hands and knees, grasping the back of Rock's shirt and pulling him above the small waves.

He didn't speak.

"Rock?" I asked. "Rock?"

He remained mute.

I pulled him onto the beach, my hands shaking. "Rock?"

I clasped his cheeks, and he finally whispered, "Yeah?"

"We made it."

I carried him again. On the beach now, water ran down from my shirt. My jean shorts clung and pinched at my thighs. Sand and small rocks stuck and poked at the bottoms of my bare feet. With each step, I felt uncertain that my shaky and tired legs would continue to carry us.

I only had to walk behind several cottages before I found one that had its lights on. I knocked and yelled for them to call an ambulance. "It's okay if you don't want to open the door," I shouted. "Just call an ambulance. And the police. We need medical attention. We're Rock Payne and Dalia Smith. We're from Sandusky, Ohio. We need the police to contact Detective Wilhelm and Charlotte Payne." I repeated my request three times before I collapsed on the sand. I cradled Rock, praying they'd done what I asked.

Soon, the flashing lights approached along a dark, deserted road beyond the houses. I tried to stand to meet the first ambulance, but my legs shook too much, and I fell. The EMTs walked out to meet us, ready to ask questions and to check our vitals. In the flashing lights, I struggled to make my eyes focus enough to read the city names labeled on the vehicles. Eventually, I deciphered, *Cleveland*.

I'd learn later Alex *had* sped us far from home when he'd dropped us to die. Even so, the police had already been searching for Rock. Charlotte had woken hours ago and had called the police when she couldn't find Rock or Alex. An Amber Alert had been put in effect throughout Northern Ohio.

Voices asked questions, and I tried to answer them, and sometimes, I had to say, "Wait, no," and change my words to be true in all the truth's complexity and many knots. And I warned them about Alex. And, oh wait, he might have had an accomplice. No, I didn't know who. And I signed forms. I asked how Rock was. I told people to call Charlotte. And my parents. And Copper. And Steve. But wait, no. Steve would be in rehab by now. No, I didn't know the name or where it was located.

I asked about Rock over and over again after they separated us when we arrived at the hospital. I signed something saying they could tell my parents everything. *Everything.* "Yes, tell them," I said. And I asked about Rock again. Even though I knew they'd updated me a few minutes ago. But I didn't quite remember what they had said. And I knew they'd called my parents. And I knew my limbs started to hurt and ache worse as I warmed and as they gave me fluids through an IV.

And then I knew nothing.

CHAPTER THIRTY

D alia. Dalia."
I opened my eyes.

Mom. Close. Her gaze traveled across my face, studying me the way she'd done when we were in elementary school, and we'd asked her to guess who was who before she'd dress Lyla in purple skirts and me in blue shorts.

"You...you called me Dalia." I swallowed, and my dry throat hurt. I tried to clear it and coughed instead.

"Yeah." She sniffed and brushed some hair away from my face.

"Rock okay?" I asked.

She nodded. "Oh, Sho-Sho. You tied yourself up in knots, and I didn't notice." She hadn't called me *Sho-Sho, short for Shorty*, in years. Not since before the arguments, before I'd told her I liked girls, before I'd told her I'd destroy every pink skirt and dress she'd ever bought me.

"Mommy?" I hadn't called her that in years either.

She leaned over the plastic railing of the hospital bed and hugged me as best she could. As I tried to wrap my arms around her, I realized that wires and tubes connected me to various devices, including a line of clear liquid that went into a vein on my hand. I didn't let any of the equipment stop me from hugging her though.

"I'm sorry," I said. "I'm sorry. I'm sorry."

"No, no, no." Her words overlapped with mine. "It's my fault. I should have seen it. I should have noticed."

"I didn't want you to. That's why I left. I didn't want you to lose Lyla."

Mom pulled back to wipe her eyes. "I can't believe you did that. I love you. And sometimes, I don't understand you." She touched my arm as though making sure I remained here. "But I really want to learn."

A sob shuddered through me, and I gasped. I gasped deep. I gasped as though I'd been underwater, and this was my first breath. The weight on my chest had dissipated, and I could finally fill my lungs with air.

Mom cried with me, leaning forward again to hold me close. "Do you want some ice chips?" she finally asked, pulling back to brush my hair away from a bandage at the side of my head.

I touched the dressing, my fingers tentative.

Mom swiped under her nose before picking up a Styrofoam cup and looking into it. "Oh, they've melted."

"That's okay," I said, my breath finally calming and my tears slowing. "Tell me more details. Is Rock really okay?"

"He's fine. They're keeping him for observation, and they're taking the opportunity to check on the cut in his mouth and make sure that the stitches are dissolving. But he should be fine."

"Good," I said.

"Copper wants to enlist a psychiatrist to meet with him a few times to make sure he'll recover from the trauma."

"He's resilient." I smiled.

"Charlotte hasn't left his side, and Copper arrived an hour ago. Steve's also been checking in on the phone. He's not allowed to leave the facility he's in for a whole month. No emergency exceptions." Mom swished the water around in the cup. "I sat with them for a few minutes. Rock said he was sending an *anvil* to watch over you?"

"Invisible friend and brother," I explained.

"Ah," Mom said. "You and your sister used to have an imaginary triplet, Calia. Do you remember her?"

I shook my head.

"She was the *troublemaker* of the group, apparently. She got the blame for everything bad that happened." She smiled wistfully and touched the fingers of my left hand. They looked bruised and puffy, but I was guessing I didn't have any broken bones. My pointer and middle fingers had dressings on them. I could see hints of dark blood under the layers of white gauze. It'd probably be months before my nails would be long enough to trim.

"Charlotte and Copper said they wanted to thank you when you feel up to it," Mom said.

"They don't have to," I said before remembering. "Oh, Mom, there's a letter in the picture book I brought home. We need to take it to the police. If I have to stay here for observation or whatever, when you and Dad go home, can you read it and call Detective Wilhelm and show it to him?"

"Yeah, whatever you need, Sho-Sho."

"Thanks. Where's Dad?"

"Downstairs…getting something for you from the cafeteria," she said, setting her cup aside. "He insisted."

I suspected he would return with hot chocolate instead of lemonade. My favorite instead of Skirty's. The thought renewed my tears.

"No, no, no more crying," Mom said. "You're dehydrated."

The idea made me chuckle. "Dehydrated?"

"You need all the water you can get," she explained and then laughed at her own logic while wiping at her tears and then mine. "Did you know, when you were babies, we couldn't tell who was who for an entire day."

"Really?"

"Yeah, having a baby is hard. Having twins is harder. And I was so tired. It was maybe three weeks after you were born. I didn't remember which of you I'd dressed in the yellow striped onesie and which of you wore the polka dots."

"*Yellow?*"

"Despite what you always thought, dressing you in pink and Lyla in purple was not for my entertainment. It made life manageable."

"So how'd you figure out who was who? When you were still allowing us to wear other colors."

"Your weight. At the time, you weighed a couple of ounces more."

"Oh, clever."

"No, I panicked for hours. I didn't think to weigh you until hour six. I just kept saying each of your names, praying one of you would turn your head. Maybe magically learn to speak English early, say, that's me, and raise your hand."

I tittered.

"That was the day that I learned to color-code *everything*. It was a few weeks before I confused who was who again."

We kept talking. It was the most we'd said to each other in months, maybe years. We wondered what was taking Dad so long. Mom told me about how I'd thrown up on Mrs. Payne when she'd come to see us for the first time after our birth. Mostly, we talked about what the doctor had reported about my health. Mom said that *technically*, there wasn't much wrong with me now. It'd taken twelve stitches to close the cut in my head. They'd removed mug shards. The sutures and bald patch where they'd shaved off some hair wouldn't be noticeable if I wore my hair down. They'd watch me for post-concussive symptoms. I'd have a lot of sore muscles since I hadn't swum for so long or so far in...*ever*. Mom said I'd remain here a bit longer because the doctor thought I should meet with a psychiatrist for assessment. Apparently, it was concerning to impersonate your deceased sister for over two months. I understood.

Mom said that if they wanted me to keep meeting with someone, we'd find the money to make it work. "Maybe each of us could do with some counseling after the last couple of months." When our conversation finally lulled, she pulled *my* phone from her purse and said, "You can't look at the screen, but here. I hadn't ended your phone contract yet."

"You…you kept my phone."

She nodded. "It was a piece of you."

"I don't have Lyla's anymore. Alex threw it into the lake."

She waved her hand dismissively. "I can't expect you to be able to control what a homicidal asshole does with phones. And you should let me dial your girlfriend for you. She's lovely, and she's missing you."

I started at the word *girlfriend.* Mom had never acknowledged Rose as being my actual *girlfriend.* Not in the whole year that we'd been together or the several years of flirting and friendship that had led up to our dating. One time, when I'd been really vengeful, I'd demanded to know if it was because we were both girls, because Rose was half-Jewish or half-black, or because of all three. I'd called Mom a bigot. That night had cemented the ice age between us. I'd been too ashamed to ever mention what had happened to anyone else.

Mom patted my hand again and placed the phone—still wearing its protective case of an underwater view—on my palm. "Rose keeps calling." She gestured at the phone. "I think to hear your voice prompting the caller to leave a message." She said the words in a way that told me she'd done the same. "Sometimes, I'd answer, and we'd talk."

"What?"

"The first time I did it, I think I traumatized her." She laughed. "Sorry," she said but couldn't hold back another chortle.

"I don't know how to tell her, how to explain. She suspected at the cemetery, and I ran."

"Just tell her you're still all in."

"Wha—how did…"

"I'm a mom. I know things."

I stared at her.

"Ly—" She took a shaky breath. "Lyla would tell me about you. And your dad. And now, Rose does. Just because we didn't always talk the way we should doesn't mean I don't have my sources."

I glared at her but only for a moment.

"Sho-Sho," she said. "You've almost unknotted yourself and gotten free. Don't stop now."

I looked at the phone and could feel the small sting of the rope burn on my right ankle under the hospital blankets. *Sometimes, that last knot is the most difficult to loosen. Sometimes, it's the easiest.*

Mom sniffled, and I looked up, letting the phone fall to my side on top of the thin, white, bedsheet. "Shit, not again," she said, waving at the sides of her face as though that would stop her tears. "I just, just keep asking myself. Did she cry out for me or for you… in the lake? Was that how she used her last breath? I shouldn't have let you two go alone. I shouldn't have pressured you to take care of her. You're a strong swimmer, but a riptide…that wasn't fair. Or I should have insisted you go to a nicer beach where there'd be a lifeguard."

And I shook because this dark thought spiral matched the ones I'd been torturing myself with since the moment I'd realized I couldn't see Lyla's head above the waves.

We both blamed ourselves.

My breath shuddered through me. Mom's thoughts, her pain, were the *same* as mine. And here I was being an angsty teen, thinking this was my suffering and mine alone. When this woman sat right there. Just as twisty and weird as her weirdest and twistiest daughter.

"Mom," I said, the only word I had to say. I opened my arms to her again and pulled her close over the bed's railing. She was there. With me. A *we*. An *our* in our shared grief and love. An *us* that would heal. *Together.*

Now would have been the perfect time for Dad to walk into the room carrying a hot chocolate for me and a cup of ice for Mom. But that wasn't what happened. Someone did knock. And they opened the sliding door and shifted aside a privacy curtain without waiting.

Mom pulled away to wipe at her eyes and nose.

"Oh, sorry," Gwen said. "Charlotte called me. I just got here from Sandusky. I wanted to check on the heroine."

"Who are you?" Mom asked.

"This is Gwen," I explained. "You saw her on the island. We work together."

"Oh, right." Mom looked back and forth between us, her back stiffening, her tone icy, like she wanted to tell Gwen I already had a girlfriend. "I remember."

"Can I talk to her alone for a minute?" Gwen asked.

"I suppose." Mom climbed to her feet. "I'll be back with some more ice…and to find where your father went," she said before stepping around Gwen and sliding the glass door and curtain closed as she left.

Gwen waited for the door to shut completely before she clapped and sang a few familiar lines from a musical. Skirty would have known the title. I cringed, but Gwen smiled and finished singing about a boat rocking, posing with her arms spread wide. "Too soon?" she asked.

"Yes," I said. *Way too soon.*

"How are you feeling?" she asked, climbing onto the foot of my bed. She rested her hand on the blanket just over my shin.

"Um, okay," I said. "A little weak…I was too out of shape to do a swim like that." I looked at her hand on me and thought of Rose. I shifted my leg away. "So," I started.

"Alex is dead."

"What?"

"Yeah."

"When? How?" I tried to sit up more on my angled bed, but my muscles protested.

"Um, well, he'd had a bad night," Gwen said. "Apparently, he was very upset. I guess Ms. Eldonforth was his mom. And Gerald Payne was his father."

"Wait, did the police tell you all that? Did they—"

"No, that's not how I know that, *Lyla*." Her voice sharpened. She rested her hands on either side of my legs and leaned toward me. Her weight caused my cell phone to shift and slide off the edge of the bed and fall to the floor. "Oops," she said, looking at where the phone sat well out of reach. "*Lyla*." She spoke in a lowered tone now, but that didn't mask the anger in her glare. "I heard Charlotte and Copper talking about you downstairs, *Lyla*. You little liar." And she winked.

Shit.

If I hadn't already felt my pulse increase, I could have tracked it on the monitor beside the bed. I said, "You...you *did* take the photo with the message on the camera." I tried to sit higher, but there was nowhere for me to go.

"Yep, at the time, it was just a little bit of fun." She smiled. "Turns out, you're more interesting than I thought." Her expression darkened. "You really fucked up my plans."

I slid my hands into the sheets, feeling around. Wasn't there a call button somewhere in the bed? I knew I had seen those in movies.

"See, someone killed Ms. Eldonforth." Gwen shrugged and looked around as though thinking, Who could it have been? "But before that *someone* could speak to Ryan—oh, I mean Alex—and calmly explain how Ms. Eldonforth couldn't be trusted and how she had to die since she *still* hadn't delivered the evidence that proved Ryan was a Payne...well, what do you think happened, Lyla?"

I gulped. I couldn't find the button.

"Well?" She grabbed my legs through the blankets and lifted them and then slammed them down. "Well, *Lyla*. What did you do?"

I cringed and slipped a hand out to feel along the railing for a button. "I went back to the island, and I told him." I didn't dare mention that I'd also taken Ms. Eldonforth's letter. Did this mean

Gwen had killed her because of me? I felt numb at the thought, as though I'd once again sunk into the cold depths.

"Yeah, you did. You told him. And that idiot beat in your head in front of a witness." She shook her head and *tsked*. "He has some rage issues. But you're lucky. He usually plays with fire. Well, *had. Played.*" She giggled. "I think you can probably connect the dots from there."

"You're the person he called from the boat."

"Yeah, Lyla. I am." She climbed on top of the bed and jumped up and down a few times, not caring if she landed on my shins.

I cried out but struggled to move my legs out of her way. Gwen stuck something to the ceiling. Then pressed a button on a small remote as she continued to jump on me. I was ready before the shadows of dancing seaweed and Smoky Shadow appeared.

"Why, Gwen?" I held my arms up as high as I could, ready to slap her if she got any closer.

She paused her jumping and wrinkled her nose at me. "Don't call me that anymore. I'm shedding that skin. Just like you."

I didn't know what to say. The undulating shadows reawakened my nausea. I had to close my eyes.

"Why are you being so stupid right now? Do you not get it?" I forced my eyes open, and she smiled wickedly at me.

"All of this has been my art. My name is not Gwen Verden. I'm so much more than an actress."

I could smell her perfume, and I struck out, but she grasped my wrist, digging her nails in.

"When we sent a letter months ago to that bitch Crystal stating that Ryan was one of Gerald's heirs, she threatened legal action," she continued, wrenching my wrist. I cried out again, and she slapped her free hand against my dressing and stitches. "Shut up," she said. "This is my favorite monologue."

I reeled, setting off explosions of pain behind my own eyes.

"We knew she wouldn't give, so I told Ryan to make nice with his long-lost mommy. Dropped hints that all he needed was a fresh start under a new name to finally have a good and decent life with her. All while knowing that Crystal the Bitch had to die if we were going to get anywhere. The oleander was *my* idea."

I could feel her hot breath on my cheek, and I cringed.

She cackled and resumed jumping. "*I'm* the one who finally made the puppets dance." She enunciated each word with another jump.

"Stop," I begged.

She leaned in close. "The old Eldonforth crone could give Ryan the proof he needed to show that he deserved to be a rich asshole too. But she fucked up that plan too."

The letter. My gut twisted, and I gagged. Gwen sprang away. I'd given her a reason to kill Ms. Eldonforth when I'd taken it. No, not a reason. An *excuse*. But taking it had stopped her and Alex from causing more suffering to the Paynes. I wouldn't torture myself over this, not with an actual serial killer staring at me.

After realizing I had nothing in me to throw up, Gwen cackled and demanded, "Well?"

I shrugged.

She mimicked my shrug. "What is that supposed to mean?"

Guess she didn't know me well.

"Want to know what Ryan did this morning? On his last morning?" she continued. "He poisoned himself."

"With oleander?"

"The student gets an A," Gwen confirmed, raising her hand as though she was going to slap me again but stopped and pointed at me, her fingernails millimeters from my nose. "Made you flinch." She lowered her hand. "He ate my whole stash in my hotel room. For me to find. You know that plant not only causes the victim to vomit, it also causes diarrhea." She waved her hand. "The more you know."

"I'm sorry," I said automatically as I searched for an escape. There was a room phone on a nearby table. With the push of a button, I could call a nurse, but I didn't trust my muscles to allow me to reach it before Gwen. I needed a plan, or she'd make me her next victim.

"Lyla." She straddled my thighs. "You better fucking apologize for real. Because I didn't like coming back to my room to find that. The hotel staff asked some uncomfortable questions."

"I'm...I'm sorry." My throat ached, and the room and shadows spun.

"Selfish asshole," she shouted.

I wasn't certain if she was referring to me or to Alex. But I prayed she'd gotten loud enough to get the attention of a nurse or Mom.

Gwen rolled her eyes and sighed, taking my face in her hands, running her thumbs over my lips. "I want to dance with you," she whispered and smiled her sharp-edged, ruby-iced smile before her gaze hardened. "And now I'm the one who is going to kill you." She laughed. "Because you see, I could run, flee, and live to slay another day. I've done all that before. Or I could admit that planning and conspiring and waiting just doesn't get me off." She smiled; her gaze turned to where her thumbs touched my lips. "I'd much rather be close and stare into your eyes, my hands around your neck, and feel the exact moment when the life leaves your stupid body. Yeah, I think that moment's going to make me tingly all over." She twisted her hold so her thumbnail dug into my lip.

I turned my head, but her grip tightened. It was right to hide the letter, I thought. *I'll do anything to ruin her plans.*

"Now, now," she said. "Play along."

I gulped as my pointer finger connected with a raised piece in the plastic along the side of the railing. I pushed on it, praying it'd bring help.

And the bed lowered a few inches.

Fuck.

"Really? Is my story putting you to sleep?" Gwen smiled. "I guess we'll just have to race to the climax then." And she lunged, one hand going around my neck, her fingernails digging into my skin.

"Mo—" I called as Gwen slapped her other hand over my mouth. I tried to bite at the skin of her palm. I raised my arms to shove her off me, but they felt rubbery and heavy.

Stop her, stop her, stop her.

I kicked, the blankets preventing me from getting any real force behind the action. My arms became tangled in the wires and tubing. I screamed again, but it was only a muffled sound. The call button, I thought. *Find it.*

I shifted my hips up, trying to force her off me. *Stop her.* I bit at her again, tearing skin with my teeth. This time I heard an, "Ouch," and she pulled her hand away, only to have it join the first around my neck. "Bitch."

The pressure increased. I couldn't breathe. *Stop her. Stop her. For Ms. Eldonforth. For me. For whoever she'd kill after me if I couldn't end this now.*

I slapped at her, tried to poke her eyes. Her grip slackened, and I breathed and screamed and screamed and screamed as best I could, feeling as though something tore in the back of my throat. Her grip loosened more, and my head fell back as she took the pillow from under me and shoved it against my face.

I turned my head to a side, seeking air, trying to kick and claw. I felt something wet and hot cascade down my side and run along my arms.

Blood. She has a knife.

The weight and the pressure lifted, and I flung the pillow off. Mom, Dad, and two nurses had pulled Gwen off the bed and were dragging her across the room. She cursed, spat, and bit at them. "Call security," one of the nurses yelled toward the hall. "What the hell is going on with the lights in this room?"

"Remote," I croaked. "Make the shadows stop. I'm bleeding."

But I tasted a drop of sweetness on my lips, and I squinted at the hot, sticky, brown liquid covering me. I could see where a to-go cup had fallen open by my side. *Hot chocolate.*

In Dad's rush to help, he hadn't put down the hot chocolate he'd brought me. I collapsed against the bed in relief.

More people rushed in to restrain Gwen, and someone managed to get the projection off. My stomach twisted again, and I gagged over the side of the bed. When I looked up, my parents stood between me and the scrum that had formed to pin Gwen to the floor. One nurse came over to check on my tubes and connections.

"She okay?" Dad asked.

The nurse nodded, and my father opened his arms wide to hug me. "I'm a mess," I warned him.

"Shorty, if you were breathing fire right now, I'd still hug you."

Mom wasn't far behind.

CHAPTER THIRTY-ONE

Two days later, I went to the graveyard. It turned out informing the world—and, in particular, the U.S. government—that I hadn't died and that my twin sister had was a bureaucratic nightmare. But I wanted to mourn properly now. Somebody had crossed out my name on the temporary grave marker and corrected it to say *Lyla*.

There you have it.

I took a deep breath. A brief morning rain had left the grass damp, but I sat anyway, grimacing as some of my muscles and scrapes protested. It felt good to be in my favorite pair of blue basketball jersey shorts again and not having to worry if they got a little wet.

I gently scratched around my temple, carefully avoiding the suture area before repositioning my hair around the shaved spot. I'd sat for almost fifteen minutes when I heard the swish, swish, swish, of someone walking through the grass.

Rose.

I didn't feel a kaleidoscope of butterflies so much as a flowering garden of kaleidoscopes upon kaleidoscopes of butterflies.

"Your mom told me where to find you." She held two to-go hot drink cups from Crimson Cup. *Hot chocolate.* I knew the heart-shaped marshmallows would be all melty underneath the lid.

"It's really weird that you two are best buddies now."

"Well, you don't get to comment about my friendship with Lauren." She sat beside me, keeping her grip on both the cups.

"And you're using her first name? Weird."

"She asked me to," Rose said, getting comfortable in the grass but still not offering either cup to me. She took a sip from one before saying, "Mmm, good." She licked whipped cream from her lip.

I thought it best to stay silent and stare at the grass. The first time we'd splurged on buying fancy hot chocolate together, it had been after we'd spent an entire wintery Saturday playing poker with a few members of the girls' swim and diving team. Rose had won a café gift card off a diver named Kelly. We'd plodded through the snow to the mall, Rose trying to get me to make rhyming couplets to go with her observations of the slush and snow. Sharing one large cup of hot chocolate and kissing away whipped cream from her smiling lips had warmed us.

"Hey," she said.

I looked up. "Hey."

"I'm so fucking mad at you," she said in a rush, looking at the cups. "And I'm also so fucking happy to see you. Why the hell would you do that?" she demanded. "What kind of ridiculous, white girl, cliched, teen-movie bullshit was that to pose as your sister?" She shook her head.

With every ounce of my being, I stopped myself from shrugging. "I don't know," I finally said. "Things got twisted."

She shook her head at me, then drank deeply from one of the hot chocolates, maintaining eye contact as she did.

"So that's how it is?"

"Mmm-hmm," she said before licking her lips.

I forced myself to look away before asking, "Is it the anger or the love that caused you to bring the hot chocolate?" I extended my hand to take one of the cups. "I ask because I've recently witnessed a murderer poison a few people's drinks."

Rose pulled the cup out of reach. "No. No poison. These are my fucking hot chocolates. And I will drink them both in front of you, and you will suffer through it."

"Okay."

"But, like…" She stared at the sky like she was fighting off tears. "For the last two-ish months, I thought I'd never be able to make or buy you a drink again. And that made me so fucking sad." She set one of the cups down so she could twist and play with her braids. I didn't recognize the gesture as a tell. Maybe this was how sad-Rose coped. "And I'd been telling myself that all I wanted was to be able to hand you a fucking hot chocolate and hear you say 'All in,' again because I know you only say that whenever you're super happy with me."

I sighed. Having this conversation terrified me. "I'm sorry. It wasn't really planned, pretending to be Lyla. It just happened. And I didn't know how to fix it without being accused of being insane or of being a murderer."

"Did you literally play dead to break up with me?"

"No." I climbed to my feet and paced beside her. It helped to remain in motion. "Being away from you was one of the hardest parts." *No lie.* "I love you."

Her face softened, and she released her braid. She moved both hot chocolates closer to her to rest on the ground, like I was going to lunge and try to steal one. Like that was what mattered most to me in this moment.

"It wasn't…*intentional* at first," I said. "I'd gotten Skirty—the body…out of the water, and I was panting and crying, and I just couldn't bring myself to say what was happening out loud." I spoke in a rush, trying to get all the words said before I ran out of air. "When the police arrived, they got it wrong when they looked at our IDs. I didn't really get that they had called me Lyla. Or that in the panic of trying to get our things, I'd put on her *A Midsummer Night's Dream* hoodie instead of mine. It was…it was…."

I took a deep breath, and Rose watched me closely, the way she had watched me before we'd gotten together. It was the same way she looked when she was assessing a new poem for inclusion in the school's poetry zine or when we played poker.

"It was only when I heard Dad call me *Lyla* that I understood. They thought I was her." My voice cracked. "And I thought…it'd be worse if they knew she was the one who died and not me. That everyone loved her more. Mom. Derek. I could…I could just… save them." My voice trembled. "From the pain."

"That's not true," Rose interrupted. "Not me." She spoke with her hands, bumping one of the cups, and some hot chocolate flew out through the drinking hole at the top of the lid. "Shit," she said as we observed the liquid rolling down a blade of grass. "That cup's yours." She picked both up again. But she still didn't hand either of them to me. "If you earn it."

"I wasn't exactly being logical," I admitted, continuing to pace. "And after I hadn't said anything, I didn't know how to fix it." I broke down. "And that's why I had to leave. Because I knew you or Dad or Mom would figure it out. And you'd look at me like I was a freak. I had images of being committed to a mental institution and never being let out again. I thought…" I struggled. "I thought everything would be worse if I told the truth." I cried.

Rose stood to hug me as I shook and seemed to realize it'd be difficult with the cups. She set them down in the grass carefully and then pulled me to her. She held me until I ran out of tears.

"Don't look," I said as I pulled away to swipe at my runny nose. "I'm a fucking mess."

She watched me, not letting go.

"I said, don't look." I sniffled.

"I didn't see a thing." She told the best kind of lie and pulled me close for a kiss. "All in," she said.

"All in," I promised.

Eventually, we sat side by side in the grass, and she passed me a hot chocolate. "Thanks," I said.

"Anyone who swims as far as you did and as hard as you did to take a kid to shore deserves all the hot chocolate the world has to offer."

I took my first sip. So much better than lemonade.

"You still swam your way free. You are still a fucking badass." She shifted closer and kissed me on my temple, the one without the sutures.

"Tell me about U of M," I said, changing the topic.

"I don't want to tell you about it. I'd rather take you there." She glanced at me, seeing if the door was open to talk about THE PLAN.

I sighed. "I don't deserve it. But can we take baby steps?"

Rose kissed my temple again. "All in," she confirmed.

I couldn't imagine moving so far away from my parents. *Not yet.* We had a lot of healing to do together. I also knew—now that I was literally myself once more—I had my people, and I could breathe. At some point, I would be up for making plans again.

And I knew that was an idea that Skirty would approve with a joyful gaze and a double thumbs-up in my direction.

CHAPTER THIRTY-TWO

On the Sandusky beach, our faces were beautiful: hair windblown, cheeks red, smiles exposing white teeth. My eyes closed, I pulled my hair back into a ponytail. The small waves only hit my shins, and I shouted, "Marco."

I heard a splash of the Erie water to my right that had nothing to do with the surf going in or out and a whispered, "Polo," as Rock readied for me to lunge at him.

I sloshed among the stones, wishing for nothing but this. "Marco," I repeated.

"Polo!" My parents, Rose, and Charlotte yelled from the beach where Steve toasted a marshmallow over a campfire for Rock. I peeked at them. Rose had stolen and wore my *Future University of Michigan Plant Biology Major. Planting the Future*, sweatshirt to guard against the cool spring breeze as she smiled in our direction. I closed my eyes again.

"You guys aren't playing," I shouted at them.

As Charlotte and Rose's laughter carried on the wind to me, I turned in a circle, my arms outstretched. "Where's Rock?"

I heard a giggle to my left.

When I finally caught him in my arms, I opened my eyes once more, and we danced in the shining surf. I didn't hesitate to giggle along with him. I knew what was true. It was no secret, and it was not a bluff: We were breathing.

About the Author

Although originally from Grand Rapids, MI, Michele Castleman has been calling rural Ohio home for over a decade now. She received her MFA in writing for children from Chatham University and earned her doctorate in Education from The Ohio State University. She is a professor at Heidelberg University in Tiffin, Ohio. She can't resist a good mystery, a cat, or an eerie setting.

Books Available from Bold Strokes Books

And Then There Was One by Michele Castleman. Plagued by strange memories and drowning in the guilt she tried to leave behind, Lyla Smith escapes her small Ohio town to work as a nanny and becomes trapped with an unknown killer. (978-1-63679-688-8)

Digging for Destiny by Jenna Jarvis. The war between nations forces Litz to make a choice. Her country, career, and family, or the chance of making a better world with the woman she can't forget. (978-1-63679-575-1)

Hot Hires by Nan Campbell, Alaina Erdell, Jesse J. Thoma. In these three romance novellas, when business turns to pleasure, romance ignites. (978-1-63679-651-2)

McCall by Patricia Evans. Sam and Sara found love on the water, but can they build a future amid the ghosts of the past that surround them on dry land? (978-1-63679-769-4)

One and Done by Fredrick Smith. One day can lead to a night of passion...and possibly a chance at love. (978-1-63679-564-5)

Promises to Protect by Jo Hemmingwood. Park ranger Maxine Ward's commitment to protect Tree City is put to the test when social worker Skylar Austen takes a special interest in the commune and in Max. (978-1-63679-626-0)

Sacred Ground by Missouri Vaun. Jordan Price, a conflicted demon hunter, falls for Grace Jameson who has no idea she's been bitten by a vampire. (978-1-63679-485-3)

The Land of Death and Devil's Club by Bailey Bridgewater. Special Liaison to the FBI Louisa Linebach may have defied all odds by identifying the bodies of three missing men in the Kenai Peninsula, but she won't be satisfied until the man she's sure is responsible for their murders is behind bars. (978-1-63679-659-8)

When You Smile by Melissa Brayden. Taryn Ross never thought the babysitter she once crushed on would show up as a grad student at the same university she attends. (978-1-63679-671-0)

A Heart Divided by Angie Williams. Emma is the most beautiful woman Jackson has ever seen, but being a veteran of the Confederate army that killed her husband isn't the only thing keeping them apart. (978-1-63679-537-9)

Adrift by Sam Ledel. Two women whose lives are anchored by guilt and obligation find romance amidst the tumultuous Prohibition movement in 1920s California. (978-1-63679-577-5)

Cabin Fever by Tagan Shepard. The longer Morgan and Shelby are stranded together, the more their feelings grow, but is it real, or just cabin fever? (978-1-63679-632-1)

Clean Kill by Anne Laughlin. When someone starts killing people she knows in the recovery world, former detective Nicky Sullivan must race to stop the killer and keep herself from being arrested for the crimes. (978-1-63679-634-5)

Only a Bridesmaid by Haley Donnell. A fake bridesmaid, a socially anxious bride, and an unexpected love—what could go wrong? (978-1-63679-642-0)

Primal Hunt by L.L. Raand. Anya, a young wolf warrior, finds herself paired with Rafe, one of the most powerful Vampires in the Americas, in an erotic union of blood and sex. (978-1-63679-561-4)

Puzzles Can Be Deadly by David S. Pederson. Skip loves a good puzzle. Little does he know that a simple phone call will lead him and his boyfriend Henry to the deadliest puzzle he's ever encountered. (978-1-63679-615-4)

Snake Charming by Genevieve McCluer. Playgirl vampire Freddie is on the run and a chance encounter with lamia Phoebe makes them both realize that they may have found the love they'd given up on. (978-1-63679-628-4)

Spirits and Sirens by Kelly and Tana Fireside. When rumored ghost whisperer Elena Murphy and very skeptical assistant fire chief Allison Jones have to work together to solve a 70-year-old mystery, sparks fly—will it be enough to melt the ice between them and let love ignite? (978-1-63679-607-9)

A Case for Discretion by Ashley Moore. Will Gwen, a prominent Atlanta attorney, choose Etta, the law student she's clandestinely dating, or is her political future too important to sacrifice? (978-1-63679-617-8)

Aubrey McFadden Is Never Getting Married by Georgia Beers. Aubrey McFadden is never getting married, but she does have five weddings to attend, and she'll be avoiding Monica Wallace, the woman who ruined her happily ever after, at every single one. (978-1-63679-613-0)

Flowers for Dead Girls by Abigail Collins. Isla might be just the right kind of girl to bring Astra out of her shell—and maybe more. The only problem? She's dead. (978-1-63679-584-3)

Good Bones by Aurora Rey. Designer and contractor Logan Barrow can give Kathleen Kenney the house of her dreams, but can she convince the cynical romance writer to take a chance on love? (978-1-63679-589-8)

Leather, Lace, and Locs by Anne Shade. Three friends, each on their own path in life, with one obstacle…finding room in their busy lives for a love that will give them their happily ever afters. (978-1-63679-529-4)

Rainbow Overalls by Maggie Fortuna. Arriving in Vermont for her first year of college, an introverted bookworm forms a friendship with an outgoing artist and finds what comes after the classic coming out story: a being out story. (978-1-63679-606-2)

Revisiting Summer Nights by Ashley Bartlett. PJ Addison and Wylie Parsons have been called back to film the most recent Dangerous Summer Nights installment. Only this time they're not in love and it's going to stay that way. (978-1-63679-551-5)

The Broken Lines of Us by Shia Woods. Charlie Dawson returns to the city she left behind and she meets an unexpected stranger on her first night back, discovering that coming home might not be as hard as she thought. (978-1-63679-585-0)

Triad Magic by 'Nathan Burgoine. Face-to-face against forces set in motion hundreds of years ago, Luc, Anders, and Curtis—vampire, demon, and wizard—must draw on the power of blood, soul, and magic to stop a killer. (978-1-63679-505-8)

All This Time by Sage Donnell. Erin and Jodi share a complicated past, but a very different present. Will they ever be able to make a future together work? (978-1-63679-622-2)

Crossing Bridges by Chelsey Lynford. When a one-night stand between a snowboard instructor and a business executive becomes more, one has to overcome her past, while the other must let go of her planned future. (978-1-63679-646-8)

Dancing Toward Stardust by Julia Underwood. Age has nothing to do with becoming the person you were meant to be, taking a chance, and finding love. (978-1-63679-588-1)

Evacuation to Love by CA Popovich. As a hurricane rips through Florida, so too are Joanne and Shanna's lives upended. It'll take a force of nature to show them the love it takes to rebuild. (978-1-63679-493-8)

Lean in to Love by Catherine Lane. Will badly behaving celebrities, erotic sex tapes, and steamy scandals prevent Rory and Ellis from leaning in to love? (978-1-63679-582-9)

Searching for Someday by Renee Roman. For loner Rayne Thomas, her only goal for working out is to build her confidence, but Maggie Flanders has another idea, and neither are prepared for the outcome. (978-1-63679-568-3)

The Romance Lovers Book Club by MA Binfield and Toni Logan. After their book club reads a romance about an American tourist falling in love with an English princess, Harper and her best friend, Alice, book an impulsive trip to London hoping they'll each fall for the women of their dreams. (978-1-63679-501-0)

Truly Home by J.J. Hale. Ruth and Olivia discover home is more than a four-letter word. (978-1-63679-579-9)

View from the Top by Morgan Adams. When it comes to love, sometimes the higher you climb, the harder you fall. (978-1-63679-604-8)